Make Believe

Books by Ed Ifkovic

The Edna Ferber Mysteries
Lone Star
Escape Artist
Make Believe

Make Believe

An Edna Ferber Mystery

Ed Ifkovic

Poisoned Pen Press

Copyright © 2012 by Ed Ifkovic

First Edition 2012

10 9 8 7 6 5 4 3 2 1

Library of Congress Catalog Card Number: 2012910469

ISBN: 9781464200809   Hardcover
        9781464200823   Trade Paperback

Poisoned Pen Press
6962 E. First Ave., Ste. 103
Scottsdale, AZ 85251
www.poisonedpenpress.com
info@poisonedpenpress.com

Printed in the United States of America

for Manda,
with my love

Acknowledgments

I'd like to offer a note of thanks to my two editors at Poisoned Pen Press, Barbara Peters and Annette Rogers. I am very fortunate to work with two women who are as passionately committed to my sleuth Edna Ferber as I am. They inspire and prod with insight, sensitivity, and, above all, wit and grace.

Chapter One

Five days ago I stepped off an American Airlines plane into blinding Los Angeles sunshine. It was a hot July afternoon, the air still and close. For a moment, standing there, I experienced a wave of panic. This was a foreign country, this vast landscape of hungry dreams under an unrelenting pale blue sky.

Five days ago I checked into the Ambassador Hotel on Wilshire, coolly regarded the bouquet of lush yellow roses already there, and immediately dialed my good friend Max Jeffries, the man I'd traveled across the country to see…to support. Max, a Hollywood insider, a man who could always make me smile, a man who now needed his friends nearby to buffer against a menacing world of accusation and condemnation.

Five days ago, the beginning of a whirlwind of lunches, cocktail parties, and Hollywood madness and tomfoolery, Max squiring me gallantly and cynically through the blather that passes for movieland hospitality. Max, the North Star in a western sky speckled with disappearing stars. Or hopeful stars.

Last night Max Jeffries was murdered.

While I socialized with his wife Alice and her friend Lorena Marr—the simple act of taking in an early dinner and a delightful movie—someone invaded his cherished bungalow and shot him in the back of the head.

Max, murdered. Impossible to grasp.

Late last night after the movie, settled in my hotel suite, I'd dropped off into a deep sleep with images of men in dark broad-loom suits pointing gnarled fingers at a hapless Max. When the telephone rang, too loud in the quiet room, I yelped, sprang up in bed. Fumbling, I peered through the shadowy darkness. For a moment I imagined I was in my own Manhattan bed, snoozing in front of my apple-green headboard. The last traces of the nightmare slipped away: gun-metal shards of hot cinder rained down on a stark, endless landscape where I sat and called out to Max…But I could not remember the rest, except that I was cold and clammy and utterly abandoned. My mouth was dry, my eyes ached.

The ringing stopped. I fell back onto the pillow. Then it began again.

I was in L.A. in a suite on the top floor of the Ambassador. Outside everything was lost in darkness.

And the clock on the nightstand told me it was just after midnight. 12:05. That registered with me.

The voice on the other end sounded tiny, mechanical, and far away.

"What?" I yelled.

"It's Sol, Edna. Sol Remnick. Max's friend."

"I know." I'd met Max's best friend at Max's home just days before. I breathed in. "Tell me."

Silence.

"Max is dead."

"Tell me."

"He was murdered."

"Tell me."

"I don't know." The sound of sobbing now, halting gulps, sloppy. "Alice phoned me, hysterical. The police are there now." Another sob, thick and raw.

The line went dead.

All night long I lay in my bed, numb, eyes wide in the dark. But I must have drifted off because I started awake as sunlight streamed through the windows. I sat up, sobbing in raspy gasps like a beaten child.

Mechanically, I splashed water on my face, pulled clothing from a closet, then fiddled with the dial on the radio until I found a newscast at the top of the hour. Six in the morning, a beastly hour to be awake, lethal to the body. I rarely violated my longstanding regimen: eight hours of uninterrupted sleep, up promptly at eight, fully dressed, breakfast of coffee with whipped milk and fresh-squeezed orange juice, and then out the door for an invigorating walk. But you didn't walk in L.A. No, instead, you found yourself wide-awake in bed after a restless, nightmare-laden sleep, grappling with the bizarre fact that an old friend had been savagely murdered. Six in the morning, sitting fully dressed in a chair, trying to make sense of a phantasmagoric world by searching for answers on local radio stations that played "Good Night, Irene" every five minutes.

It couldn't work, of course, this search for answers, but what other recourse did I have? Room service delivered a pot of coffee, orange juice, and buttered English muffins—the man nodded at my generous tip but stepped back, doubtless startled by the gaunt face of the old and trembling woman.

Max, dead. Max, murdered. Dead. My Max. That puckish, lively soul singing "Make Believe" to me in a restaurant years back. Where? In Pittsburgh? In Philadelphia? A *Show Boat* tryout. I knew that. Of course. Whenever someone did *Show Boat*, he'd be there…and I would be, too. The two of us, giddy in the aisles. And now another *Show Boat*, in Technicolor. Metro's splashy version with Ava Gardner. But Max was dead. There'd be no more revivals with him. His musical genius would be missing.

Yes, it was Pittsburgh. That greasy spoon. Manny's Deli Delight. Preposterous. Max sang to me, that twinkle in his eye. Silly and foolish, in a parody of ingénue Magnolia Ravenal's arch soprano from the deck of the showboat. Everyone in the restaurant laughed. We got free coffee. I remembered that. *Sing for your supper*, Max warbled at the waitress, *and you'll get breakfast.*

Why was this memory coming to me now?

Max, dead.

The news at the top of the hour. The lead-off story featured Max Jeffries, Hollywood agent and most recently musical arranger for Metro's celebrated extravaganza *Show Boat*. I winced: even news of murder out here in Hollywood arrived with a requisite commercial endorsement. Max "was found murdered at his home on Wilshire Boulevard." Police reports were sketchy, but early information indicated his wife, Alice, as leading suspect, "a woman once married to mobster Lenny Pannis." Alice Jeffries, cleared of charges of murder in the Pannis case. Police were investigating. In the news recently, "Max Jeffries, champion of the Hollywood Ten, faced accusations of Communist leanings when he sent a letter to..." I switched off the radio and sat there, shaking my head. A few simple lines of questionable reportage—innuendo and suspicion and accusation. A few throwaway lines, and both Max and Alice—in fact, the world of the blacklist—were skewered and found guilty. Treason and murder.

At ten o'clock, after repeated attempts to reach Alice or Sol, I decided to take a taxi to his bungalow. I had to do something. The walls of my suite were closing in on me. I'd paced the carpet back and forth and watched L.A. wake up from my high window: the white buildings on the boulevard lost their night shadows and emerged into brilliant sunlight. A normal day in Los Angeles. All the days in L.A. were normal, except for...for what? The day when a close friend was shot to death. When the phone rang, I expected Sol, lunged for it, but was startled by a gruff though sleepy voice. Detective Marv Tilden would like to speak to me. He was downstairs. Could he please...respectfully...? Of course. After all, I spent last evening with Alice, the alleged but impossible killer of her husband. We watched a Jimmy Stewart movie and roared at his antics. Alice's preamble to a deliberate killing when she returned home?

Detective Tilden apologized for the intrusion in a drifting, beachcomber voice that suggested we'd be sharing mai tais at the pool shortly. He even leaned on the doorjamb, slouching, one hand rustling his trim blond hair. Dark tanned, with small squirrel eyes in a long face, he towered above me, a pencil-thin man in a gray linen suit. He shouldn't be standing there, pad at the ready, a sober look on his face. A young man, late twenties, he belonged on a surfboard waiting religiously for that elusive ninth wave.

"Miss Ferber, forgive the hour. An honor to meet you."

I nodded. A good beginning. An apology and a courtesy.

But he wasted no time. Yes, I was with Alice and Lorena Marr last night. We had an early dinner at the Paradise Bar & Grill just up the street, then took in a movie nearby. "Which movie?" Was that important: Well, yes. It was *Harvey*.

He smiled. "Did you like it, ma'am? My wife liked it but I didn't. I'm not into imaginary rabbits. Although now and then, as a detective, I try to pull one out of a hat." He chuckled at his own joke. Movie reviews and an interrogation? Quietly, I waited as his face hardened. "Then?" He looked sharply into my face.

"Then we stopped back at the Paradise for a nightcap. A glass of sherry. That is, Lorena and I did. Alice was worried about Max and hurried home."

"What time?"

"Perhaps ten. Maybe a little later. I know I was back here just after eleven and asleep soon after."

"Alice Jeffries went right home?"

"So far as I know. Where else would she go?"

"She drove herself?"

"No, she had walked to the bar. It's close. We said goodbye in the parking lot."

"Do you believe she murdered her husband? Max?"

"Of course not, young man."

"Why not?"

"People I know don't kill one another."

He smiled. "She was a suspect in the killing of her mobster husband, Lenny Pannis. His brothers still want her charged."

"Absurd," I snapped.

"Absurd?"

I didn't answer him. I'd already stated my opinion.

On and on, a detailed recounting of an eventless evening, the small bits and pieces of a lovely time in the company of two women who made me laugh—one of whom was happily married to a man I cherished. Max, now murdered.

"Any tension?"

"Among us? Of course not."

"Any hint of trouble with her husband?"

"Of course not."

"Are you sure?"

I was piqued. "Young man, I've already answered that question. Do you think I'd revise my answer in my very next breath?"

He stared. "It's been known to happen." He grinned. I saw gleaming white teeth, too many of them.

"Then you don't know me, sir."

He nodded. "I do now, Miss Ferber."

"Then you're obviously quicker than others of your generation."

His eyes twinkled. "I like to think so."

I was starting to like him. "No," I concluded, "nothing struck me as odd. Alice was devoted to Max, who was a decent man…"

"What about this Commie business?" he broke in, his eyes darkening. "The Hollywood Ten, pinko sympathies. He seems to have had some questionable associates."

I breathed in…Perhaps my liking of this young man was premature. I didn't like it when my snap judgments proved wrong. "Scurrilous nonsense. A man who exercised his First Amendment rights…"

His face tightened. "I hear you, ma'am."

I doubted that he did, but his investigative instincts told him to back off.

He got nowhere with me and finally snapped his pad shut abruptly. He stood and stretched. He'd get back to me, if necessary. I was in town for another week, right? I nodded. "How did you know that?"

"I checked the hotel registration."

"Of course."

"Thank you, Miss Ferber." He turned away.

"A second, Detective Tilden." He paused, folded his long, lanky arms around his chest. "The radio said Alice was a suspect."

"Yes, she is."

"Based on what?"

He hesitated, then sighed. "Well, I'll tell you. A gun was found in his workroom, dropped onto his desk. Her fingerprints were on it."

"Surely…"

He held up his hand, and I got quiet. "No harm telling you, Miss Ferber, I suppose." A pause. "Two small fingerprints on the handle, which suggests she gingerly picked it up between thumb and index finger, someone not used to handling a gun. Not *liking* to handle a gun. So she's a suspect, but…sort of."

"Sort of? Young man, I don't trust sloppy qualifications."

He paused for a second. "Her story is that she arrived home, opened the front door—it was locked—and spotted the .32 laying on the side table where she keeps her mail. She was surprised, thinking Max had left *his* gun there and forgot it before going to bed. I gather he'd taken his gun out of a drawer recently. A nervous habit. Death threats and all. But she always insisted it be out of sight."

"Max had a gun?"

He nodded. "A .38 that was found in his desk drawer under some papers. His wife couldn't tell the difference. She picked the gun up and was carrying it into the workroom, angry that he'd been so careless. She found him slumped over his desk, a bullet hole in the back of his head. He'd been shot from behind, surprised perhaps. She says she dropped the gun on the desk."

"So she's innocent." I was ready to dismiss the officer.

He gave me the indulgent smile you'd bestow on a child, and one not very clever at that. "As I said, she's still a suspect. Sort of. She could have *planned* it to look like that. You know, wipe the gun off, and then pick it up with two fingers and drop it."

"Rather elaborate planning, no?"

"Nothing compared to some of the stuff I come across."

"But she was gone for the evening. He planned on going to bed."

"Well, somehow during that long evening, he was murdered. Maybe before she left for dinner with you. No way of knowing. We figure it didn't happen when she got back home sometime before eleven."

"She called him from the Paradise Bar. He didn't answer."

"Maybe because he was conveniently dead. And she knew it."

"Impossible." I remembered something. "As I'm certain you've found out already, Lorena Marr phoned the house from the bar. She was making certain Alice was on her way, but Alice had already left. Max said someone was at the door and he couldn't talk."

"Maybe Alice was returning, surprising him. She was late getting to the Paradise, I've heard."

"Impossible."

"Nothing is impossible when it comes to murder, Miss Ferber." Finished, he nodded a goodbye and walked out.

"Impossible," I announced to myself.

Within seconds, someone rapped on the door, and I suspected that Detective Tilden had returned, sheepish, apologizing again for his intrusion but peppering me with more questions. But a lanky young man in a bellman's outfit mumbled something about Western Union, thrust an envelope into my hands, bowed, waited for a tip, and then retreated. Inside an envelope marked "Deliver Immediately" was a telegram from George S. Kaufman in New York. EDNA. JUST HEARD. SO SAD. A GOOD MAN. CAN I HELP? GEORGE.

So the calamitous news had been carried to the East Coast, where Max's many friends, settling into their lunches at midday, now grieved at the loss. I sat at the edge of a chair, the telegram crumpled in my hands, and reread it. A GOOD MAN. Succinct, perfect: the bittersweet epitaph.

In that moment, gazing out the window, I thought of my last days here—all the frenzied activity surrounding my visit to Max, who'd been hounded in the press for his defense of the Hollywood Ten. Even my name had been mentioned in the press. And in that same moment, my spine rigid, a flash of lightning electrified me: there was a good chance I'd encountered Max's murderer. After all, Max and I had discussed the way his old friends had betrayed him...how industry types had turned him into a leper. At dinners, lunches, cocktail parties, I'd met the folks who loved or hated him. Straw patriots hurling barbs his way. Chilled now, I stood, antsy: someone I'd talked with most likely killed my friend.

Again, the rapping on the door. Anxious, I rushed to open it and found the same bellman, red faced now and jittery. "My apologies," he murmured. "Another telegram was delivered minutes after..." His voice trailed off.

I grabbed it from him, reached for my purse for some change, but he backed away, disappearing down the hallway.

Inside the envelope another telegram from Kaufman. EDNA. DO SOMETHING ABOUT THIS. G.

Typical of George, I thought, to order me about—and, as usual, after the fact. Because, quite frankly, I'd already decided that I *would* do something. I really had no choice. No one murders my friends and gets away with it. That's not the way my universe works. That's never the way my heart beats.

Chapter Two

Five days ago Max Jeffries had answered the door before I had a chance to press the bell. He stood there, this tiny slip of a man, his face wide in a sloppy grin, and then, wordless, performed an exaggerated two-step. I grinned and bowed. He glanced over my shoulder at the departing taxi and squinted. "Too far to walk, Edna?"

"I didn't want to be taken in by the police."

It was one of our running jokes. Years back, visiting Los Angeles, I'd left the Bel-Air Hotel for my obligatory early morning stroll but was summarily stopped by a cop who seemed stunned that I wanted to *walk* the streets. "Madam," he kept saying as he wagged his finger. I soon learned that walking was suspect behavior here, enclosing oneself in a shiny new car was *de rigueur*, and nothing else would do. Folks drove to the corner store, and considered it a worthy journey.

Max's snug bungalow, situated perhaps a quarter mile from my top-floor suite at the Ambassador, was an easy stroll, though one likely forbidden by local ordinance and rigorous custom. I'd hailed a taxi. A New York cabbie would have balked at such a piddling trek—indeed, would have cursed me roundly in salty Neapolitan or robust Gallic dialect—but here in the land of wide boulevards and constant sunshine I garnered a half-hearted smile. Everyone in L.A. smiles too much. Incessant sunlight makes folks giddy, of course, maddened like buzzing horse flies near a cottage porch light.

Max laughed and ushered me inside. "I could have picked you up."

"Don't be foolish, dear Max. It's bad enough that I'm mooching supper from you."

We sat in a small living room, which I recalled fondly from a visit years back. A shadowy room, too dark, despite thick velvet burgundy curtains pulled back to allow sunlight in. It was early evening, still light outside, yet you'd never know it. The bungalow—one of a row of similar white stucco homes, each with narrow white columns banking the front doors—was nestled under the intimidating presence of a towering skyscraper cruelly built yards away, relegating the quaint homes to darkness and isolation.

Max had switched on too many table lamps that did nothing more than exaggerate the long drifting shadows on the walls. I settled into a deep, worn sofa. A lived-in room, comfortable, inviting. A home. Max's home. Every space from table top to wall, even a paneled door, held black-and-white photographs chronicling Max's long career in Broadway theater, on the road during interminable tryouts, and, for the past couple of decades, life in Hollywood as a freelance musical arranger as well as small-time talent agent.

A quick glance gave me shots of Max with Clark Gable, Gary Cooper, Ginger Rogers, Jerome Kern, among so many others. Max grinning with Fred Allen at the Chi Chi Club in Palm Springs. Max playfully sparring with Mickey Rooney. Max doing an exaggerated soft shoe with Marge and Gower Champion, the two veteran hoofers now in the new *Show Boat*. I admit I didn't recognize many of the celebrities in the photos. Despite my being enthralled, begrudgingly, with movieland magic, I always declared an abiding dislike of Hollywood's trashy output. How many doomsday pronouncements had I made to the press on the unsavory effects of movies while at the same time demanding Hollywood moguls buy the rights to my novels? Jack Warner was now wooing me for the rights to *Giant*, a novel not yet published. Carl Laemmele used to send me boxes of Belgian chocolates. Max and I had long, intense talks on *that* subject, let me tell you.

Max's face got serious. "Edna, you didn't have to fly to L.A. to see me, you know. I don't need…"

I held up my hand. "Don't be ridiculous, Max. My indignation over the way you've been treated fueled my journey, truth to tell."

He laughed. "It is wonderful to see you after so many years. It's been so long."

He walked to a black-lacquered art deco sideboard and poured red wine into two glasses. "Still merlot?"

"You know me, Max. The little tippler."

"Yeah, I recall your insistence that one glass of anything is worthy and healthful. Two glasses makes you say and do foolish things."

"Well, it's true."

"Edna, you've never said a foolish thing in your life." He raised his glass to me.

We clinked glasses. "I'm an old lady now. Maybe it's time to be foolish." I sat back, sipping the delicious wine. I smiled back at him, the two of us silent for a moment, lost in the comfortable space that old friends fall into so neatly and deliciously, some reflective touchstone. A peaceful kingdom, this little bungalow.

Max had aged. He was a small compact man, so slender of build he seemed an undernourished adolescent boy. He had a bony face with jutting chin covered in a slight stubble, grayish. Balding now, his once straw-like honey-blond hair was sketchy and stringy. But those eyes, metallic steel gray, always—and still—giving his face a mischievous, impish look, the boy who steals the crab apples from your neighbor's yard. Those deep-set eyes made the utterly drab face burst alive, rivet, demand your attention. As a young man, he'd been a dancer in a chorus line back in New York, a live-off-the-cuff gypsy. But when his dancing days were over, he became a back-of-the-chorus baritone in Broadway musicals. Then, for his final passion, a mighty fine arranger of musical scores, with a growing reputation for originality and cleverness. In time he became an intimate of Jerome Kern, a man I knew well, a man notoriously hard to befriend.

"You're staring at me, Edna."

"I know. I'm not sorry. I like looking at you."

He shook his head. "My wife'll be jealous…for the first time."

I took a deep breath. "Max, a married man."

"Hard to believe, no?" He pointed to a corner china cabinet with scalloped trim and chalk-white finish, something that rightly belonged in a colonial home on Cape Cod. "Your gift of the Baccarat vases was excessive."

Four years back—Max, fiftyish then—the inveterate bachelor and summer nomad who trekked alone across the Alps, had surprised everyone by marrying a local widow, whom I'd never met. No one had—at least none of the New York circle that knew Max. Fond of Max, our serendipitous court jester, we were tickled—and talked of nothing else for days. George S. Kaufman famously quipped, "Some men have to reach that half-century mark before they make their first mistake." Max's letter to me, intimate and cozy, had gushed—a squirming emotion I dislike in nearly everyone—his absolute devotion to the mysterious Alice.

"And where is Alice?" I asked now.

"She's dressing—keeps changing her dress." He slapped the side of his face, a silly gesture. "Oh, perhaps I shouldn't tell you that. She's so nervous about meeting you that she's been fretting all day. You're Edna Ferber. You're *Show Boat*…"

"Good Lord," I interrupted him. "I'm hardly some massive pleasure craft lumbering down Wilshire Boulevard."

"You know what I mean." He grinned sheepishly. "She'll be out in a second."

It was almost a stage cue because, with a squeak of an unseen door and a very audible titter, the woman appeared in the hallway. She stood there, statue-like, one hand extended out for no apparent reason, a paralyzed smile on her face. I was reminded of the indomitable Katherine Cornell and her usual preposterous stage entrances, whether called for or not in the script. Max made the introductions while Alice slid into a canary-yellow wing chair opposite me. I wondered when she planned to start blinking.

I didn't know what I expected, but not this prim, matronly-looking woman, dressed now in a simple floral-print housedress with two rather ungainly red bows stuck indecorously to her bodice, a dress that clashed with the yellow of her chair. Hardly Hollywood—more Emporia, Kansas, the farmer's wife at a Grange supper of pork-and-beans that followed a Methodist quilting bee. George Kaufman, always privy to transcontinental gossip though most was spurious and definitely scurrilous, had informed me that she was a notorious black widow whose rich gangland husband had died under mysterious circumstances. I'd expected some slicked-over movie confection, much too young for Max, a vacuum slathered in a harlot's glossy lipstick and dime-store rouge.

Alice, to the contrary, wore no makeup save the dimmest hint of light powder on her cheeks and a faint tint of apricot lipstick, decorous and flattering. With my own bright red lipstick and rouged cheeks, my head of permed white curls, I played the madam. The near-septuagenarian out on the town. Not only that, but Alice was small and chubby, with a cherubic face that held round walnut-brown eyes, a little too large, so that she seemed startled awake. She was the kind of woman you'd see depicted on a box of laundry detergent or baking powder. Or the friendly if annoying neighbor in an Andy Hardy movie. Mickey Rooney would beg her for candy.

I found myself liking her. She had a thin, sweet smile that reminded me of friends connecting after long absence.

"We finally meet," she whispered.

"Can you believe I got married, Edna?" Max got up to pour his wife a drink. Not wine, I noticed, but iced tea from a pitcher.

"I *was* a tad surprised." I was stunned, truth be told.

Alice looked at him with affection. "I had to convince him."

"She asked *me*," Max confided.

Alice grinned. "Otherwise we'd still be going Dutch after late Friday night suppers at Chasen's. Or still standing at the juke box at Sneaky Pete's on Sunset Strip, dropping nickels in to hear 'I'm Looking Over a Four-Leaf Clover' for the hundredth time."

"No, it was 'Baby, It's Cold Outside.' Esther Williams." His eyes gleamed. "I love that song." He took a sip of wine, rolled his tongue over his lips. A deep sigh. "Edna, seriously, this visit, though a pleasure, wasn't...necessary."

"Of course it was." Emphatic, quick.

"I'm small potatoes in this whole political mess..."

"Well, you're my potato." I grinned. "Though these days a very hot potato."

Max had long been involved with different productions of *Show Boat* dating back to the Hammerstein and Kern Broadway hit of 1927 that ran for 572 performances and was almost immediately revived. He'd been hired to perform his wonderful magic on MGM's latest Technicolor extravaganza, the much-touted remake starring screen heartthrobs Howard Keel and Kathryn Grayson, as well as, scandalously, Ava Gardner as Julie LaVerne, the tragic mulatto. The movie was now finished and eagerly anticipated. Previews in April and May in out-of-the-way theaters throughout California had been favorable, indeed, downright rapturous.

I was cynical, of course—the two earlier films had made me squirm, and I fully expected the same reaction this time around. Bowdlerized, slapdash renderings of my romantic saga, piecemeal and suspect. With his history, Max had been hired to orchestrate the music, and, typical of Max, he'd worked tirelessly on this new Metro release, his loving touch all over the production. In a letter he claimed it would be a superb movie, though I winced at that—but finally Max had written that L. B. Mayer or Dore Schary—he didn't know which blustery mogul—had quietly removed his name from the film credits. In fact, he'd been cruelly walked off the grounds.

"I've been blacklisted," Max wrote me. "I'm the new Hollywood leper in fantasy land."

Hollywood, sadly, was awash in fear and reprisal, a noisome cancer eating into the rarefied industry of make believe. Back in 1947 the House Un-American Activities Committee in Washington, under the leadership of a pudgy martinet named J. Parnell Thomas, had begun investigating Communist influence in the movie industry, particularly among scriptwriters. Hollywood folks, stunned, had been compelled to head East to testify to past or present affiliation with the Communist Party. A garish public-relations nightmare. *Are you now or have you ever been a member of the Communist Party?* was the nightmarish mantra.

At first Hollywood fought back with protests and meetings, buoyed by support from the studios. But then public opinion shifted as the gossip columnists roared their disapproval, and Hollywood bigwigs ran scared. Heads tumbled. Careers died. Lives ruined. What resulted was the Hollywood Ten, now bound for prison and career suicide.

Just this past year, with the specter of jowly and stentorian Senator Joe McCarthy waving undocumented lists of Reds in government before Republican women's clubs in the heartland, as well as a new round of attacks from a reconstituted HUAC, Max reacted. Bothered by the spectacle, he had to say something. Of course, he knew Communists, men who'd joined when it was a party dedicated to fighting fascism in Germany and Italy, idealistic souls who'd recanted after the Stalin purges. In fact, he was a close friend of two of the Hollywood Ten: John Howard Lawson, whom I knew as a serious if windbaggish playwright, and Dalton Trumbo, a brilliant scriptwriter we all called Doc." Good men, and loyal Americans.

Max had penned an indignant but I thought beautifully crafted letter to the *Hollywood Reporter*, articulating the case for First Amendment rights of the accused, a heartfelt cry for balance and fairness and—well, it didn't matter. That simple letter, forceful and intelligent, earned him the label of Communist, fifth columnist, fellow traveler, card-carrying Red, a betrayer of American democracy. An endless stream of glib, dismissive phrases. A brutal attack in Myron Fagan's muckraking *Red Treason in Hollywood.*

Reprinted here and there, quoted by a slap-happy, Red-baiting Walter Winchell, referred to by Jack Warner before some committee, the letter branded Max a danger. His timing was bad. The Rosenberg trial was bold-face, front-page news. The Alger Hiss debacle still sizzled. The Russian A-bomb threat frightened everyone. No matter that Max was a good man; condemned in the local press, named by *Red Channels* in their muckraking columns, he became estranged from both friends and foes. Clients drifted away. Phones went unanswered. Max became the unwitting poster boy of the moment: the veteran entertainment insider who supposedly answered the phone when Moscow called.

I'd written that I'd be visiting him—to lend support.

Max now seemed eager to change the subject. "Metro asked you to the premiere of *Show Boat*?"

I swelled up, indignant. "Not exactly a heartfelt invitation… just a courtesy. No thank you! I've already refused. I made a *point* of it. I don't like their treatment of you, and I've told them so loud and clear. I came to see *you*. Spend time with you, go out for dinner. *Show Boat* has nothing to do with my visit." The West Coast premiere was scarcely a week away, and MGM knew I was in town. I'd heard they were worried I'd make a scene. Some of the scenes I'd made over the years were the stuff of legend.

Alice spoke up. "They'll hound you. Their rep, a guy named Desmond Peake, the man who axed Max from the studio, called *here* to get information from *us.*"

"I know. There are phone messages filling up my cubby hole at the Ambassador."

"He's a real shark, that one," Max noted.

"I will see them, of course, whoever *them* is. They've scheduled a private showing of the movie." I bristled. "Max, I simply don't like the fact that your considerable contribution to *Show Boat* is going uncredited. A horrible word: 'uncredited.' So dismissive and unfair."

"It doesn't matter to me." Max shrugged.

Hotly. "Oh, but it does."

Alice nodded. "Justice." She wagged her finger at her husband.

"Exactly," I echoed. "I detest a witch-hunt, and this one is lasting too long and is too insidious. I don't understand this… this madness. I gather that gossip queen Hedda Hopper is on an anti-Red tear, even smearing you in her columns. 'Moscow Max'—right? Snide and catty."

"I'm famous." Max raised his eyebrows. "Edna, everyone in Hollywood is desperate to be wildly famous." A half-bow. "I did it effortlessly."

"Infamous," Alice muttered. She reached over and gently touched her husband's hand. It was a sudden gesture, instinctive, but it seemed so necessary at the moment, a lover's reassuring pat, sheltering. Just for a second they glanced at each other, excluding me, and in that instant I witnessed real affection, love, concern. And, to my horror, a little fear. I felt a lump in my throat because I realized, like a blow to the face, how treacherous and precarious their peaceful life had become. Trouble in a sun-drenched paradise.

Max breathed in, once again anxious to shift the conversation. A thin smile, teasing. "Ava Gardner can't wait to meet you."

I gasped, a histrionic Victorian reflex I detested in myself, though these days the grim specter of humanity seemed to warrant it more and more. "Whatever for?"

"Think about it, Edna. You wrote *Show Boat*, the movie she thinks will define her career, showcase her as a real actress. The movie that, like *The Killers* a while back, will finally convince the world she's more than long legs, curvy body, and sex-goddess appeal. A breakthrough movie, that one. Hemingway himself sent her roses. But Metro has a track record of dumping her into grade B movies. They don't *believe* her power. Both Hedda Hopper and Louella Parsons wrote wildly insane columns protesting Metro's casting, can you believe? Keep her *out* of the classic. '*Show Boat* is America…Ava is…cheesecake.' But she can act, you know."

Alice chimed in, "She's mentioned you a number of times."

"Ava Gardner?"

They both laughed. "Edna, Edna." Max leaned forward. "She's not what you think."

Frankly, I never liked it when people told me what I was thinking. A little too arrogant, such a presumption. Max, however, I'd forgive. "Well, to be honest, she doesn't strike me as… dimensional. I mean…" I faltered. "Sex goddess, hellcat, those nightclub scenes that make the papers…" I suddenly realized my narrow image of the beautiful woman was the product of George Kaufman and Marc Connelly blathering their puerile adoration for the voluptuous woman. George, I knew, regularly devoured *Photoplay* and *Modern Screen*, though not in front of me. He knew better.

"You'll love her," Alice confided with certainty. She wrapped her arms around her chest, twisted her body into the cushions of the chair. "She gives the greatest hugs."

"I don't allow strangers to hug me," I announced, imperious.

"You won't have a choice." Alice giggled like a schoolgirl.

"And she won't be a stranger very long," Max added.

Now I changed the subject. "Tell me, is the movie atrocious, Max?"

"God, no." He laughed out loud. "It's…Technicolor."

I sighed. "Oh, joy. A splashy cartoon. Magnolia Ravenal dancing with Donald Duck."

Max hedged, glanced over my shoulder. "Well, it's different from the Hammerstein and Kern version. The director Pop Sidney didn't want to use Hammerstein's libretto. He did leave off that ugly word for Negroes in 'Ol' Man River'…"

"Thank God for that. In my novel only the lowlife characters use *that* word."

"But they've rewritten most of the dialogue which is…"

"Juvenile, insipid…" I interrupted.

"A little bit, in places. But the music is pure Jerome Kern. Otherwise I wouldn't have worked on it."

"Thank God." I paused. "You know, I make no money from this production. Not a red cent. Hollywood hacks can willy-nilly run amok with my work. I've sent off letters to MGM, in fact. Letters ignored, for the most part. They run from me like the plague. *Show Boat* is meant to be a simple story, a romantic look at life on a Mississippi floating theater, though with an underbelly of darkness—the mixed-blood tragedy of the South. Cap'n Andy and his wife Parthy shelter their innocent daughter Magnolia who falls for a ne'er-do-well gambler Gaylord Ravenal, marries him, and leads a life of sadness and penury until she returns to her home on the *Cotton Blossom*."

"It's a slice of Americana." Max was nodding. "Melodrama, vaudeville, minstrel show, song and dance."

"Remember that early script I got my hands on, thankfully abandoned?" I grinned. "I believe it may have come from *you*. Ingénue Magnolia blames *herself* for Ravenal deserting her and their baby. 'I must have done something very wrong.' *Her* fault, the failed wife, not the wastrel gambler and huckster. Lord! In my novel Magnolia grows as a strong, purposeful woman, not a simpering, weak-kneed woman fawning before a prodigal husband." My voice was rising, my cheeks flushed, so I stopped. "I'm sorry. I'll never be happy with what they do to my work."

"It's a different movie now. Romance, yes, and sweeping ballads and dance, but with a dark thread of sadness, discrimination, loss. A lot of the movie now focuses on Ava Gardner, the doomed siren exiled from the boat because she's mixed blood and married to a white man. Julie LaVerne frames the movie, the tragic mulatto who has a heart of gold, sacrificing her career for her childhood friend, Magnolia. Ava's damned good…"

My spine rigid, I stared at Max. "That remains to be seen." I shook my head slowly. "Max, you've made a life of helping the enemy destroy my work." But I smiled, and so did he.

"Hey, I've done my best."

As a young man in Manhattan, Max had apprenticed on the Broadway hit with Jerome Kern and became the great composer's protégé. I didn't know Max then, of course, though I'd faithfully haunted the rehearsals of *Show Boat* at the Ziegfeld Theater. A clever, gifted young man, he'd migrated to music from dance, even writing a ragtime hit for Sophie Tucker that no one now remembered. Jerome Kern liked him—a rarity, given the composer's notorious isolation. Over the years Max found his most comfortable place with the frequent versions of *Show Boat*—in one excruciating form or another.

Alice cleared her throat. "Edna, tell me how you two became friends. Max tells me a silly version…"

Max had started to sip his wine but stopped, eyeing me over the rim of the glass, a twinkle in his eyes. "Absurd but true. Tell her, Edna."

"A preposterous beginning, I suppose," I began. "The tryouts for *Show Boat* were in Washington D.C. A freezing November. Everyone was a nervous wreck. After all, Ziegfeld had done a slew of zany, popular musical revues, with leggy chorus girls and madcap vaudeville comedy skits. Here was a novelty—a musical *play*, with the music and routines built around a real story, in fact, based on genuine American history. We had no idea how it would go over. We didn't anticipate the…the hysteria. A jam-packed play, too long, too much music, opening night it ran hours over, with people stamping their feet and roaring. 'Ol' Man River' had them screaming out loud. When the audience left, exhausted, at nearly one in the morning, we were stunned. No one had left the theater early. The next morning the line for tickets wound around the block, and we knew we had a smash hit. But they had to slash music, dialogue, scenes."

Max jumped in. "I was inside cutting a scene, debating which music had to go, listening to Hammerstein curse us out and Kern tinkling the keys of a piano like a bratty child, so I took a break, strolling outside. And there, wrapped in a puffy shocking-red scarf, buried in a full-length mink coat, was Edna Ferber, the wide-eyed and flabbergasted author, standing on a corner staring at the snake-like line."

I laughed. "And Max, a stranger, sidled up to me and whispered, 'This is all your fault, Madame *Show Boat.*'"

Max saluted me, laughing. "And a wonderful friendship was born."

"And he has had to hear me whine and kvetch with each new production. He reports in, dutifully, and I go off like a mad woman." I grunted. "Especially the first movie in 1929."

"The joke was that I was hired to help with the music for a *silent* picture, Alice. You know, piano introductions. But then talkies came with *The Jazz Singer* and suddenly we had to do it over—half silent, half talkie. And then we had to do a *third* version, all talkie now, finally with Kern's music rights secured."

"A hodgepodge of nonsense."

"Oh, yes, a mess. Unwatchable. Laura La Plante looking frail and helpless and not certain what continent she was on." Max got up to refill his glass. I held my hand over my empty glass. "Then the 1936 version with Paul Robeson and Irene Dunne. Beautiful."

"Well, Robeson, yes. And now MGM with little of the Hammerstein dialogue intact. Barbaric, infantile."

"Now, now, Edna."

"Don't 'Now, Edna' me," I said in my best Parthenia Hawks spinster's voice, arch and shrill, delivered from the deck of the *Cotton Blossom*.

"Wait and see, Edna."

"I'm too old to be patient…or even tolerant of fools."

"I bet you were always like that, Edna," Alice said.

"It's a talent I developed early in life." I sighed. "Frankly, it saves time in an imperfect world."

◇◇◇

Alice served an elaborate supper. Max had decided we'd have a *Show Boat* feast, a meal described in my book—Queenie's sure-fire, bang-up sensation, a ham stuffed with cloves and cinnamon and peppercorns and a host of other aromatic herbs, all jammed in with a sharp knife so that the swollen meat, baked, glazed, sliced, formed an ornate mosaic of color and design. Luscious, tasty, and gratefully savored by me. I allowed myself another glass of wine. Alice served coffee and homemade pecan pie smothered in whipped cream spiked with brandy. Succulent, rich. I groaned under the pleasure. There was little talk during supper, idle chatter, catching up with news of old friends.

Max was especially fond of George Kaufman, who'd recently been on the West Coast, and he recounted George's scandalous caper with some frivolous and gaudy studio starlet. "George the saturnine puritan," I babbled. A character flaw in an otherwise exemplary man.

While we were still at the dining room table, the doorbell chimed, and Max invited in a short, stocky man, a shock of spun-white hair curling over tiny ears, a pale ashy face, and a thin hard mouth that seemed shaped by a razor. A cigarette bobbed in the corner of his mouth, the ash long and unchecked. Barney Google eyes behind oversized eyeglasses. "This is my old friend, Sol Remnick," Max told me. "The first friend I made when I moved here from New York. He comes from the same old Brooklyn neighborhood, but I didn't know him there."

Sol nodded hello, a mumbled greeting, his eyes wary, as he pulled out a chair across from me, watching my face. Alice poured him a cup of coffee. After the greeting, he said nothing but quickly downed the coffee, almost in one hasty gulp. He sat back. "So I'm interrupting, yes?"

"It's all right." Max waved a hand at him.

"So you're Edna Ferber." Still no smile, but another respectful nod. "An honor. Max…values you." A strange remark, I thought, though true. As I did Max. Still I said nothing. He started to stand. "I'll be back tomorrow."

"No, sit, Sol," Max insisted. "For God's sake. We're all friends here."

Sol leaned into him, confidentially. "The Screen Actors Guild is meeting tonight, Max. Someone told a reporter that it's lousy with Communists. Everyone is panicking. Ronnie Reagan threatens to…something about a loyalty oath…He's been talking to the FBI in secret, they say." He paused and glanced at me. "I'm sorry."

Max grinned at me. "Sol and I stay up all night discussing Hollywood and the witch-hunt."

He shrugged his shoulders. "It's my only story, I'm afraid. Miss Ferber, I helped organize the Committee for the First Amendment to fight back. We need to do battle. I'm…driven." For the first time he grinned, and his face came alive, wrinkled, rutted, but filled with vitality and force. You saw a man who seemed a hard-boiled sort but was really a softie out of a Dashiell Hammett novel, a stocky man in a baggy double-breasted seersucker suit with a Hoover collar, an ex-boxer type, the pugnacious man who stops to play with children. But a man who could not disguise his nervousness.

Alice pointed at him. "Your Cousin Irving."

That made little sense to me. "What?" I had no cousins named Irving. I'd know. I did have a pesky older sister named Fanny, and she was trial enough.

Max explained, "Sol plays Cousin Irving on *The Goldbergs*. You know, Gertrude Berg's wildly popular television show. He started when it was on the radio, but now he's on television. A star, can you imagine? Molly Goldberg. You know, the nosy woman hanging out of the tenement window, yelling, 'Yoo hoo, come in, you'll have a nice glass tea and we'll talk some.' Irving is her nebbish cousin, the sad sack in an unpressed, oversized suit, a blunderer…"

"I don't have a television. Never will. A full meal of no nourishment."

Sol burst out laughing, enjoying the moment. "For that, all Hollywood moguls like Louis B. Mayer will applaud you."

"Cousin Irving's hugely popular, Edna," Alice added. "He fights with his son, Moshe the doctor."

"I'll bet." I spoke too quickly and, I feared, too snarkily. I could envision the hapless Sol with his Borscht Belt vaudeville slapstick, all buffoon and droopy face.

"Did you read Max's letter?" Sol suddenly asked me.

"Of course," I answered. "I can recite parts by heart." Max wrote of being an American, and deeply proud of it, and the need for a voice of reason in the savage wilderness of accusation and calumny. By law, he stressed, American citizens could not be forced to disclose their political viewpoints, and yet, perversely, these poor men were commanded to do so. "My favorite line: 'Now we will create American concentration camps for the honest naysayers.'" I liked that. "Noble."

"They want him to recant," Sol told me.

"What does that mean?"

"To join a patriotic organization like the American Legion, I guess. To sign a loyalty pledge. To apologize. He should admit any errors he made. Penance." Sol turned to Max. "But he's unrepentant."

Max shrugged, the Yiddish comic by way of Jack Benny. "So what's to repent?"

"Metro unloaded Doc Trumbo, others. Fox booted out Ring Lardner, Jr. Hollywood has few heroes these days. But Max is one." He saluted him.

"For God's sake, Solly, I'm not a saint. I said what I had to say. You got to speak up for your friends. I'm not Thomas Paine." He grinned. "Just your garden-variety pain in the *tuckus*."

"A hero." Sol looked at me, awe in his voice. "I couldn't have written that letter." Then, slowly, "Max's touch is all over *Show Boat* but his name has been erased."

I harrumphed, grandly. "I aim to see about that."

"Edna, don't. Not for me." From Max, pleading.

"You'll be blacklisted, Miss Ferber, and branded a Commie sympathizer," Sol said.

"I've been called a lot of things, sir, but I think my American-ism speaks for itself."

Max hesitated. "I thought mine did, too." A gleam in his eye. "Though I did cast a vote for FDR."

Sol added, "America has become a dangerous place."

Silence: the weight of the declaration, awful and raw.

I sat there, staring from one to the other, my gaze taking in these decent folks, good people, earnest, hard-working, loyal, trustworthy. For a split second my pulse raced, wildly. My heart fluttered. In this modest home, drinking coffee with an old friend, I was hit suddenly, as if by a lightning bolt. Fear flooded my soul.

"Are you in danger, Max?" Fear gripped me.

Max didn't answer.

Alice looked worried. "Well, there have been threats. Some phone calls, nasty hate mail. Death threats."

"Dear God!"

"Witch-hunt," Sol muttered.

"What about your friends?" I prodded him. "Years of work in town. In New York. On the road. Your agency, respected. Your tradition with *Show Boat*—all those crews you worked with. Your name *means* something in this town. Your friends?"

"You." Max had a wispy smile on his face.

"You're exaggerating, no?"

Serious: "Edna, there are days I seem only to have enemies. Just enemies."

Chapter Three

The next day Max and I sat at noontime in the crowded coffee shop adjacent to the Cocoanut Grove ballroom at the Ambassador. We'd been there a half hour, fiddling with empty coffee cups, Max twisting a napkin into shredded bits while I ceremoniously checked my lipstick and hair in a compact mirror. I was nervous. Ava Gardner, of course, was late in arriving, but Max told me to expect that.

"Max, why are *you* so nervous?"

He grinned. "I'm not. You are."

"You shredded a napkin into confetti."

"You know I always do that. You're the nervous one, you, the peripatetic novelist who's interviewed presidents and battled with Ethel Barrymore."

"Don't remind me of that battle-ax. And I always check my lipstick twenty times a day. A minute. A second. I'm hopelessly vain." I started to withdraw my compact from my purse but thought better of it.

"Edna, you're *Show Boat*."

"If you call me that one more time, Max, I'll scrape the barnacles off your hide myself."

He scoffed. "Don't believe Hedda Hopper's vicious sniping at poor Ava."

"Well, frankly, I've never read a word of that harridan's incendiary columns. I leave that to the worshipers at the Hollywood shrine. Like moon-eyed George Kaufman, who has told me that Ava's been known to hurl dinner plates across a dining room and curse like a fishwife at quivering souls…and…"

"All true, Edna. A hellion, to be sure. A bottle of booze in one hand, a Coca Cola in the other."

"I've little patience with…"

"But she wants to meet you, Edna."

"I don't tolerate bad behavior unless I'm doing it."

"She's had more than her share of bad press, Edna. That's true. Hedda Hopper and Louella Parsons, two destructive women, choose their victims and then go for the jugular. Hedda with her outlandish hats. She lives in Beverly Hills in a house she calls 'the house that fear built.' They expect you to be afraid, to tremble. But with Ava, they misjudged her."

"And why's that?"

"She doesn't *care*. Her career, her public image, what Metro thinks, what *you* think about her. She's a fierce woman, strong. You want to know something? Edna, she's out of one of your novels, one of your determined heroines. She's like you—a savvy soul who speaks her mind. She's you with more makeup, higher cheekbones, and an MGM contract."

"And she's called the most beautiful woman in the world."

"She is *that*." He tapped me on the wrist. "The artist Man Ray said she could only be truly experienced in person—such is her beauty. It's not important to her, though. Her looks. Hedda Hopper labeled her a home wrecker because of the affair she's having with a married man, and lots of souls can't forgive her. She shows me piles of hate mail calling her a hussy and a snake. The seducer of the boyish Frank Sinatra. You've heard of him?"

"You say his name with such derision, Max."

"Well, I don't care for him. He's an annoying gnat with a blustery ego. Downright nasty at times, especially to waiters and clerks."

"A pleasant voice, I think. Too honey-toned for my taste. He sang 'Ol' Man River' in that horrible movie, *Till the Clouds Roll By*, Sinatra perched up on a white Grecian column, that skinny man lost in that oversized white tuxedo…a travesty. People in the theater laughed out loud. What was MGM thinking?"

"Laughable. Truly. Frankie going on about toting that barge, lifting that bale. Only the part about drinking and ending up in jail rang true to some. And Metro now knows it. That finished him. He's out of a contract now, his career *kaput*."

"A disgrace." I went on. "I knew Jerome Kern. He played his songs on *my* grand piano. Thank God he died before the release of that grotesquerie." I bit my lip and announced, happily, "I'm prepared to dislike Sinatra."

Max smiled. "You won't be disappointed."

The waiter refilled our cups, paused, and then swept up the shredded napkin Max scattered on the table. The young man whistled softly, clicked his heels deliberately, and shuffled off, looking back over his shoulder.

"A bad habit." Max shrugged. "Sorry."

Suddenly Max called out to a man strolling across the lobby. "Larry. Larry." He waited. The man paused, deliberated, seemed ready to bolt out the door, and then thought better of it. Hurriedly, he glanced around the crowded lobby, eyes narrowed, searching, then hesitantly moved toward us. He wasn't happy. "Larry, you've been a stranger."

"Max," the man mumbled, as his icy stare took me in.

"Larry Calhoun," Max told me. "My oldest friend in Hollywood."

A strange line, considering Max's assertion last night that Sol Remnick was his oldest West Coast crony. Yet the words betrayed a hint of sarcasm, bitterness I'd never heard before from Max.

"Mr. Calhoun, a pleasure," I smiled, though I added, "except for the fact that you seem a jumpy rabbit ready for the bush."

He didn't smile back, though Max chuckled. "Larry, sit down." A command, out of character from the soft-spoken man, though Larry—again with the furtive glance around the small room, peering out the French doors into the lobby—slid into a chair. "This is Edna Ferber."

"I know."

"You do?"

Again, the sour frown. "Everyone knows you're in town. You're...*Show Boat.*"

I glanced at Max. "I really need to reassess my public image."

Larry sat there, dutiful, hands folded neatly in his lap, a penitent schoolboy. "How are you, Max?"

"Getting more famous by the hour, it seems."

"I mean..."

Max addressed me, warmth in his voice. "When I first came to L.A., Larry, Sol, and I were inseparable, happy-go-lucky young guys, the three musketeers, tackling Hollywood, making money, climbing up the tinsel ladder, dreaming, dreaming. Back then we invested in an apartment house or two in the valley, some property in the hills, too. Retirement planning, we called it. The three of us shared the little money we had. Years back, of course...when Hollywood was an uncharted Eden and we were three Adams thrashing through the undergrowth. There were no snakes in the garden."

Larry looked into his face and said in a small voice, "That was then."

"And now we have a paradise...if not lost, well, at least in the hands of creditors."

Larry snapped at him, "I don't see you refusing the monthly check from the real estate folks."

"True." Max shrugged. "Edna, Larry was in a few Betty Grable movies. One movie, if I remember, with Myrna Loy. Bit parts, but a line or two. God, how we cheered him on back then! Our friend on the movie screen. The handsome cad. The suave hidalgo, the continental gigolo." He smiled innocently. "Typecasting."

Larry squirmed in his seat. He looked the faded actor, the square-jawed juvenile lead, romantic, with his tall lithe body, the chiseled bronzed face, the full head of carefully combed black-gray hair, an elegant Roman nose a little too red these days with blood vessel speckles. Yet he sported unfashionable sideburns, a pirate's affectation, as though he'd just tottered off the set of an Errol Flynn movie. I imagined he inflamed a few fluttering hearts, even these days, this man with the matinee idol carriage. But his eyes betrayed callowness, a grubbing meanness. They darted too much, the caged animal; their blackness was dull and flat. I didn't like him, though I didn't know him.

"I gave up acting, though I get called for parts—small parts—now and then."

"Are you his agent?" I asked Max.

"God no," Max said. "Larry set his sights on high ground—his first wife knew somebody who knew Paulette Goddard…"

Larry started to stand, then slipped back into the chair. "Sorry to hear about your troubles, Max."

Max shrugged his shoulders. "So I'll live."

"These are tough times." He sucked in his breath and glanced away. "But you *asked* for trouble when you fired off that foolish letter. Christ, what were you thinking?"

Max's voice was rushed. "I was thinking about my friends."

"And you signed that petition against that mouthy senator, and *Red Channels* listed your name…" He seemed to be checking off a list in his head.

"I didn't see your name on it."

Larry snarled, "Nor will you ever. I don't want to lose my job. I got three ex-wives to support."

"Just what do you do, Mr. Calhoun?"

My question seemed to take him by surprise, a puzzler, because he furrowed his brow and seemed unable to answer. Then, with pride, "I'm a manager at Grauman's Egyptian Theatre, where, by the way, *Show Boat* will shortly hold its West Coast premiere. It's a real coup for us."

Max interrupted. "You don't come around the house any more."

Larry stood now, rocked on one leg. "And you wonder why?"

"I know why." But Max was looking at me.

"You can't bring us down with you, Max. You have to understand that. The hint of scandal these days, names bandied about like crazy, the mere suggestion of Communist stuff, sympathies—you know, a death sentence." He swallowed the last two words. "Miss Ferber, good day."

He hurried into the lobby and he didn't look back. Pausing at the registration desk, he seemed to be asking for someone, and then idly glanced back at us. For a second my eyes locked with his. Even from that distance, I could detect fear there, palpable, stark. He turned away, his shoulders hunched as he leaned on the desk.

"A coward," Max grumbled. "The older he's gotten the more frightened he's become. He used to be a roustabout soul like the rest of us. I mean—the three of us had the times of our lives. Then he got scared. Now he plasters photos of Joe McCarthy into a scrapbook."

"I'm so sorry. Some friend."

Max reached across the table and held my hand, tightened his fingers. His touch was oddly cold, stiff.

A low hum swept through the lobby and into the lunch-room. People walking by stopped, their steps frozen, heads tilted. Everyone seemed to be in motion yet, strangely, no one moved. Nearby a busboy, a freckled, red-faced lad with a hawk nose, had been refilling a water glass from a pitcher but now, oblivious, poured water sloppily onto the table. A comic scene, some foolish Marx brothers routine, but the hum got louder still, almost a titter, until I wondered…earthquake?

When I looked at Max, he was grinning.

Every head had turned, as though on oiled ball bearings, toward the center of the lobby where Ava Gardner, striding across the floor, momentarily stopped and looked around. As epicenter of that seismic shift in the earth's rotation, she stood there, checking her watch, as all those around her seemed to lose their minds.

It was, frankly, awesome. This presence one woman could have, electric, galvanizing, stupendous. Everyone was smiling, wide-eyed, like little children surprised by a treat. Only Ava herself, standing there naturally in the center of that space, bringing one hand up to check on her hair, seemed unaware of the rumbling sensation she caused. This was Movies, writ large; this was melodrama on the wicked showboat stage; this was Theater; this was, perforce, a blinding of the noontime sun.

I held my breath, enthralled.

She spotted us and smiled, gave a slight, tentative wave that struck me as oddly insecure. The lonely girl in town who spots an old friend at the bus station.

As she approached our table, the busboy dropped the pitcher, and was immediately admonished by the truculent patron whose lap now was sopping wet. The boy didn't seem to care.

She held out a hand to me, and I shook it. Politely, she'd first slipped off her elbow-length white cotton gloves before she gave me her hand. A nice gesture, and correct. She dazzled, truly, but I was unprepared for her…radiance. A run of movie-magazine catchphrases sailed into my head, and I smiled at them all.

Now I've never favored my own plain looks, not back as a young woman with bushel-barrel hair, and certainly not as I approached my seventies. A part of me had always irrationally resented the easy and fashionable beauties who glided through life. But now, slack-jawed, I found myself watching her. The most beautiful woman in the world, they called her, Hollywood exaggeration and utter blather. Now, frankly, I didn't know who else came close, Helen of Troy having long departed from the world stage.

You saw a woman put together with exquisite care, a black-and-white ensemble of geometric patterns, a white lacy blouse under a sleek black silk jacket with green oriental stitching, over a tight black skirt that hugged her curves at the hip but dramatically flared out at the knee, lampshade style. It was her face that arrested yet excited: those high cheekbones, lightly rouged; the emerald almond-shaped eyes with a slight yellow mote that caught the overhead light; that seductive dimple on her chin, a face encased in a swirl of chestnut curls. Wide, sensual lips, coated in a deep passion crimson, a color so bloodlike it seemed enamel. Luminous porcelain skin with an opalescent cast, vaguely foreign.

"Miss Ferber, I'm sorry I'm late." A low, husky voice, and I thought of Greta Garbo speaking in *Anna Christie*. She leaned in and I smelled exotic perfume, pungent jasmine perhaps, a sweet elixir, heady as thick wine.

Such women were dangerous.

Deadly, but they compelled one to draw close. Ships were wrecked on the coasts of their attention. You had no choice.

I smiled, stammered, "So you're the new Julie LaVerne."

Those green eyes gleamed, catlike. "It's a wonderful part, Miss Ferber. I don't have to show my long legs, and there's even a scene where I'm allowed to look haggard, worn, without makeup. I don't have to look like the glossy prints in *Photoplay*." She struck a model's artificial pose, held it, and then burst out laughing. Her roar was raucous, whiskey husky, a late-night voice, closing time at the bar.

"When Max"—she reached over and touched his cheek, and I swear he blushed—"told me you were his old friend and would be coming out here, I *demanded* a meeting." She winked. "Men don't refuse me anything." She narrowed her eyes. "Except, of course, loyalty. Fidelity. Men seem to be missing those parts of their character."

Somehow I found my voice. "I've never married…"

But she spoke over my words. "And I've married two times and will probably marry over and over and over, like a punch-drunk sailor looking for one more open tavern."

"Why?" I asked.

The question surprised her, so she didn't respond.

Max looked into her face. "So how's Frankie?" His tone was not friendly, and Ava picked up on it, wagging her enameled finger at him.

"Now, now. Francis is Francis, you know. The boy who would be a menace to society. Read Louella Parsons who has her spies working overtime at Ciro's and the Trocadero. Every time we have our spitfire public battles, I read a different version of it the next day in the Hearst tabloids. Frankly, her version of my life is much more interesting than mine."

"Fiction usually is more interesting than real life."

She leaned into me. "Max finds Francis an irritant. Which, of course, he is. But Max doesn't love the scrawny singer. I do. Sadly. Max keeps telling me—Ava, he's a married man. Separated, I say. I may stretch the morals clause in my Metro contract but I don't fully snap it apart." She reached for a cigarette, and, out of nowhere, a waiter bounded across the room to light it.

We ordered lunch—she had chicken salad on rye and a pineapple and cottage cheese salad, and scarcely picked at both, though she ordered two martinis—as I quietly contemplated this Hollywood siren. No fool, this beauty, I realized. In fact, she struck me as quite smart, even witty, a woman in full possession. No, that's wrong—not *full* possession because there was something amiss here, some little-girl desire to be noticed. Helen of Troy with a tragic flaw: insecurity. Vulnerability. Because her stream of words, delightful to listen to, dominated the conversation while laced with something else: she was hellbent on making me *like* her. She had no way of knowing that I already did.

I sat back, the warm spray of her words covering me. She and Max gabbed about the industry, inside gossip, internecine warfare, who was sleeping with whom, who'd lost favor with Louis B. Mayer, who passed out on the dance floor of the Mocambo last night, the night Howard Keel got juiced on martinis, her photo in that girlie magazine *Wink*. The day before, she'd bumped into Mickey Rooney, her first husband, who begged her to go home with him. She'd walked away. I took it all in, delighted by her words. With her flashing eyes and infectious laugh, she was, emphatically, my tragic heroine Julie LaVerne, exiled from the *Cotton Blossom*.

The meal finished, she sat back, stirred her black coffee with a shot of brandy poured in. "I'm reading *So Big*, Edna. You know, when I met my second husband Artie Shaw, well, I'd only read *Gone with the Wind*. I *am* from the South, Edna. You *had* to read that book. Every parlor had a copy placed next to the Bible. We all told our boyfriends we'd…think about it tomorrow. Artie insisted I read Darwin's *Origin of Species* on our honeymoon. I'm not making this up. Quite the aphrodisiac, let me tell you. Can you imagine? Talk about your survival of the fittest. And Thomas Mann, *The Magic Mountain*. One page of that and I'm asleep. No magic there, just a mountain of a book. Too thick a book. My arms sagged…"

I volunteered, "Frankly, a strain on the stomach muscles, such a book."

She laughed. "You said it. To this day I cringe when I see the spine of *Buddenbrooks* in my bookcase. But he did make me into a reader. Sometimes husbands can actually be good for a marriage." Then her voice dipped. "But, unfortunately, he also made me a divorced woman out on the town." She sat up straight and held my eye. "Edna, I'm talking a blue streak, dizzy with being here with you, when I only want to ask you one thing. How can we help Max? This brouhaha about that letter to the *Reporter*. This nonsense of the blacklists. Metro knocking him out."

Taken aback by the sudden shift in conversation, I shrugged my shoulders. "I've been thinking about it…"

That didn't satisfy her. "Too many good souls crushed by this Red menace nonsense. Max a Commie? Preposterous. I've known him for years. Lord, he voted for FDR." She grinned widely. "We all did. Hedda Hopper called my Francis a pinko last week, right after she named me the new tramp in town." She stopped, out of breath.

I fumed. "She should be blacklisted for wrecking the English language."

We all laughed, Ava choking on cigarette smoke.

"We have to think of something." Her fingernail with the red polish tapped her lower lip.

"Enough," Max implored. "Let's talk of *Show Boat*, my *real* passion."

"No, it's *my* real passion, Max. Yes, you've certainly left your mark on each new version, but this movie is my chance of a lifetime." She reached into her purse. "But I have something here to share with Edna. You know what it is already, Max, but keep quiet." She winked at him. "Something that trumps your *Show Boat* stories, dear Max. Even that dried flower you keep from Helen Morgan." She shrugged. "A weed stuck in the pages of your diary. Such a sentimental fool."

Max teased her. "What is it now? An autographed picture of Rita Hayworth?"

She gently tapped him on the cheek. "Fresh boy. Now, Edna, I come from a small dirt town in North Carolina called Grabtown, a desolate red-dirt tobacco town with a whole lot of poverty. Dirt roads, no running water, no electricity. I was a scrappy tomboy who picked the worms off the bright-leaf tobacco and washed the black sap off with lye soap. Back in 1924, when I was two years old, my mama's cousin Minnie worked at a boardinghouse over to Bath by the Pamlico River where a certain lady novelist came to board Charles Hunter's James Adams Floating Theater. Do you remember that?"

I sat up, caught by her words.

A fond memory, of course. I nodded, smiling. "I remember my stay on that wonderful boat, selling tickets, hauling props around, spooning out food, and listening to Charley's amazing memories of life on a showboat as we sailed to Belhaven. It was a goldmine of information and lore from a great storyteller." I grinned. "But when I lit a cigarette in town at lunch, I saw shock on everyone's faces. Women don't smoke in tobacco country. My *Show Boat* grew out of that visit." I scrunched up my face purposely. "But I remember that boardinghouse, Ormond's—the boat was delayed two days in Elizabeth City. I had to rent a room. A smelly place, an old brick house that took in transients, moldy with mice and indigestible food. Gray, grim sheets on the bed that…" I shuddered.

Ava was laughing. "Cousin Minnie delivered eggs and milk daily to that place. She got your autograph." Ava slid a slip of paper across the table, a sheet torn from a school tablet, stained in one corner, wrinkled, but prominently in the center was my thick-inked name: Edna Ferber, followed by a resolute period after the "r."

Edna Ferber period. Always a statement.

I shook my head and passed it to Max.

"When she died," Ava went on, "I got it. My treasure. And now I'm Julie, the best goddamn Julie there will ever be. Helen Morgan and Broadway my foot." She reached out and took the slip from Max and tucked it back into her purse. "An omen, Edna. In the stars, you know. I was crawling through tobacco fields, barefoot and snotty, while in Bath you were creating an empire." She bowed.

Max groaned. "Ah, barefoot girl with cheek of tan. Barefoot girl with plenty of cheek."

"You said it, brother."

"I don't remember Minnie."

"Of course not. No reason to. You hopped around town in an old Ford driven by a Negro boy, plodding through the overgrown graveyard. Everyone *watched* you. Minnie was scared to death of you, she told my mama. You were…famous."

"Well, now you're famous."

She sat silent a long time. "True, but fame isn't what it's cracked up to be, is it, Edna?" Those gleaming green eyes held me.

"No, it isn't."

She was getting ready to leave. "Let me see more of you while you're here, Edna. Max told me you'll skip the premiere—you're a sensible woman—but I'm gonna make you my Southern fried chicken one night. I'm a dammed good cook, though no one believes that. In ten years I'll weigh three hundred pounds, and love it. Not only that but…"

A flash of blinding light, disorienting. I turned to see a photographer bent on one knee, a few feet from the table, his camera aimed at us.

"Damned fool," Ava screamed.

Within seconds a reporter in a wrinkled white linen suit, pad open, pencil at the ready, was next to her. "Ava," he blurted out, "lunch with a Commie?"

Max started to rise but Ava's hand held him down. Her eyes flared, furious, her neck muscles pronounced, scarlet. "Leave us alone."

The hotel manager, alerted, scurried over, frantic, dragging on the reporter's sleeve, blocking the photographer. "Out, out," he yelled.

The reporter announced to no one in particular, "Max Jeffries and Ava Gardner…and some old lady."

I bristled at that. Well, this old lady had a few things to say, so I threw back my head and snarled, "You and your simian crony have the manners of barnyard swine."

Ava looked at me and giggled.

The manager shooed them away, though the gawky reporter, his hat askew and his tie undone, yelled over his shoulder, "Read the *Examiner* tomorrow. Commie at lunch at the Ambassador. Sex goddess turning pink before our eyes…"

Ava, to my horror, stuck out a tongue at him, and the flash went off again.

Watching their retreating backs, I spotted Max's old friend Larry Calhoun still standing by the registration desk, shielded partly by a garish potted palm, one hand pulling a frond across his face.

"I'm so sorry, Ava," Max began.

She stopped him. "I have lunch with whoever I want."

"But your career…this photo…tomorrow…"

"What are they going to do? Fire me?"

His eyes got dull, tired. "Yes."

"Of course not." A ripple in her laughing voice. "After all, I'm their resident love goddess."

"Ava…"

She turned to me. "Edna, I'm a superficial woman. Truly. I see things black and white. I like my friends. I don't like reporters. And I like Max. So it's simple for me. Black and white. I'm …superficial."

Chapter Four

On the phone later that day Ava insisted drinks that night at her home would be fun. "Just a few friends. Alice and Max, of course."

"I'm not good at cocktail parties," I told her.

"I swear I won't throw anything, Edna. I'll behave."

I hesitated, uncertain. I planned a quiet evening in my suite, reading Kathleen Winsor's *Star Money*, though I fully planned to despise it. I'd avoided *Forever Amber*, but I found her newest potboiler at the airport, and for some reason I bought it. I'd already dipped into it and didn't like it. Sentimental balderdash, overwrought emotions, but, said Kitty Carlyle, a boiling read. I'd see about that. "No, Ava, I'm planning to order a pot of coffee with whipped cream and…"

Someone grabbed the phone from her. "I promise I'll behave." Frank Sinatra spoke rapidly. "It's time we met, Miss Ferber. Don't believe what the gossip sheets say about me." Ava said something to him that I couldn't catch. "I'll send a car with my personal bodyguard."

An image of some simian lug head flashed into my mind, some monster with greasy-black hair, his knuckles dragging the ground. A vocabulary of four-letter words grunted at me. A toothpick stuck between his missing front teeth and an odoriferous cigar dancing merrily from his drooling lips.

"Sounds like fun to me." My voice was a little too sarcastic.

"You will?" Ava was surprised.

A small cocktail party at her Nichols Canyon home, a few friends. Three or four people. George Sidney, the director of *Show Boat*, promised to attend but I wasn't to believe that. He always promised and then never showed up. Howard Keel and Kathryn Grayson, possibly. "Edna," Ava said in what sounded like an afterthought, "I live in the country. You have to see my yard."

"Sounds like fun to me," I repeated, softening my voice.

"Edna, don't be mean to me."

"I'm mean to everyone, especially my friends." But I was beaming.

"So you'll come?"

I breathed in, eyed the already dog-eared copy of *Star Money* lying on the nightstand. "I'll come."

◇◇◇

Ava's small house nestled among towering palm trees on a knoll above a wooded canyon beyond Ogden Drive, high up a steep chaparral-banked hillside, a quirky pink stucco house that seemed a prop in a Disney cartoon: a splash of brilliant color against a fantasyland grove of impossibly well-positioned tropical foliage. A white-washed picket fence, incongruous as a frilly bonnet on a streetwalker, surrounded the place, with clumps of brilliant purple and yellow ice plants dotting the landscape. Yellow roses climbed the picket fence, pungent honeysuckle covered a trellis, and beds of petunias lined the driveway.

Odder still, I spied a clothesline behind the small house on which some lace blouses flapped and bellowed in the slight early-evening breeze.

Who was the bizarre woman, Ava Gardner? None of these trappings struck me as *femme fatale* accoutrements, the battler in the nightclubs. Well…maybe the pink stucco. A Negro maid opened the door, and Ava rushed over and introduced her as Mearene. "My Reenie." For some reason Ava squeezed her shoulder, an affectionate gesture that brought a smile to the maid's face, though she scurried away into another room.

"Max and Alice are already here," Ava told me. "Come in."

The walls of the front rooms were painted a daffodil yellow, a burst of springtime that jolted, yet oddly soothed. I expected sleek, chrome-studded Italian sofas and polished glass tables with *faux* Archipenko statues. I discovered overstuffed sofas and armchairs, and stolid wooden tables that I'd expect to find in some old-guard oceanview cottage in Massachusetts. Ava the night owl, always out on the town, doubtless found sanctuary here when she straggled back home, exhausted, at four in the morning.

"I chose *everything*," she stressed. And she pointed to a row of exquisite Degas prints gracing the walls, ballerinas silhouetted against pastel backgrounds. I complimented her.

She led me to the hallway in back—I waved at Alice and Max, sitting on the huge charcoal sofa with drinks in hand—where one wall had floor-to-ceiling walnut bookcases filled, most likely, with Thomas Mann and Charles Darwin. My fingertips grazed volumes of Sinclair Lewis and Hemingway. *Madame Bovary*.

The opposing wall held a succession of black-and-white photographs mounted in simple black frames: stills from earlier productions of *Show Boat*. There was Helen Morgan sitting atop an upright piano, looking forlorn; a doe-eyed Laura La Plante emoting before a handsome Joseph Schildkraut; Jules Bledsoe on a cotton bale chanting the universal dirge, "Ol' Man River"; a stern Edna May Oliver admonishing a rapscallion Charles Winninger, the irascible Cap'n Andy. A kaleidoscope of Julie and Joe and Queenie and Magnolia and Gaylord Ravenal and Parthenia Hawks and Cap'n Andy. On and on, an awesome collection.

"A gift from Max," Ava whispered. Then she winked. "More good omens, Edna."

By the time I returned to the living room Max and Alice were talking to a newly arrived guest. Max stood. "Edna, this is Lorena Marr."

The woman rushed over and grasped my hands. "I only came because Ava said you'd be here. Cocktail parties—even Ava's—made me take to my bed, so much posing and…" She stopped. "Just as I'm doing right now, the first culprit."

Alice spoke up. "Lorena is a reader at Paramount."

Ava added, "And the ex of Ethan Pannis. One of Francis' Hoboken buddies."

A slender woman in a gold lamé cocktail dress and a small sequined hat planted to the side of her close-cropped hairdo, she dropped my hands, half-bowed, and picked up her martini with one hand, a cigarette in the other.

"Shaking hands, Miss Ferber, gets in the way of my cultivating my only two vices." She bowed deferentially. "I've read *Show Boat* so many times there are nights when I return from Ciro's after imbibing too much bubbly that I swear I can hear the iron-throated calliope all the way from the mighty Mississippi."

Ava handed me a martini that I gingerly sipped. Ice cold, perfect.

"That calliope is the sound of coins being deposited in my bank account," I quipped.

"Lord, Miss Ferber, you searched for a gold mine in the muddy river beds while foolish men hammered at rocks in the Rockies."

"Pure luck."

"I doubt that." She grinned. "You've played with the big boys—and won. I admire that."

I liked her, I decided: sharp, quick, clever, attractive. A slick Hollywood concoction, perhaps, but funny. Something about her words seemed practiced and nervous—a desire for my approval?—but the clipped words couldn't disguise the warmth in her eyes.

Ava broke in. "Lorena is a strange Hollywood divorcée. She kicked Ethan out, but still goes out to dinner with him. They're best friends."

"Who exactly is this Ethan Pannis?" I asked.

"Ethan and Tony Pannis. Brothers," Lorena told me in a tone that suggested I should know them. "Frank Sinatra's loyal entourage. Scattering rose petals in his path."

"I was a Pannis bride, too," Alice suddenly announced.

"I don't understand."

Her voice was hesitant. "I was married to Lenny Pannis, their older brother."

Max cleared his throat and spoke rapidly, his voice hollow. "Edna, Lenny died from a fall, and his brothers blame Alice to this day. It's all foolish stuff. Lots of anger there."

Suddenly I remembered George Kaufman's description of Alice: the black widow. George had shown me a sensational clipping from a tabloid: a hollow-eyed Alice sitting in a Los Angeles squad room. Those nasty accusations of willful murder. I'd paid so little attention. Rag-tag journalism, yellow at the edges.

"Well," Lorena confided, "I had to leave darling Ethan. He's somewhat of a prig, a man who measures life with algebraic equations and a calculus disposition. I found him delightful... for three years. Actually *two* of those three years. The third was bitter lemon. I liked his drive and ambition—at first. Cutting back the sails on his dreamboat lessened the man, I'm afraid—made him petty. Nasty." She grinned. "Now that we're divorced, I find him amusing."

Ava jumped in, grasped my elbow. "Don't you love cocktail parties, Edna? We can talk about our exes with abandon. Wait till I get started on Mickey Rooney. My first Hollywood lover. The chipmunk with bedroom eyes. The boy next door as Casanova. Love finds Andy Hardy."

Lorena raised her eyebrows. "Randy Andy by the picket fence."

Alice was the only one who didn't laugh. "Ethan was a mean drunk, Edna."

Lorena defended him, shaking her head vigorously. "That was then, Alice. A bad time. He's a teetotaler now. Ethan paints all his pictures inside the lines. A kindergarten teacher would *love* him." She sipped her drink, but I noticed she watched Alice over the rim of her glass.

Alice frowned. "It took a slap across your face to crash down your house."

Lorena looked annoyed. "All right, Alice. All right. I walked out." She shrugged her shoulders. "So now we're friends. Dinners, movies. We *like* each other. We didn't when we were married."

Alice was shaking her head. "I'd never be comfortable…"

The two women stared at each other, eyes wary, bodies tense.

"Lenny's death sobered him up—a dose of cold water in the face. But by then our marriage had crumbled." She took a drag on her cigarette. "We're different people, you and me, Alice." She glanced my way. "You'll meet Ethan…and his brother Tony." A little chuckle. "You won't be happy."

Alice smiled now. "Lorena and I have become best friends, Edna. Exiles from the Pannis clan."

Lorena grinned at her.

A yelping dog came barreling in from the kitchen, a pudgy corgi Ava introduced as Rags. The dog yipped and spun around, circling the maid who walked in with a tray of appetizers, passed them around, and then, bizarrely, sat next to Ava, chitchatting and smiling. She munched on a canapé. For a second Ava and Reenie giggled about something. Oddly pleasing, that sudden tableau, which told me a lot about Ava.

From across the room Max asked, "And where's Frank?"

Ava stood and looked out the window. "God knows. He *promised* to be here early. It's going to be the few of us. Pop Sidney backed out. So did my manager. So did Howard and Kathryn. Everyone waits for a better invitation." She bit her lip. "The last time they were here Francis insulted them all." Ava lit a cigarette and sat back down. "Max, you know you'd like it if Francis didn't show up."

Anxious now, Ava kept glancing out the front window, biting her lip, distracted. From where I sat, I could watch the driveway. Finally I heard the prolonged blare of a horn, a teenage boy's shrill announcement of arrival, and a sleek Cadillac convertible swerved off the street, breakneck speed, and slammed to a stop on the pebbly driveway alongside a privet hedge. The trellis of honeysuckle shook.

I could hear raised voices from inside the car, shrieks of laughter, someone bellowing what sounded like *barroom barroom barroom*.

Ava, her face pressed against the window, was trembling, her face hard, severe. She sucked in her breath. Her glance took in Max, then Alice, then me, a sweep that communicated apology and sadness.

"Goddamn it." Under her breath.

Frank trooped in, followed by three other souls lined up behind him. "Guess who was hiding out at mi casa, dipping into my liquor cabinet." Frank addressed all of us—all, that is, except Ava, who was fuming, arms folded, her back to the window.

So this was the bobby-soxer phenomenon, this crooner of dreamy hit-parade ballads. The Voice smoothing its way through Italian bel canto rhythms. So scrawny and bony, a pencil, emaciated, a protruding Adam's apple, his body hidden in an oversized black tuxedo jacket, a floppy red bow tie under a hard chin. He flashed an onyx pinky ring. He smiled at me while he was talking to Ava about something I didn't catch, and those riveting deep-sea blue eyes electrified the otherwise skeletal face. A skinny little man, I realized, with a pronounced receding hairline and ears that reminded me of a New York taxi cab barreling down Broadway with both doors wide open.

Ava gulped down a drink and smiled at me. "Time for the floor show, Edna."

Frank approached me. "Miss Ferber, we haven't met. A pleasure." He shook my hand with a surprisingly weak grip.

Then, betraying nervousness I didn't expect, he nodded at the two men standing near him. "Edna, my two buddies, Ethan and Tony Pannis." He didn't introduce the bizarre woman who'd flounced in behind them, now standing in a corner. Both men abruptly moved too close to me and I tried to shrink my already diminutive self. "From New Jersey. Although I knew their big brother Lenny first. He was my good old buddy from the neighborhood—and got me through some tough jams. He saved my life, really." He stopped, seemed in awe of his own words. "These two were youngsters then. Ethan"—he indicated the slender, twitchy man in a severely pressed gray linen suit—"is an accountant at Metro, a money man. And this is Tony." He pointed to a chubby man, his India-ink black hair permed into a Little Orphan Annie bowl of curls, a man dressed in a sequined tuxedo jacket that barely contained his protruding belly. "His younger brother."

"You probably know me as Tiny Sparks, the, you know, comic."

"I've never heard of you."

"You got to get out to the valley. I headline at Poncho's Comedy club."

Frank sang a line, his voice a little shaky, "Down in the valley, the valley so…so…very, very low…"

Ethan shot Frank a puzzled glance, then leaned into him, motioning toward Alice and Max. "You didn't tell us *they'd* be here." Frank shrugged and chuckled. He'd obviously had a few belts at his…casa.

I didn't know what to think of this contradictory duo. The slick accountant with the neat haircut and horn-rimmed glasses, the sensible pale-blue necktie, a conservative feathered fedora held discreetly in hand. And the carnival act, all glitter and riotous confection and blubber.

"We've been dying to meet you," Tony/Tiny said.

I said nothing.

Ava made no attempt to hide her distaste. "Francis," she began, her words low and angry, "what are they doing here?"

He didn't look at her. "They were at my place in Palm Springs when I got back." He smiled. "You said it was a party. I brought a party with me."

Ava glanced at Alice and Max, both sitting on the sofa, looking uncomfortable. "Damn you."

Tony seemed to be happy anywhere that would allow in a man who happened to be wearing a dynamited clown tuxedo covered with green and red and silver buckshot sequins. Tony, I guessed, now spent most of his offstage time as…Tiny. A Hippodrome elephant in a Groucho Marx fright wig.

Ethan looked as though he wanted to be home adding up a column of figures, far from the maddening brother, though, as his brother's resident sheriff, he immediately frowned as Tony walked to the liquor cabinet and poured himself a martini from the pitcher resting there.

"Christ, Tony," he muttered. He nodded at me. "A pleasure to meet you, Miss Ferber."

He nodded at his former wife when she glanced his way, and for a moment they both smiled at each other, though Ethan's quickly disappeared. Lorena, I noticed, seemed to be waiting for something. Ethan stepped closer, and the hard, set face relaxed, became almost boyish.

Oddly, he spoke now in a stilted Elizabethan voice, so lilting it compelled us all to pay attention. "'How now! What do you here alone?'"

Lorena, obviously settling into an old and familiar playfulness, became a fluttering heroine, her voice equally Elizabethan. "'Do not chide; I have a thing for you.'" She winked.

He grinned. "'A thing for me? It is a common thing—to have a foolish wife.'"

She bowed.

For some reason Ethan addressed me, and his severity had returned—that rigid jaw, those unblinking eyes. "And Hollywood said I couldn't write dialogue." He glared at Max, who was ignoring him.

"Well," I countered, "if you're going to plagiarize, you might as well go for the best."

He grumbled. "Shakespeare is over-rated."

A stupid remark, best ignored. Said by the court jester who never learned to jest.

Ethan turned away, a little flustered, but what caught my eye—and sadly so—was the look in Lorena's eyes: a lingering affection there, perhaps unwanted but unavoidable, a bond she'd refused to relinquish. It saddened me, then. I realized that Lorena, despite her feisty, tough-as-nails demeanor, that hard-bitten exterior, might be a foolish woman.

"Ethan," she announced. "You've brought the circus."

"Be nice, Lorena," he pleaded.

"Why would I go out of character?"

He laughed, a dry, brittle laugh that seemed more sardonic than celebratory. Immediately he disappeared into a corner of the sofa, and began picking a trace of Rags' generous dog hair off a pants leg. "In Arabian countries," he told no one in particular, "it's considered unclean to have dogs inside a house."

"I'm a hard-shell Baptist," Ava told him.

"Christ," he mumbled.

Ava looked toward Max and Alice, shrugged her shoulders, and mouthed the words: *I'm sorry*. Max waved back, a thin smile on his face.

Reenie circulated with more appetizers, but deliberately rolled her eyes when she approached Tony, who was mixing his drink with his index finger. For a few minutes I talked quietly with Lorena about her life in the script department of Paramount, but it was a strained conversation. Everyone seemed to be keeping a deliberate, if tense, distance from one another, the two hostile factions content to drink in corners and eye the others over the rims of their whiskey glasses. No one was happy, but maybe Tony/Tiny.

Lorena told me, "As you can tell from our opening skit, Ethan used to be a scriptwriter."

From across the room Ethan shook his head. "For God's sake, Lorena. Not really. One measly script doesn't count. I'm a numbers guy."

"You mean a racketeer," Frank joked. He was pouring himself a drink.

"Yeah, sure thing." Ethan didn't look happy.

Ethan, I noted, drank spring water, refusing liquor. And he eyed Tony who got drunker and drunker, at one point spilling his drink on his sleeve. Now and then Ethan put out his hand, protectively, admonishingly, warning in his eye. When Tony turned away, Ethan slid Tony's glass to the side, the older brother as desperate protector. He saw me looking. "I am my brother's keeper, Miss Ferber. A lot of good it does me."

Tony looked at his brother, squinted. "You won't let me have fun."

"That's because one of us goes to work in the morning, the one who pays your bills."

Tony narrowed his eyes, a trace of resentment there. "I make money at the club."

"Which you toss away."

"Now, boys," Frank began, "remember your old mama in Hoboken."

Ava spoke up. "Francis is loyal to old friends to the point of downright suffocation. Get him talking about playing kick ball with Lenny in the street and he'll get weepy on you."

Frank ignored her. He raised his glass. "To the memory of Lenny, my old boyhood friend."

I toasted someone I didn't know, but I noted that neither Max nor Alice raised their glasses. At the mention of her dead husband—I flashed to that clipping of Alice in a police station—Alice looked down into her lap. Lorena was shaking her head, unhappy. Ava sat with her arms folded, her lips drawn into a straight line.

Tony leaned into me. "Frank takes care of us. Got me the job in the valley. He *knows* people."

Ava spoke over his words. "Max used to be Tony's agent, but Tony deserted Max when…" She stopped, flustered.

Downing his drink and swaying back and forth, Tony bellowed, "When Alice murdered my brother."

The words sailed across the room. Time stopped.

Lorena had been lighting a cigarette but froze, the match burning.

Looking up, Alice gasped.

"Cool it, Tony." Frank spoke through clenched teeth.

"Don't be an idiot, Tony." Ava punched his sleeve. "Not here tonight."

Ethan was frowning. "Tony, shut up."

But Tony couldn't be stopped. "I gotta say it again. She pushed him off that balcony. She got all the money. His money. *Our* money. Lenny *promised* us, remember? She married that…

that fool Max. *Him.*" He pointed at the ashen man. "He was just…waiting."

Ava spoke to me sarcastically. "The legendary Lenny Pannis had lots of money, pots of it at the end of the Hollywood rainbow, at least his brothers believe he did. He ran shadowy businesses and played with the big boys. He was a big shot in this town. Supposedly he made a fortune."

"He did," Tony went on, his words biting. "He *did*. Alice killed him. He was gonna divorce her. The money…" He glared at Alice, who was staring down into her lap again. Max was making rumbling noises, fidgeting in his seat.

I stared at them all, stupefied by this raw and public scene.

"Stop it now," Ethan whispered.

Ava was trying to end the conversation and looked at me. Perhaps she saw disgust on my face, tempered by a little wonder. "The neighbors heard them arguing on the balcony. Lenny, agitated, toppled over. Alice was inside…"

Tony yelled, "That's the phony story the police bought."

Ethan stood abruptly and looked shame-faced. "We shouldn't have come. Tony, get up."

But there was no stopping the drunk man. "I *fired* Max. He was an accomplice to murder."

Ava sneered. "And look at the jobs you've been getting ever since."

"Hey, I'm doing all right." He pointed at Max. "You ruined all our careers, Max."

Max started to say something, but Alice put her hand on his knee. He blinked wildly at her.

"Say good night, Tony." Ethan prodded him.

I turned to Ethan. "And what do you think of Max?"

Ethan deliberated, cool, quiet, steely-eyed, turning from me to glare directly at Alice. He spoke to her. "He married the woman who murdered my brother, Miss Ferber. We just can't prove it. And on top of everything else, now we learn he's a Commie. Max is filled with surprises."

Silence. An awful silence.

Ava sidled up to Frank and watched as he poured himself a drink at the sideboard. I didn't hear what she whispered to him, though Frank, gulping down a drink, spoke loud enough for all of us to share the moment. "Hey, I got friends, too. You did say party. I only party with friends."

Ava whispered something else, but he turned away. He caught my censorious eye—a look I'd perfected and executed on even more annoying members of the lesser species—but he simply smiled that charming witchcraft smile. A hard nut to crack, this Sinatra boy, a crooner confident in his power to attract. I figured it was time he met his match.

The two Pannis brothers huddled in a corner, Ethan whispering in Tony's ear. The woman who'd followed them in—she'd stood in a corner the whole time—now tucked her arm around Tony's waist.

I sat back as Max nudged me.

"Edna." Max tried to make a joke. "You don't look like you're having fun."

"I didn't expect to." I sipped my drink. "I'm too old for these shenanigans." I pointed a narrow finger around the room. "This tinseltown soap opera."

"I expect you never liked cocktail parties…ever," Alice added.

"Like New Year's Eve parties, which I avoid like the plague, cocktail parties thrive on forced hilarity and futile dreams of new and unexpected pleasure."

"Good God," Lorena howled.

"Then what do you do for entertainment?" Alice asked.

"Well, I go to cocktail parties and New Year's parties. I like to watch people fail at their dreams."

Max shook his head during the abrupt pause that followed my comments. "Don't believe her, Alice. The people Edna watches will end up in one of her novels. She's memorizing our scintillating dialogue right now."

"Don't flatter yourself, Max," I chided. "George Kaufman you're not."

The woman who was hanging onto Tony's sequined sleeve squealed at something he said, and then apologized. She clung to Tony, sipping the drink he'd handed her, but she looked frightened, as though she couldn't understand what had just happened in the room. Now she was whispering in Tony's ear, and he didn't look happy.

"Is that Tony's keeper?" I asked Alice.

Max, listening, answered. "Liz Grable."

"Tell me about her."

Max brushed an affectionate hand across Alice's face. "See, what did I tell you? The novelist."

"Is she Betty Grable's misguided sister?" I wondered aloud.

Alice smiled as Max spoke in a soft voice. "Her name is Liz Carnecki. A fledgling actress, at least a decade ago. She thought a name change would usher her into stardom."

"Did it work?"

"She's still trying, God knows where. I was her agent for a split second, a favor to Tony way back when, but I could rarely place her. Nowadays she works in a hair salon on Hollywood Boulevard. Hair Today. Can you imagine? She's got an efficiency that's way, way out by the Hollywood Cemetery on Santa Monica Boulevard, where Tony squats these days."

Liz Grable/Carnecki was now staring at me, mouth agape, showing too many capped teeth. Had she heard us chatting about her? An impossible woman, I realized, all bamboozle and peroxide, hair so teased and puffed and platinum she looked like cotton candy at a fair. A woman in her forties—those lines could no longer be disguised by all that pancake makeup—she attempted a sweet twenty-something starlet look with that round bright red blotch on each cheek, that Clara Bow cupid's mouth, that tight cobalt-blue fringed cocktail dress slit up one leg, and a stenciled leopard pattern scarf around her shoulders. A shock of seashells—yes, they had to be seashells gathered on some California strand—circled her powdered neck. She was, I suppose, perfect for Tony/Tiny, though I hereby confess a definite orneriness in my description of the bodacious lass.

"Miss Ferber!" She came sailing across the room, and I feared a catastrophic collision. "I was telling Tony last night that I would make a *perfect* Sabra Cravat in any remake of *Cimarron*. I was *born* in Oklahoma. And I hear you're finishing your book on Texas. I *know* oil wells. My papa…"

Tony/Tiny, her sequined conquering hero, dragged her away.

Lorena leaned into me. "Are you ready to leave yet?"

"I'm always ready to leave a party."

Lorena lowered her voice. "I can't believe they all showed up here, Edna. Everyone has been so careful to…to *avoid* these encounters. And that drunken attack by Tony—well, we've heard it before."

"Is Tony always like this?"

Lorena glanced at Tony. "He's often the one everyone likes— when he's sober. He can be sweet—used to be sweet. But when he drinks…"

"Why are they here?"

"Frank brought them here on purpose—to rile Ava. He had to know. Ethan and Tony refuse to be in the same room as Alice. Frank *knows* that. And Frank can't stand Liz. To bring *her* here…"

"She's not a favorite of yours?"

Lorena shrugged her shoulders. "I'm too unglamorous for her. And of no importance. She tends to ignore the other women in the room. Liz spends her days clipping hair and waiting to be discovered like Lana Turner at the Tip Top Café on Highland Avenue."

"It's not going to happen?" I injected wonder into my words.

"Not in this lifetime, even out here in fantasy land." But Lorena seemed to regret her words. "I shouldn't mock her. She is who she is. It's the boys I should be angry with."

The two hostile camps settled into different corners of the living room, though every so often Tony hurled hostile looks at Alice. Max was mumbling about leaving, repeatedly checking his wristwatch. Alice whispered, "A little longer, Max. Just for Ava's sake."

But Ava wasn't happy. Her strides across the room were abrupt, jerky. Frank stood next to the liquor cabinet, his tongue rolled into his cheek, the wary battler, eyeing her, waiting, waiting. Lorena and I made small talk about Agnes Moorhead who played Parthy in *Show Boat*, an actress we both knew slightly and who now, Lorena informed me, was unhappy with the way her lines were cut in the movie, making her a one-dimensional harpy. We watched Liz Grable, lipstick smeared on one side of her mouth, pick her nervous path across the floor to Frank's side, where she proceeded to vamp and titter like a schoolgirl flirtation. From where I sat I could pick out her coy flattery, as her fingers grazed his sleeve. Nodding silently, Frank leaned into her, made a loud, cruel observation about cheap Woolworth's perfume and looked ready to shove her away. Hurt flooded Liz's face, her eyes blinking wildly. Any moment she'd burst into tears.

Lighting a cigarette, Ava watched the scene carefully. One false move on Frank's part, I suspected, and she'd tear across that room, nails extended, clawing Liz's powder-puff face to shreds. But Frank turned away, delicately maneuvering Liz out of his path, and Ava leaned against the wall. Her chest heaved, a spasm of utter sadness escaping her.

The party died. Voices drifted off, eyes closed, weary. Drinks slipped onto the floor, and a funereal pall settled in the room. I'd been chatting to Lorena about something Agnes Moorhead told me during her visit to New York when I became aware that my voice was the only sound in the room. Bothered, I looked up into a sea of blank, accusing faces. Tony, eyes narrowed, was glaring at Max, who stared back, bothered. Alice had leaned into her husband protectively, her fingers gripping his sleeve.

Suddenly I wondered how drunk Tony really was. His look conveyed more sloe-eyed resentment than, say, an inebriate's sloppy anger. How much of his drunken spiel was a deliberate act? There was caginess in his eyes as he surveyed the room. A sweet man? I wondered at Lorena's words. A man definitely hard to read. His severe stare moved to Alice, his former sister-in-law, and the rubbery face contorted, tightened. It was, frankly, an awful moment, rank as a battlefield wound. The room shuddered.

Ethan had been sitting next to him, moody, withdrawn, his eyes also on the black widow Alice, but now, jarred by Tony's grunting and jerky moves, he roused and reached out to grip Tony's arm. "Stop it, Tony." Words said softly, but forcefully.

"No, it ain't right. What she did."

"Not now. For God's sake."

"You take too much crap, Ethan."

"Look around. People are *watching* you."

"Who gives a damn?"

Frank spoke up. "You're acting like a creep, Tony." He motioned to Ethan, snapping his fingers. "Okay, take him home, Ethan. He's too drunk. Get him the hell outta here."

Liz Grable suddenly got protective, one of her arms cradling Tony's shoulders, drawing him in. "He's in a bad way tonight." She looked at me, apologizing. "Tony's a…lost boy. I'll take care of him."

"Take him home, Ethan. Now! Do you hear me?" Frank's words thundered in the room.

"Yeah, sure," Tony sneered. "Let's leave Adam and Ava in their little paradise." He brightened. "Isn't that what you called them, Ethan? Adam and Ava."

Ethan reddened and shot a nervous glance at Frank.

"Now!" Frank snapped his fingers again. His foot stomped on the floor. "Goddamn it all. Scram!" One of the Degas prints on the wall shifted.

Tony's voice became a plaintive howl. "She married a goddamn Commie, Ethan." He swayed, nearly fell. "We're sitting in a room with a Commie." He pointed a finger at Max. "You ain't loyal to America, Max. Ain't it enough that you ruined all—yeah, *all*—of our careers. Me and Liz and…and everyone else. But you turn your back on America. Christ Almighty, what a city. You"—he spoke at Alice—"kill my brother and then shack up with a pinko."

I stood, ready to leave, tired of this maddened scene. Outside Frank's bodyguard/driver was sitting patiently in a town car— not, I hasten to add, the monosyllabic gorilla I'd anticipated, but, rather, a gentle giant who fussed and salaamed before me, the perfect gentleman. I only saw the gun in his inside pocket when he bent to pick up some dropped car keys. He was out there now, patient, this Sir Galahad, my chariot ride back to my cocoon at the Ambassador.

"Good night." I raised my voice.

Ava pleaded. "Edna, I'm sorry."

"Delightful evening."

"I'll make it up to you."

"That's what I'm afraid of."

"Now!" Frank thundered again. I was the one who jumped and grabbed my throat.

"Commie," Tony repeated.

Alice had started to sob as Max maneuvered her from the sofa, headed to a side door. As he passed Ava, she reached out and touched his cheek, a quick, reverential gesture that reminded me suddenly of Julie, exiled from the showboat, leaving in darkness and gently touching the swarthy cheek of Joe as he mourned her expulsion. I expected strains of "Ol' Man River" to swell now, a clichéd Hollywood crescendo. But no: silence in the room. Little Rags leapt around, rattled by the tension, his noisy panting and yelping a soundtrack to the evening's ragged coda.

And then, almost as though a chapter was skipped in a book, the room emptied, everyone gone. Alice and Max left by the kitchen door, quietly. Lorena hastily shooed Ethan, Tony, and Liz into her car, taking them away. I had intended to be the first to leave, so I had no idea why I was still there, standing in the center of the room, the referee announcing the next battle between Ava and Frank. Adam and Ava in paradise my foot!

Outside my charioteer was most likely standing next to the passenger door, fingering the tattoo of MOM he doubtless had on a concealed bicep. He was probably checking his pistol in case I got feisty on the ride back.

"Good night," I said again.

Ava breathed in. "Edna, Tony isn't always like he was tonight. He's a…quiet man. Lately he's been getting worse—drunk and…" She sighed. "He has bad nights. If you meet him another time…"

"I'd rather not," I interrupted.

Frank snickered. "His life is going nowhere."

Ava readied another apology, but Frank looked at me as if I were the tidal wave that had caused such havoc in the room. I sensed he didn't like me, the old biddy come a-calling. He was looking from me to Ava, a gaze that was both dismissive and furious.

"Good ni—" I stopped. Those were the only two words left in my lexicon, starved as it now seemed to be.

Frank bit his lip and watched Ava through half-shut eyes. "Hedda Hopper called me a Hoboken has-been. On the way out of this miserable town." He swiveled around to face me. "You're a savvy old broad, Edna. Tell me, do you think I'm a Hoboken has-been?"

I waited, steamed. He shouldn't rile this admittedly savvy old broad. "Frank, I didn't know you were from Hoboken."

The line hung in the air, bloody, cruel.

Ava burst out laughing. "Edna, I love you."

"Well, I don't." Frank pulled at the goofy red bow tie and backed away. "Good night, Edna." He sneered my name, drawing it out.

"Francis," Ava started in. "This is all your fault. You drag these sorry failures to my house."

"Maybe I'm one, too."

"Maybe you *are*," she stressed. Then she spoke in a hollow, wispy voice. "I don't know why everybody has to be…enemies."

Frank turned his baleful eye on her. It was preparatory, I sensed, to an evening of battlers' rage, broken cocktail glasses, upturned tables, shoving, tears, perhaps even a Degas print smashed to the floor.

"Christ Almighty," he hissed with a sickening grimace, "You gotta have enemies, Ava. You know that. How the hell else do you know you're alive?"

Chapter Five

Frank Sinatra was not in a good mood. I knew that because, though I'd not seen his face yet, the back of his neck was crimson, his shoulders were hunched, and he was tapping his right foot nervously on the floor. Ava faced him, unsmiling. As the maitre d' escorted me to their table, she looked past him toward me and attempted a welcoming smile. The tapping of the right foot stopped suddenly.

The taxi had just dropped me off at Don the Beachcomber on North McCadden Place, and I imagined myself deposited, reluctantly, onto a movie set for some Busby Berkeley pineapple-and-luau extravaganza. Garish spotlights, some revolving from the rooftop, illuminated massive palm trees silhouetted against an ocean-blue backdrop touted as the "island of Mahuukona." Worse, the maitre d' who grasped my elbow, an obsequious gentleman who was obviously expecting me, was dressed in a flowing Hawaiian shirt so ostentatiously decorated with blood-red hibiscus blooms that it brought to mind ancient blood-letting and savage sacrifice. Maidens hurled willy-nilly into the mouth of a seething volcano, lava steaming. Yet he spoke in a flat Brooklyn accent and smelled of cheap cigars.

Ava rushed to embrace me but held on too long, whispering something in my ear I didn't catch. Frank stood, turned, that enormous toothy grin switched on; he extended his hand, performed a half-bow. He pulled a chair out for me.

"Edna, I was worried you'd abandon us," Ava said.

"Not a chance. I'm certain to be featured in some gossip sheet by morning."

Only Ava laughed. "And Alice and Max are late. After all, it's *his* birthday dinner."

They'd been drinking, I could tell, and two ashtrays already held snubbed-out cigarette butts, though a passing waiter seamlessly made both disappear, each replaced with a sparkling clean one. Frank immediately started talking of an encounter earlier with a pesky photographer as they'd pulled up in his Cadillac convertible. "You see, Miss Ferber, he was hiding behind that trellis of bougainvillea, like a night prowler, and jumped out, scaring us to death." Still seething, he sputtered to a stop.

Ava added, "Francis yelled, 'Beat it, you crumbs,' and knocked the camera out of his hand, and they…tussled. Francis scraped a knuckle." Frank held out his hand to prove she wasn't lying. Ava glanced at him. "I don't know why you have to grapple with them. It only makes it worse, you know."

Spitfire words, furious. "They're bums. All of them."

"Still…"

"Ava, not now, doll."

She shrugged. "Quite the place, no, Edna?"

My eyes swept the cavernous room. Plastic palm trees, a virtual forest of green disaster. Bizarrely, there were stuffed pudgy monkeys hidden among the lacy fronds. "Beautiful."

"They have the best rum zombies here," Ava told me.

"Zombies? Like the living dead? Why am I not surprised? That's all of Hollywood, no?"

Frank shot me a look as though I'd lapsed into dialectical Farsi. He downed his drink and brusquely signaled the waiter for another. When the waiter neared, Frank stuck a cigarette between his lips and demanded, "Match me." The waiter hurriedly lit the cigarette.

He was rubbing his bruised knuckle. I saw a trace of blood there, broken skin.

"I should sue that damn photographer hack. My knuckle's gonna swell up tomorrow, you know…"

Ava ignored him. "Edna, what are you drinking? A zombie? They got this drink they invented called the mai tai. Rum is king here."

"So I gather from the garish placards outside. I'll have a glass of red wine."

Ava insisted. "The zombies are…"

Frank rapped his good knuckle on the table. "You and those goddamned zombies. The woman can choose her own drink, Ava. Christ."

"I'm only suggesting…"

"Leave her alone."

I ordered a glass of wine.

Ava smiled at me. "We do love each other, Edna. You have to believe that."

"Thank God for that. No one else would have either one of you."

Both Ava and Frank stared at me, though Ava smiled. "Christ," Frank muttered. And I swear he mouthed something about old crazy broads.

"All right, Francis dear, let's have a pleasant evening."

"Yes," I added, "dining with stuffed monkeys watching me will be a sobering experience."

Frank seemed to notice the monkeys populating the plastic palms for the first time. "This place is a dump."

"I like the booze here," Ava said.

"You like the booze everywhere."

Somehow, through some sleight of hand I'd missed, my glass of wine appeared before me. "Cheers," Ava toasted. "To *Show Boat*."

Frank smiled. "Life on the wicked stage."

Ava checked the entrance. "Where *are* they?"

I bristled, ready to leave this boorish young man—and, I suppose, boorish young woman—both wreathed in noxious clouds of cigarette smoke, their voices strangled with whiskey. All a bit wearying, if familiar. Old ladies should be spared the sight of the next generation sinking into a quagmire of dissolution. Sort of saps one's faith in the progress of humankind.

Ava, I quietly concluded, was a tantalizing dish best savored away from the whiskey chaser that was her smarmy boyfriend.

Frank excused himself. "Call of Hoboken nature."

Ava began apologizing. "We bring out the worst in each other, Edna. But, trust me, also the best. We're so much alike—wild, jealous, craving the nightlife. Hot-headed fools, you know. We're two insomniacs, lonely night animals wandering the desert. But I didn't want *you* to see this. It's just that…that photographer set Francis off, and that set *me* off and…"

I sipped my wine. "It's all right, Ava. Years back I weathered the besotted members of the Algonquin Club in New York. After that experience—can you imagine Dottie Parker inebriated, her mouth running in top gear?—anything is bearable." I batted my eyes. "Even you…and Francis."

Frank returned, stopping to light a cigarette from one of the blazing tiki torches that speckled the room.

"Miss me?"

"We never stopped talking about you," I noted.

"I'll bet." He narrowed his eyes.

For a while the squabble subsided, a sticky truce in which both drank too much, smoking incessantly, voices subdued but edgy. Unhappy, I snatched a Chesterfield from Ava, and Frank gallantly lit it. His fingertips were stained yellow. In the flickering candlelight of the table, I noted scars on his neck and cheek. A scrapper, I concluded. The Hoboken one-hundred pound runt bullied in the schoolyard who learned the most effective offense is cruelty and crooning.

"You look gorgeous," Ava told me.

With a rose-colored shawl draped over my shoulders, accenting a polka dot black-and-white dress, I felt like someone's visiting aunt.

But of course she was the gorgeous one, dressed in a slinky cocktail dress of lavender-toned marquisette with a strapless top of shimmering green taffeta, an oversized turquoise brooch pinned on the bodice, drop earrings that went on and on, cut emeralds mounted in filigreed silver cascades that caught the glint and flash of overhead lights. Frank wore a powder blue Norfolk suit with a scarlet bow tie; his hair was slicked back, oiled.

Max and Alice bustled in, apologizing. Max was waving what he announced was a clipping from the morning's *Examiner*. "The paper has a photo of me and Ava and you having lunch yesterday. They mentioned you by name, Edna."

"What does it say?"

"No article, just a photo with a long caption. You, readers are informed, won the Pulitzer Prize for *So Big* back in 1924. I am identified as a 'Hollywood insider currently under a cloud.'" His face animated and yet ashen, he kept tapping the torn sheet.

Ava broke in. "Happy birthday, Max." She stood and approached him, enveloping him in a bear hug. "Let's be happy tonight."

He grinned back at her, but I noticed he didn't put the clipping away. He simply laid it on the table, face up, next to an ashtray.

We ordered a tableful of grotesque dishes no one seemed eager to eat, plates of Cantonese specialties that had migrated too far from the Chinese homeland: Bo Lo Gai Kew with sweet and sour sauce, chicken chow mein with water chestnuts, sesame beef with bell peppers, almond duck. Column A and column B. And everything garnished or disguised or simply destroyed with chunks of pineapple, for me the least interesting of tropical fruits.

Frank skewered a chunk of pineapple at the end of a knife, and then dropped it. It plopped onto the carpet and, again, by some magical sleight of hand, when I glanced down at the spot, the offending fruit had disappeared. Tiki voodoo, I supposed. Frank retreated into his own thoughts, his eyes scanning the room, and I noticed Ava sometimes followed his hazy gaze. If his eyes rested too long on some fluttery young beauty batting her kohl-rimmed eyelids—and they seemed to be generously

positioned throughout the room like opening-night spotlights—
Ava bit her lip and groaned.

I'd heard stories.

Ava moved her chair closer to mine and smiled. "Max, if you'll
forgive me, I want Edna to see one more…omen."

Dramatically, she reached under her chair and brought up a
small black velvet box. For a second she cradled it against her
chest, lovingly. She opened it as though it were a Christmas
present. In her palm she displayed a pair of green satin shoes,
worn, tattered, the heels blackened.

"Edna, my sister Bappie won these at a charity auction in
New York years ago. When she visited back home, she gave them
to me. 'These will take you to Hollywood.' Her exact words.
Irene Dunne wore them when she played Magnolia in the 1936
Show Boat." She thrust them at me, but I didn't take them: two
scuffed, dirty shoes, doubtless a wonderful talisman for her, but,
to me, nothing more than someone's old and bacterial slippers.

"Beautiful." I figured that would be the operative word for
this doomed evening. Beautiful. Just plain beautiful.

Ava was going on about Bappie's husband, a Manhattan
photographer who'd taken the first photo of her, displaying it
in his Fifth Avenue window where it was spotted by some scout.
Ava as virginal country girl, with sunbonnet and a faraway look
in her eyes. MGM offices, located in Times Square, called for
a screen test and…and a Hollywood contract. Fifty dollars a
week, Ava and Bappie traveling west by bus. The dream began.

Suddenly Frank's hand swept across the table and sent the
shoes flying. They landed at the foot of a blazing tiki torch.

Ava screamed. "Damn you." Leaning across the table, she
slapped Frank's face, and he recoiled, rubbing the scarlet patch
on his cheek. Immediately Ava crumbled. "Oh, Max, this is not
the evening I planned for you."

I said nothing.

Welcome to Hollywood.

Frank was unrepentant. "Ava, for Christ's sake, do I gotta
listen to that story again? You drag out those…those moldy shoes

in a restaurant…like…I don't know. It's…boring. Remember that night you babbled about showboats and tobacco fields and your mama's cooking to Louis B. Mayer? Christ, his eyes glazed over." He inhaled his cigarette. "I wanna get you on a showboat to China." He must have thought the line uproariously witty because he guffawed—and then sang it out, trilling the cadences. *I wanna get you on a showboat to China.* He rubbed his cheek.

Everyone in the restaurant was staring. Quietly, a waiter returned her shoes, and Ava tucked them away.

"Edna *understands* my…omens."

"The past is over."

"As good a definition of 'past' as I've heard," I sniped. He glared at me.

"Omens, my ass." He was still staring at me. "You think some old lady cares a damn for this claptrap."

I sat up, spine erect. "I certainly do, young man. I make my living going into the past."

Frank ignored me, though his look suggested I was a foolish old ninny, out to final pasture.

Silence, uncomfortable, the room settling back to normal, glasses clinking, laughter across the room, sporadic tinkling ukulele music suddenly piped in and obviously amplified. Tiki magic, again.

◇◇◇

Over coffee Max picked up the clipping from the *Examiner,* but now he was smiling. "I don't like being photographed from this angle. Did you know that Hedda Hopper recently called me a nervous ferret?"

I could tell he wanted to discuss the violation. His fingers drummed the sheet.

"Perhaps we shouldn't discuss it now." Alice tapped his sleeve affectionately.

Ava smiled thinly and half-waved at me, shrugging her shoulders. It was a gesture suggesting fatalism, the price you paid for living out here; but in the next moment she reached across the table and gently touched Max on the cheek. Immediately he quieted, grinned sheepishly, and closed his eyes dreamily. Lord, I thought: Circe and her exquisite charms. The ravishing Lorelei leading men to rapturous shipwreck.

The last time I touched a man's cheek it was, unfortunately, a crackerjack slap. The offending cheek was Aleck Woollcott's chubby one, just after he informed the dinner guests that one needn't call a dog a bitch when Edna Ferber was in town. Of course, I'd begun the conflagration by calling him, this three-hundred-pound mountain of sarcasm and salt-water taffy, a New Jersey Nero who mistook his pinafore for a toga. Ah, the old days at the Algonquin when our frivolous battles and repartee were chronicled in F.P.A.'s "The Conning Tower." Now my name appeared in Hollywood gossip sheets as an East Coast busybody. And Commie sympathizer, at that.

Ava's sensual touch was something I'd never acquired—nor, frankly, wanted.

"This is all getting to Max," Alice said. "I've suggested we go to New York for a visit. See friends. Some theater."

I stared into Max's beaten face, his eyes red-rimmed and tired.

"Well, I'm here another week. Fly back with me, you two. We can do theater…"

Max spoke quickly. "No. I can't leave my friends."

Frank sneered. "Why not? They've all left you."

Ava pointed her cigarette at him. "Francis, be nice."

He gave her a sickly-sweet grin and actually winked, some conspiratorial gesture that elicited a groan from her.

"I could care less about any of this nonsense in the gossip columns, especially Hedda Hopper's twaddle," I began. "The woman is trying to sell newspapers, having already surrendered her soul. What alarmed me was today's front-page article in the Los Angeles *Times* that discussed the ratcheting up going on in Washington now. Did you read that? And now this Joseph McCarthy yammering about Red infiltration in government offices. I feel as though the country I love—know to my marrow—is in danger of irreparable transgression. *More* transgression. Lord, we weathered that madman Hitler and the concentration camps and the A-bomb and now…" I waved a hand in the air, helpless.

"Does anyone really care about Hollywood?" Alice asked.

"I don't," Ava announced, midway through lighting a cigarette.

I reached for a cigarette and Frank cavalierly lit it for me. As he leaned in, I smelled musky cologne that reminded me of wood shavings. The blue-gray smoke oddly calmed me as I went on. "According to the article, when the Hollywood Ten went to Washington in 1947, they left L.A. with a crowd cheering them on at the airport but, arrived there, they realized how *alone* they were in Washington, once removed from this…this celluloid cocoon out here. The rest of America—all those *Saturday Evening Post* and *Coronet* readers in the heartland—think Hollywood and imagine scandal, deception, intrigue, unbridled sex, infiltration, Commie this, pinko that."

"If you want to know what I think…" Ava started.

But I wasn't finished and raised my voice. "But it's a contradiction, don't you see? Hollywood is, perversely, America itself. The studios *invent* an America for the world to look at. Not a real place but a movie hall oasis—*The Wizard of Oz, Gone with the Wind*, John Wayne's *Rio Grande*, the Busby Berkeley dance spectaculars. *Cinderella*. Even *Show Boat*, a fantastic portrait of an America that's sugar-coated and inviting." I stopped. "The capital of the United States is not Washington D.C. In some bizarre sense it's Hollywood." I crushed out my cigarette and sat back.

Listening to me, Frank sat back, a cigarette bobbing between his lips. He had a wise-guy smirk on that skinny face, and those marble-blue eyes twinkled. Suddenly, mockingly, he began a slow handclap: one two three four. Space between each resounding clap.

Ava squirmed. "Francis, for God's sake."

"I think it's a bang-up speech," he protested. "Worthy of that bastard Louis B. Mayer. Jack Warner couldn't have topped it—better than that weepy apology he delivered before the HUAC, in fact."

Max looked at me with utter admiration. "You said it, sister."

I roared. Max's clipped voice, exaggerated now with a squeak in it, had the same amused tone he'd employed, years before, at the National Theater in Washington D.C. at the *Show Boat* tryout. Echoes of: "This is all your fault, Madame *Show Boat*." At that moment we must have been thinking the same thing, for he mouthed the very words at me: Madame *Show Boat*. Only I noticed. I tilted back my head and winked at him.

Ava turned to Alice and nodded toward us. "Darling, those two have something going on."

"I hope so," Alice answered. "And I'm happy about it."

Ava put down the cigarette she'd been toying with for a minute or so. "This'll all blow over."

"What will?" Frank asked, testily.

"You know, this Commie stuff. Every so often a bunch of dizzy gnats swirl around the picnic table, irritating everyone, making everyone think it's a plague of Biblical locusts. Then the sun shines and they're gone. America is like that—we got good people here."

"Yeah, Ava." Frank sucked in his cheeks. Unexpectedly, he got reflective. "My agent told me to back off public statements. In fact, he said it's time to join a pro-America organization. You know, *Red Channels* will remove your name from their list of pinkos if you publicly take a loyalty oath and join, say, some flag-waving group."

Max groaned. "You're not serious, Frank."

"I'm just saying…"

I drew my tongue into my cheek, waited a moment. "Have you considered the Daughters of the American Revolution?"

"The Sons of Italy," Ava giggled.

Frank was taking this all too seriously. "No, it's got to have 'America' in the name."

"You're kidding." From Alice.

Ava chuckled. 'The American Sons of the Italian Revolution."

Everyone laughed, especially Frank, laughing at himself.

The conversation drifted away from the explosive topic as Ava shared an anecdote about Howard Keel sneaking tequila into his dressing room. Keel, I gathered, a show-business trooper with matinee-idol looks, was a bit of a character, a rollicking scamp who enjoyed his late-night revelries.

I nursed my glass of merlot, while Ava and Frank finished off their zombies. But what alarmed me was that Max, famously an infrequent drinker, a man who joked that he got tipsy on rum cake, seemed hell-bent on getting drunk. Not pretty, that picture, though I sensed that the morning's photograph in the *Examiner* had wound him up. Here was the birthday boy in the land of the zombies. Avoiding Alice's disapproving eye, he kept signaling for another drink. At one point he sloshed liquor onto the tablecloth and seemed surprised that someone had behaved so indecorously.

The mood at the table shifted when Louella Parsons led an entourage to a nearby table. The Hearst gossip columnist glared at our table as she passed, and she emitted a raspy harrumph that would do justice to the hectoring Parthenia Hawks as she watched the sleight-of-hand gambler Gaylord Ravenal step onto the showboat. Max laughed out loud, a hiccoughed titter, and seemed unable to stop.

Dressed in a muddy red dress that exaggerated her small, chunky build, Louella Parsons kept looking over, particularly at me, the shrinking violet at the table; and I wondered whether she knew who I was. Doubtless, given my photo in the *Examiner*, chummy with Ava and the Commie. Perhaps she was feeling scooped, and now, perforce, was hoping I'd execute some egregious *faux pas*—an unseemly belch, a toppling onto the floor, swooning at Frank's knee and revived by ammonia salts held under my nose—that would enliven tomorrow's mean-spirited diatribe for the Hearst readership.

On my best behavior—I do have a few of those moments, Aleck Woollcott notwithstanding—I smiled back at her, even tilted my head. The dreadful tyrant—a squat fireplug wrapped in that ill-chosen dress, perching on a chair and sipping some grotesque concoction that looked like cough medicine—shared a second, though *sotto voce*, harrumph, and turned away. I was immensely happy.

I didn't notice the young man approaching our table. Ava, of course, did, attuned as she most likely always was to the serendipitous attention of all the men in the world, whether he was a hayseed boy or a tottering codger. Men zigzagged through her life, giddy and ready to blather inanities at her. So Ava had already turned, the huge smile at the ready, as the young man tentatively neared. Perhaps late twenties or early thirties, he was a dark-complected man in a pristine Army uniform, his cap held tightly in his hand. On his face a puppyish grin, two pinpoints of red dotting his cheeks. He looked the wholesome farm boy, athletic and sturdy, that new American breed, the extra for a World War Two propaganda newsreel.

"Miss Gardner," he stammered. "I hate to disturb you but…" He stopped, and from under the Army cap he withdraw a slip of paper and a pen. His hand shook. "I'm rude, I know, but…" The sloppy Peck's bad boy grin. Andy Hardy from the front lines. D-Day boy, now delivered safely home.

Ava waved him closer. "You're not disturbing me, handsome."

The man shuffled close to her and he was visibly trembling, which amused me. Who was this Hollywood Helen of Troy who could easily topple the topless towers of Ilium and make men immortal with a kiss? Which, to my horror, she did. She quietly signed her name, handed it back, but as he bent forward, she half-rose and cupped his face between her hands. She kissed his forehead lightly. "What's your name?"

"Harold Porter, Junior." But the space between "Porter" and "Junior" was so long—I swear it had to be five seconds—that she laughed. We all did, and his face got beet red, as he tried to back away.

"Were you in the war?" she asked him.

He nodded.

"That's why I kissed you. You're a hero."

"I ain't a hero. I just served."

"No, you're a hero." But she had already turned away, and Harold Porter (space) Junior was himself backing away, delirious and punch drunk. For me, watching, rapt, it was an illuminating moment, and a touching one. With a seamlessly graceful gesture, Ava the sultry siren became, for one moment, the girl next door.

Frank glared at her. "Was that necessary, Ava?"

"Of course."

"I don't think so."

"Not now, Francis."

"If I kissed a girl…like the waitress…"

"I wouldn't be surprised," she blurted out.

"It seems to me…"

"Not now, Francis."

He reached for his pack of cigarettes, angrily tapped one out, and it flipped off the table onto the carpet. While we watched, mesmerized by his jerky movements, he ground it under his shoe. He lit another and puffs of smoke clouded the table. One hand was a fist, the knuckles white. We sat there, silent, silent.

Alice cleared her throat. For some reason, she started talking about Sol Remnick in a twittering, birdlike voice. "Sol mentioned that Larry Calhoun wants to sell his shares in the property they all own together…He needs cash. He knows Max won't give him money and…" She breathed in. "Sol said…" She stopped, looked down.

No one was listening.

Well, I was, of course, but something else was happening at the table. The cigarette vender, a pretty girl in a colorful Polynesian wrap, her case suspended around her neck, had paused at the table, but was waved off. As she moved away, Frank grasped her arm. For a second she paused, uncertain, because Frank's touch lingered a little too long. She turned, smiled vacuously at him, and then, rattled, scurried away.

Ava burst out laughing. "Now we're even, Francis."

"Christ, Ava."

From a table some yards away, the young man we now knew as Harold Porter (space) Junior was passing around the autograph, preening before an older couple I assumed were his smiling parents. Now and then he glanced over, as though to make certain he'd actually met the goddess, or, perhaps, to imprint the magical image on his lifelong memory. I smiled, tickled. I doubted whether my autograph, sometimes requested, though not so much any more, garnered such attention. I doubted it.

Max had been mumbling, but I couldn't understand him, his words running together, swallowed. His hand slipped on the glass he held. Alice watched him, concern and fear in her eyes. This was not the Max any of us knew, this suddenly libidinous man, giggling and hiccoughing, downing glass after glass of the sinful zombies. His face was flushed, with half-shut lazy eyes, his movements slow and languid. A turned-over glass.

Frank kept twisting in his chair, scanning the room, his eyes narrowed. When he spoke, he slurred his words. He breathed with short, quick gasps that reminded me of a scolded child. None of us at the table mattered, I realized, save the beautiful Ava. A man possessed, intoxicated, paralyzed by a stunning woman—a man cowed and yet emboldened by a fierce and awful jealousy. The spotlight focused solely on Ava and her unpardonable transgression.

For a moment, startled, I let my mind play with images of Julie and Steve and Pete on the showboat. Julie, the beautiful mulatto with the melodious voice, a doomed woman, hungered after by men like Pete, a lowlife towboat worker, himself haunted and driven. And Steve, the possessive husband, jealous of any man's attention to his wife, pledging a love that was to last forever but would crumble on the mean Chicago streets after exile from the *Cotton Blossom*. Two men, maddened by jealousy and lust. Pete who squeals to the local sheriff to punish her—punish *them*. He would destroy her if he can't have her. Frank and Ava, jealous and possessive and…destructive.

Ava singing her dirge as night shadows covered her. Can't stop lovin' dat man of mine…fish gotta swim…birds gotta…

I came out of this idle reverie with a start: something was happening at the table. Max, tipsy, was flirting stupidly with Ava, half-serious and a little self-mocking. He rolled back and forth in his seat, a pale dervish, and babbled something about Harold Porter (space…now ten seconds, though no one laughed) Junior getting a chaste kiss from Ava, a young man who fantasized about kissing the screen goddess.

"Dreams to last a lifetime," he babbled.

Ava looked amused, though she kept shaking her head. "Max, what's got into you?" She tapped the back of his wrist.

Alice whispered, "Okay, Max, you've had enough to drink." Idly, she fiddled with her purse, snapping it open and shut.

And then, bouncing in his seat, Max whooped like a moon-besotted Indian and leaned over and kissed Ava on the mouth. It happened so suddenly that nothing seemed to register immediately. Watching the violation, I thought how innocent it was, passionless, perfunctory, the ah-shucks apple-cheeked boy kissing the pretty girl in school on a frivolous dare.

Ava pulled back, wide-eyed, and waved a schoolmarm finger at him. She giggled, "Now, now, young man, do I have to tell your mother?" She winked at Alice.

I was laughing.

Max slumped back into his seat, eyes nearly closed now, a simpering smile plastered to his face. I thought he'd drifted off into a catnap.

A sudden grunt, mean, thick, as Frank shot out of his seat and lurched around the table, his arm brushing my sleeve. He hovered over the drowsy Max as Ava squealed, "Francis, what are…"

She got no further. Another coarse grunt as Frank's fist flew out, a missile, and slammed hard into Max's jaw. The crack of bone on bone. Max's head revolved like a puppet's head unhinged. A spurt of purple blood splattered on the white tablecloth.

Alice screamed. She started to stand but slipped back into her seat.

Surprised and wounded, Max toppled backwards, the chair crashing onto the floor and spilling him onto the carpet. He lay in an ungainly heap, doubled over, his hands cupping the bleeding jaw. He hunched there, looking up at Frank who rocked back and forth, his eyes flashing, his hard blue eyes now brilliant purple. He hadn't unclenched his fist, smeared now with blood.

"I never liked you," Frank sputtered.

Max opened his mouth to speak but he dissolved into a fit of nonsense giggling. Blood oozed through his fingers, down his neck, onto his shirt. "Thump thump thump," he burbled. I had no idea what that meant. He gave a drunkard's idiotic smile. "Happy birthday to me. Happy birthday to me."

Thump thump thump.

Giggling.

Alice and Ava crouched on the floor next to him. Whimpering, Alice cradled his head in her lap while Ava dabbed the blood with a linen napkin. Ava's fingertips glistened with Max's blood.

"Damn you, Francis." She looked up at him.

Silence in the restaurant.

Someone screamed, a woman, hysterical.

Frank looked around, his eyes zooming in on the screaming woman.

He looked down at Max.

"I could kill you in a heartbeat."

"Francis…"

"A goddamn heartbeat."

He stormed away.

At the nearby table the anonymous woman screamed and screamed. And Louella Parsons smiled.

Chapter Six

My day began, of course, with Louella Parsons' insidious but tremendously entertaining column.

The gossip queen devoted her entire column to our sad escapade, given the fact that she had a front-row seat and, to use her words, "was close enough to see spittle at the corners of Frank's mouth." Obviously she'd been dizzy with delight, fueled by her own intake of zombies, tottering to her typewriter minutes after Frank's outburst, her column probably delivered by midnight to the yellow journalistic presses. Her prose dripped with giddiness, though she loaded her paragraphs with *tut-tut* phraseology—"ignominious shame," "truly a sad spectacle," "a waste of talent," a "wanton disregard of civilized behavior," "a low point in Hollywood history."

On and on, an endless and platitudinous array of admonishment. "And then, while we all watched, Frank threatened *to kill* the hapless man." She italicized the infinitive.

But in her stream of consciousness narrative, she most likely rued her use of the word "hapless," for in the next paragraph she described Max Jeffries as a "lamentable pinko" who "defends the indefensible." Oddly, her easy condemnation of Frank, though over the top with venom, then paled by comparison to her depiction of Max, whose treasonous behavior clearly trumped Frank's gangland fisticuffs.

Louella Parsons, I realized, carelessly assigned folks to various rungs of her own perversely conceived hell. She knew who should suffer the most heat in Hades. Like Dante, she buried the traitors at the bottom.

My phone never stopped ringing, yet I never answered. Slips of paper in my cubbyhole mailbox downstairs identified the writers as reporters from the *Los Angeles Times*, the *Examiner*, and even, to my horror, the *New York Times*. Someone provided me with clippings from the *Examiner*. My name was mentioned, which surprised me. I was labeled the activist writer, some latter-day Upton Sinclair or Ida Tarbell. "Edna Ferber, whose *Show Boat* is to be premiered July 17, is an intimate of Max Jeffries."

Hmmm, I considered: MGM just shuddered. Walls shook. All of it made very little sense.

I hid away.

When I called, Alice informed me that Max was nestled in bed, sipping orange juice. His doctor had patched him up, and would be returning shortly. Max, whimpering, kept asking for more pain medication. He was, she insisted, impossible to be with. Lorena Marr, checking in, invited her out and Max, over-hearing the invitation, insisted Alice leave him be. He'd hole up with the radio on—"*Burns and Allen*," she said, "will shut him up"—and drift into a hazy, drug-induced slumber. Girl's night out. Alice consented, though Ava begged off. She wanted no limelight this evening, secluded in her Nichols Canyon home where, she told Alice, Francis knew he was not wanted.

"Lorena has convinced me to go out," Alice told me.

"Good idea," I told her. "Men who are ill believe the earth's rotation must immediately be adjusted to suit their desires."

She laughed. "Oh, I know. Poor Max. I love him dearly, but…" She stopped. "We're catching a movie. Please join us, Edna," Alice pleaded. "An early dinner at the Paradise. You can see it from your hotel. A movie. The three of us."

So I found myself strolling a half-block up from the Ambassador and opening the doors of the Paradise Bar & Grill: Steaks and Chops! A modest eatery with the capitalized "d" of "Paradise" blacked out on the neon sign. The "i" of "Grill" flickered madly. PARA ISE. Lorena and Alice were already there, and waved me over.

"Everything is free," Lorena announced. "I own the place. Well, *we* own the place. My ex-husband Ethan and I. We've yet to make a penny off the place and I'm intent on unloading it."

Alice looked sheepish. "I haven't been here since my marriage." She looked around. "I didn't really want to come here. Ethan and Tony don't want me here…"

Lorena broke in. "Look here, Alice. I own *half* of this place. You're my good friend." Then she laughed. "As I say, the food and drinks are *free*."

But I noticed Alice looking around, uncomfortable. The apple-dumpling widow of Lenny Pannis, accused of murder by Ethan and Tony, now back behind enemy lines.

Anyone looking for paradise would not locate it in that dimly lit dining room with red-and-white checkered tablecloths on wobbly tables, circled by wrought-iron ice-cream parlor chairs. A line of booths hugged the kitchen wall. At the back an old walnut-stained bar with red-leather-and-chrome stools. As we settled in, a burly waiter placed a bud vase on each table. Each one contained a white carnation tied with a red ribbon. A red wicker-covered bottle held a lit candle.

The Paradise Bar & Grill was one step up from the Automat. Archie and Veronica holding hands over a New York strip steak, medium rare. Which, of course, was what I ordered, and it was surprisingly good—toothsome, robust, tender, though served with canned green peas and onions, alongside a baked potato unnaturally titanic, stuffed with chives and slathered in sour cream. Alice, I noticed, barely picked at her grilled Catalina swordfish. Lorena ordered an avocado salad, the turkey club, and a pitcher of martinis.

Lorena had brought five clippings of Louella's nasty column. She bubbled over, and in seconds she had Alice and me laughing, though I'd resisted. Last night's melee at the Beachcomber still upset me…Max's bloody jaw and Frank's feral eyes. Lorena glibly termed it the "Mai tai Massacre." A natural mimic, she assumed a haughty, imperious tone last heard, I supposed, from the throat of stuffy Margaret Dumont in the Marx brothers' films. She arched her back, trilled her r's, imagined a pince-nez slipping off an aggressive Roman nose, and oozed condescension. I laughed like a schoolgirl on holiday.

Yes, Lorena kept saying, she felt sorry for the poor bruised Max. Yes, as she patted Alice's wrist, she was happy he was on the mend, luckily nothing broken, just an ego sorely compromised, a man who now insisted it (and everyone) go away.

"Thank God Max can't hear us carrying on," Alice said. Then, smiling, she mimicked Max with affection: "'Please leave me alone to lick my wounds.'"

Lorena raised her voice. "Poor Louella. Tsk, tsk. It was all very sad for her to witness. Wasn't Frank Sinatra a downright thug and a bounder? She worked herself into a Victorian lather over the blood-splattered white napkin—'An affront to the refined Polynesian eatery, an elegant watering hole.'" Lorena's voice cracked, and we all erupted into gales of silly hilarity.

She'd underlined the particularly enlightening phrases and insisted on reading aloud. "She saved the *coup de grace* for the last paragraph," Lorena added, even though I'd already read the tripe more times than I cared to acknowledge. In her Margaret Dumont operatic singsong, "'I had to *witness* this travesty. I'm used to sophisticated dining, with candlelight and crystal, not gladiator bloodletting and profane language. Dear Reader, I now draw a discreet Edwardian curtain over that crude farce.'" Lorena raised a glass. "To Louella, the best show in town."

Alice bit her lip and confided in a low tone, "You know, Frank carries a gun on him."

A chill swept up my spine. "What?"

"It's hidden."

"But why?"

"Ava told me."

"But he sometimes travels with a bodyguard." I thought of the gentle giant I'd met, the dapper thug in a double-breasted suit, gun hidden.

"Yeah, that same bodyguard threatened to kill a photographer unless he handed over the film in his camera. But Frank likes his own gun. No one knows."

I whispered. "Has he ever used it?"

Alice shrugged. "He's shot it off a few times. He likes to play cowboy. Once, in New York, when he and Ava battled, he called Ava to say he was killing himself, and then fired two shots into a mattress, holding the phone close. She came running, hysterical. And in Indio, outside L.A., Frank and Ava, both drunk as skunks, shot up the town's streetlights with two .38 caliber Smith & Wessons, his guns, and…Frank grazed this man and…"

I raised my hand. "Enough. No more. This is frontier out here, no man's land. Barbaric."

"Welcome to the wild west, Edna," Lorena quipped.

I looked at Alice. "So Max is all right?"

"Right now he's sleeping like a baby. What the doctor ordered."

"Poor Max." But I smiled. Poor Max, that performance so out of character last night. Well, a man who could still surprise me.

"He should never have kissed Ava," Alice whispered. Then she grinned. "I didn't like the drinking, of course, but I've never seen him so…frivolous, flirtatious. It was…delightful. Until the end."

Lorena chuckled. "I used to hope Ethan would do something spontaneous. During the three years of our fragmented marriage, even his husbandly kisses seemed measured out, charted on a military map. It was *maddening*. A drunk with a slide rule." She leaned into Alice. "I didn't tell you that I called your home a little while ago. To make sure you were coming."

"I decided to walk over." Alice looked perplexed. "Max answered?"

"Yes, but he said he was feeling queasy and was headed for bed. He said you'd just left." A pause. "He told me something interesting. He mentioned that he'd heard through the grapevine that Tony lost his stand-up job at Poncho's. Lord, I just heard about it late last night. Ethan called me. But just like Max to worry about others! He told me he'll get Tony a job."

"Sounds like Max," Alice said. "Turn the other cheek. Did you tell Tony?"

Lorena nodded. "I was calling just as Ethan and Tony came in. Ethan whispered to me that Tony started drinking early this afternoon—he's so depressed. When I told Tony about Max's kindness, he refused to believe it—said Max was playing a game. Imagine! God, you can't please him. But a few minutes later I saw Tony on the phone, so I thought he was calling Max. No, he told me when he hung up, he was calling Liz to tell her what Max was up to."

"How did she react?"

"She wasn't home, which bothered him. Ethan told me— 'What does it matter?' he said. 'He'll only lose that one, too.'"

Alice looked pleased. "Max'll do what he says."

"Ethan is right—Tony will lose another job." Lorena tilted her head to the side. "You know, Max didn't hang on the phone. He said someone was knocking at the door."

Alice looked worried. "What? He wasn't expecting anyone."

"He thought it might be his doctor."

Alice glanced toward the pay phone near the entrance. "Well, maybe…"

"It's all right, Alice," Lorena assured her. "He's probably asleep now." She pointed across the room. "Well, speak of the devil-may-care. The co-owner of Paradise. Adam is here…with, of course, the sequined snake."

We watched Ethan and Tony Pannis walk in from the kitchen, settle into the corner booth near the kitchen. Ethan spotted us, nodded formally to me, but avoided looking at Alice. He purposely turned his back on us. Tony seemed lost in his own world, leaning into his brother and blubbering about something.

Lorena whispered a little too loudly. "I feel for Ethan, frankly. This is gonna be a long evening, I mean, with Tony/Tiny fired from that club. He's already soused. It was just a matter of time. Lately he's only been filling in a couple nights a week. He's lost his steam, really. That, and the fact that he is just not funny."

Alice fidgeted. "Ethan is not happy I'm here, Lorena."

Lorena lit a cigarette and blew sloppy rings in the air. "Who cares? You're my friend. He's begrudgingly accepted that fact."

"Still…"

"Forget it, dear."

Lorena leaned into me, confidentially. "On nights like this, Ethan's sole purpose is to keep Tony from getting too drunk and staggering crazily down Wilshire Boulevard. Ethan works on his account books and plots out his burgeoning real estate empire while Tony drinks and gets loud and unruly. Then Ethan drives him home to Liz Grable's waiting arms. A sad spectacle. Ethan doesn't know what to do, I guess."

Alice broke in. "Tony seems to be getting worse, no?"

Lorena bit her lip. "A shame, really. Two or three times a week he's here getting plastered. It never was like that before. Liz won't be around him when he's drunk, so Ethan takes over."

"Brotherly love?" Alice offered.

She smirked. "Yes, loyalty to a dead brother."

Alice whispered, "Lenny."

The name hung in the air, filled the room, explosive.

Lorena eyed her. "Sorry, honey…didn't mean to bring *that* up."

"I don't understand the power of Lenny's ghost over everyone." I glanced at Alice, who wasn't happy.

Lorena also glanced at Alice but answered me. "You see, Ethan, well, *created* the problem. Sorry, Alice, but I want Edna to understand. When Lenny died—the so-called murder at the hands of the lovely Alice"—she reached out and caressed Alice's hand—"one chapter of the universe ended. Ethan was a drunk who got slapped awake. Lenny had said he'd be divorcing Alice here and bringing the boys into the business. Whatever that meant. Untold riches. Tony was a decent comic, mildly funny with his offbeat humor, endearing at times, a little dumb but cagey enough about his career. Sarcasm and dumbness sometimes go hand in hand. A social drinker, that's all."

Alice spoke up. "I remember Tony as a cheerful sort, a jokester." She glanced toward Tony. "And quiet."

Lorena went on. "A nice guy. But somehow, maybe inadvertently, Ethan played Dr. Frankenstein and created the monster we have before us. Ethan hammered on and on about the murder, the money, the power they were now deprived of. The Hollywood triptych: gold, glory, clout. Lost now. Tony, depressed, started eating and drinking. Now he's a mess—and sad."

"And the insult comic was born," Alice added.

"Tony stopped being the bumbling, goofy comic onstage, so Ethan talked him into becoming an insult comic. The chubby guy in the sequined outfits attacking his audience."

"And a drinker," Alice said.

"In here, mostly," Lorena insisted. "Guarded by Ethan who, I suspect, feels guilty for his creation. His cookie-cutter mind can't deal with the new and vastly deteriorated version of a harmless brother. Ethan is afraid because Tony—now Tiny Sparks—has these spurts of anger, out of control. So he plays...warden at the prison he built."

"And Liz?" I asked.

"She loved him—the old Tony. She can't understand what's happened these past few years. So she makes him stay away when he's—like *this*." She pointed to Tony slouched in his booth.

"Watching Tony at Ava's the other night—that drunken spiel—bothered me. He struck me as an overgrown child, but a beaten child—an innocuous lad given to pouting. The brother who always expected to be duped, to be hurt, so he tries to be cagey. He ends up—miserable."

Alice was nodding at me. "Now, grownup, he hides behind a bottle."

Lorena clicked her tongue. "Ethan doesn't know what to do. He's not good with sloppy emotion."

"It's a wonderful life," I commented, wryly.

Ethan had taken a sheaf of papers from a portfolio and was circling numbers with a pencil, ignoring his restless brother. Tony, suddenly staring back at us, was calling out to the bartender. Ethan looked up and frowned.

"Absurd," I said.

"The bartender," Lorena informed us, "knows to bring a drink only when Ethan nods at him. That way…"

I surveyed the vaudeville duo. "There is something wrong with those two. They're…clowns."

"Of course there's something wrong," Lorena roared. She threw back her head. "And yet it took me three long years to realize it."

I was disturbed by noise behind me. Turning, I watched a group of chattering women sit down at a table. They all seemed to be talking at once. Alice and Lorena glanced at each other. "Lord," Lorena muttered.

Alice whispered to me. "Sophie Barnes." She indicated the woman nearest to me.

Lorena spoke softly. "Ah, Max's infatuated secretary. Ex-secretary, I should say. She's seen Alice but is ignoring her."

I shifted in my seat, watching.

Sophie Barnes and her three friends were celebrating one of their birthdays. Sixtyish, bosomy, showy in flowered summer dresses with enormous brooches, they seemed unhappy to see Alice, who avoided their stares. Poor Alice, I thought: Ethan and Tony, and now Sophie Barnes. The nondescript housewife, so roundly maligned. One woman carried a bunch of flowers and a balloon, a tableau that seemed incongruous in a place called PARA ISE BAR & GRILL. Loudly, she ordered a bottle of house champagne while another talked shrilly of her boss, a martinet worthy of slaughter; and they all roared. I noticed a white pastry box placed at the edge of the table. I was glad we'd be gone when the candles were lit and a shaky chorus of Happy Birthday depressed the already dismal room.

A buxom woman now fiddling with the contents of an enormous black patent-leather purse, Sophie was probably early sixties, with a long horse face containing small bird-like eyes, her graying wispy hair coifed into a helmet of Shirley Temple spit curls. A rhinestone-studded pair of eyeglasses were suspended from a chain around her neck. She dipped into her purse and took out a handkerchief. As she drew it to her nose, she glanced toward us.

Our eyes locked. A flash of naked cruelty covered her face, the lips curled as her eyes darkened. I swear she mouthed those tantalizing words: *Louella Parsons.*

Good for you, Sophie. Fight back.

But I'm not an enemy you should make.

By the time we left to take in a movie, Tony could be heard arguing with Ethan, who seemed resigned to Tony's attempts to put himself into a drunken stupor. "Do what you want," Ethan hissed, disgusted. "Drink yourself into an early death. Die for all I care. One more brother of mine dead…"

Tony was yelling something to the bartender.

Lorena leaned into my neck as I walked in front of her. "Did I tell you that Ethan has a histrionic streak? He's good at playing martyr."

"It's a thankless pursuit," I offered.

"Yes," Lorena agreed, "but martyrdom has a way of enslaving everyone in its path."

"Let me call Max first," Alice said as we passed a pay phone at the entrance. We waited. Finally she replaced the receiver. "He's not picking up. Good. He's asleep."

"Or not answering," Lorena teased. "I imagine his friends are having a field day with this."

Alice pursed her lips. "What friends? Sol Remnick? Everyone else has disappeared. Max is a man without a country."

"I'm his friend," I insisted.

"I know, I know. And folks like George Kaufman. S. J. Perelman called. But…out here among the natives…you know."

I did know.

On the sidewalk, headed to Lorena's car, I began, "So that's the redoubtable Sophie Barnes." I'd spoken to her on the phone over the years, and Max had often commented on her importance to his office. "She runs the place like a military base," he once told me. But I'd never met her. She looked exactly as I'd imagined her.

Alice chimed in. "His one and only secretary, from day one of his agency. A bulldozer of a woman, efficient as all get out. A prickly spinster, that one, and wildly, madly, insanely in love with the oblivious little Max. They were a team, the two of them."

"I remember her. So friendly on the phone. Not chatty…but kind. Max hasn't mentioned her in years, and I never thought to ask about her." I looked back at the Paradise. "What happened?"

"Well, simple story, Edna. Max married me. The earthquake that rocked California. It was a big surprise for everyone, including the woman who quietly adored him. Sophie collapsed, hysterical, took to her bed. Suddenly she quit her job and hasn't spoken to Max since that day. That's when Max closed his office on Melrose Avenue to work out of his home. He wasn't taking on new clients, and he'd meet the old ones in the bungalow. A month later Sophie wrote him a weepy letter that talked of his betrayal. A befuddled and miserable Max tried to reach her but to no avail. It still breaks his heart. He talks of her with such… melancholy. Whenever they cross paths in town, she makes a grunting sound, heaves those determined shoulders and storms away." She glanced back toward the bar. "Max still worries about her."

"What can Max do?"

"Well, nothing. Since the blacklist troubles erupted, she sent a brief note, along the lines of—'I warned you, Max. I would have stopped you from sending out that letter. You reap what you sow. The Bible warns you, too.'"

"Another soul who has abandoned Max," I lamented.

"Friends disappearing." Alice touched me on the wrist. "You know, Edna, the disappearing act is the most popular form of entertainment in Hollywood these days."

The movie delighted the three of us. Jimmy Stewart in *Harvey*, a new showing at the Wiltern Theater down the street. Only Lorena had seen it when it was released by Universal back in October. I'd relished the stage version, and I had invited the delightful ingénue Josephine Hull to my apartment for a dinner with George Kaufman and playwright Mary Chase. Happily, Josephine reprised her Broadway role in the movie, garnered a

Best Supporting Actress Oscar this past March, and I welcomed the chance to see the talented woman playing the sister of daffy Elwood P. Dowd, a man whose imaginary best friend is a pooka named Harvey.

Jimmy Stewart's antics were a welcome tonic after the last couple of tense days, an antidote to the Hollywood wars I'd encountered. Weak from laughter, I realized how much I needed that diversion. I rarely went to the movies. Stage plays, yes, on the arm of George Kaufman or Noel Coward or Moss Hart. But Times Square movies held little attraction for me. I'd never seen the film version of my *Cimarron*, winner of an Oscar for Best Picture, though I'd told no one that. I didn't want to go. Perhaps I was the mother who didn't want to see her children leave home. And yet here I was, a frequent visitor to Hollywood, having lunch with the likes of Carl Lammaele or Louis B. Mayer, watching avariciously as they cut enormous checks with my name on them.

Strolling out of the Wiltern, we bumped into one another, silly and giggly, malt shop girls. It felt good, that feeling: getting old somehow meant that it was too easy to forget how to laugh. A rabbit everyone was hungry to see taught me a lesson.

Not wanting the evening to end, Lorena insisted we return to the Paradise for a nightcap, but Alice was anxious about Max and begged off, waving goodbye to us. "Please, Edna," Lorena insisted. "Join me." So…yes, why not? One drink. A little sherry. "It will help you sleep."

A few stragglers lounged at the bar, but all the dining tables were empty, some of the chairs upended on them. Ethan was packing away the ledgers, capping his fountain pen, but seemed glad to see us. He called out to the bartender, "Harry, tell them about Sophie." He pushed an empty high-ball glass to the edge of the table.

Harry walked out from behind the bar, a broad smile covering his face. He placed tumblers of sherry before us. Yawning, stretching, Ethan yawned and nudged a snoring Tony, his body slumped back in the booth. Harry was a large pot-bellied man with a walrus-moustache and side-of-beef hands, and he seemed eager to share his tale. "By the time the birthday cake was lit, this woman—Sophie, Ethan told me she was—is in a huff with this other gray-haired lady, the two swearing back and forth like combat troops. And Sophie starts grunting and heaving and springs forward, and, you know, she takes her huge black pocket book and swings it over the table." He shook his head as he demonstrated the move. "Like *this*. She knocked all those lit candles all over the room and a whole lot of frosting on the other lady's puss. Then she made for the door, pushing chairs out of the way. This Sophie was steaming mad." He bowed. "Like out of a movie."

Ethan stood. "Close up, Harry. Lorena, take care of the safe, okay? I gotta get Tiny Sparks home to his lovely."

Tony opened his eyes, a wistful smile on his lips. He let out a chuckle, and I wondered whether he'd heard Harry's story about Sophie. Harry helped Ethan hoist him out of the booth, and Tony, spotting us sipping sherry, wanted to know if we'd read what Louella Parsons had written. Or at least that is what I believed he muttered at us—a mess of syllables strung together. Harry held onto his shoulders, while Ethan secured his ledgers behind the bar.

"Yes," Ethan told him, "they've read it. I have. We have. All of L.A. has. Even, I gather, Sophie has."

"Why?" I asked Tony, who ignored me.

Harry was grinning. "You should have seen it, ladies."

"What got her so mad?" I asked Ethan.

He started pushing Tony toward the door, his fist in the small of his brother's back. Harry balanced him. "From what I could hear, one of her friends made a catty remark about Max making a fool of her, stringing her along. Something real foolish. All it took was the mention of Louella's name to start the fireworks." He shoved his brother forward. "You can walk on your own, Tony. I'm not gonna carry you." He pulled on his sleeve. "You're not the first person to lose a job."

I said good night, thanks for everything, lovely, lovely, and insisted I could walk the half-block back to my hotel. Outside, my sweater pulled tight against the night chill, my clutch held securely against my side, I heard a horn blare. Ethan passed by, Tony in the passenger seat, his head thrown back in blissful sleep. I watched as Ethan waved his hand in the darkness.

At 12:05 that night, roused from by bed at the Ambassador by a call from a sputtering Sol Remnick, I heard those awful words. "Max is dead." Then: "He was murdered."

Chapter Seven

I sat with Alice and Sol in the living room of the bungalow. Sol had let me in and told me that Alice had asked him to call me because she wanted me there. The dark room was darker now, the burgundy curtains closed. A table lamp was switched on. From where I sat, I could see the closed door of the workroom, a Do Not Enter notice sealing it off. I shuddered but couldn't take my eyes off it.

"Max let the person in," Sol was saying.

"What?" I roused myself.

"The door was locked, not smashed in. The windows were all locked. The police checked. Max was in his study, probably talking to someone."

Alice mumbled, "He was supposed to be sleeping in bed."

"Someone knocked on his door when Lorena was talking to him. He must have let that person in then." A pause. "Someone he knew."

Alice was frowning. "Maybe not. He could have opened the door, and the person forced him into the workroom. They had a gun."

No, I thought. That was impossible. Max would not allow his own execution. He was too careful after receiving death threats. Alice was thinking like a Mafia bride.

I brewed tea in the kitchen, carried it in on a tray, and handed filled cups to Alice and Sol. Sol placed his on a small end table while Alice, wrapping her fingers around the cup, sipped hers slowly. She was waking up, her eyes looking at me, red-rimmed, blank.

Sitting mutely on the sofa, she was still dressed in the frilly summer dress she'd worn last night to the movies. She'd slept in it—or maybe she hadn't slept at all. Now it was rumpled, one sleeve slipping off her shoulder so that the strap of her slip showed. A ravaged face, tear streaked, her evening makeup splotchy on her cheeks and under her tired eyes.

"Alice, I'm so sorry," I mumbled again.

She held out her hand and I took it. I settled in next to her, cradling her body.

She trembled, her teeth chattering, but then, facing me, she said in a mechanical voice, "They didn't have to kill him."

Sol jerked his head up and down. "Alice, the police will take care of this."

Sol's face looked haggard, his eyes moist. Every so often a shiver passed through his body, his sighs deep and scary.

"'They'?" I asked her.

She gripped my wrist. "He had too many enemies. How will they know who did it?"

Sol stood and paced the floor, finally stopping in front of us. We both looked up at him, this squat bulky man who started to tremble. Something was on his mind as he rubbed his chin with an index finger.

"Alice, why did you call Larry Calhoun last night?"

An untoward question, so far as I was concerned, and it struck Alice the same way. "What?"

"When you called me last night, you told me you had tried to reach Larry, but he wasn't home. Then you called me. I told you to call the police." His raspy voice was oddly petulant, questioning.

She shrugged and glanced at me. "Really, I don't know, Sol. I saw Max lying there, I dropped the gun, and I...I thought first he was sleeping and then there was that hole in his head, the clot of blood on his hair, and...I got numb...I had to reach someone."

"But Larry?"

Alice looked perplexed. "Suddenly I couldn't remember your number, or Larry's, or anyone's. I wasn't even thinking about the police—I don't know why. I searched for an old address book that I never use and his was the first number…" Wide-eyed, bewildered. "I didn't know what to do. I should have called the police. Does it matter?"

"He wasn't home." Sol bent down, staring into her face. "Did he call today?"

"The phone has been ringing but I won't answer it. The police were here all morning and they answered it. So I don't know…"

I rattled my teacup, annoyed. "Sol, what is the meaning of this?"

"No meaning." He made a clicking sound, annoyed. "Max is my best friend and…" Again he trembled as he turned away. A fierce edge to his voice. "Larry stopped being a friend sometime ago."

"Why bring it up now? Do you think Larry killed Max?" I was blunt.

A deep intake of breath. "No, God, no. No." He closed his eyes a second, his face becoming a grid of deep wrinkles. "No. No. Well, I don't think so."

"Then what?"

"He was one of Max's *enemies.*"

Alice sucked in her breath. "Sol, not now."

Sol looked ready to sob. "Someone has to answer for this."

Room service delivered dinner to my room at eight o'clock, but I barely touched the poached salmon. Parched, I downed glass after glass of water and pushed the plates away. I kept dropping ice cubes into my glass and refilling it, but the water was never icy enough.

I stared out the window, down at Wilshire Boulevard. Headlights were popping on, like fireflies appearing across a grassy field.

L.A. was empty for me now, a wasteland of wide boulevards and endless palm trees and redundant convertibles cruising up and down Wilshire Boulevard. Everyone in L.A. had to keep moving, driving, driving, afraid perhaps to stop. To stop was to realize that there really was nowhere to go. To escape you drove to the water's edge or into the desert. Both landscapes dwarfed a soul. Endless palm trees. Endless turquoise cars and jade-green station wagons. Maddening.

New York had tunnels with rickety and smelly subways, a whole world underground. I'd never been on one, nor would I ever; but there must be a cold comfort in being buried down there. No sky to remind you that the sun would soon set. That night had fallen. That one more day of your life was gone. There was no time down there. You stopped counting the hours down there. Time in a vacuum.

Restless, I decided to walk outside the hotel, though I avoided the manicured grounds and the robin's-egg blue pool. And, of course, I didn't venture too far away on the boulevard lest Detective Tilden, idly dreaming of Malibu surf, send a squad car to rescue me from the noxious yellow smog and careening bumper-to-bumper traffic.

I needed to set something in motion—if only my body. I needed answers. Let me retrace the steps I'd taken this past week. Someone, I knew, had something to tell me. But what?

I stopped by the door of the Paradise Bar & Grill and noticed that the flickering "i" had abandoned its struggle to illuminate. Perhaps during my remaining week in L.A., I'd witness the complete disappearing act of the eatery—why not? Everything disappeared in L.A.

Yesterday I sat in this restaurant with Alice and Lorena. A wonderful evening filled with laughter and silliness. While I enjoyed their company, someone was murdering Max.

I shivered.

I needed to think about the people out here. I needed a plan of action. A glass of red wine, I thought. Quiet, alone.

The dingy room was nearly empty, a few drinkers hunched over the bar, the same portly bartender Harry polishing a glass as he took my order. He sat me at a table by the door, recognizing me. "Lorena's taking this hard," he murmured in a kind voice. "Real hard. She won't get out of bed, Ethan told me. She can't believe it."

"Well, no one can."

One of the bar patrons, a shriveled old man with hair tied into a careless ponytail, weathered sandals on his bare feet, sauntered to the juke box. Nat King Cole's "Mona Lisa" came on, staticky but lovely, and the barfly swayed back and forth, humming along.

In a booth by the kitchen, Tony huddled with Liz Grable, Tony in the same seat he occupied last night with Ethan, who was nowhere in sight. Though they sat in shadows, I could see Liz leaning across the table, her hand resting on top of Tony's, a comforting gesture. Gazing around the room, he spotted me. For a second he looked confused, squinting, and he whispered something to Liz. She watched me surreptitiously, her hand shielding her face; but the gesture was transparent, a child playing hide-and-seek. Then they both gave up and simply gaped at me, brazenly.

I finished my wine, laid a five-dollar bill on the table, and stood; but Harry, coming from behind the bar, refilled my glass, tapped the rim, and mumbled, "On the house." He grinned. "Slow night in town and you're my favorite customer." I slid back into my seat.

"I doubt that, sir. But thank you."

"It's been a rough day, right?"

I took a couple sips, decided I'd had enough, and pushed the glass aside. At that moment, Ethan Pannis strolled out of the back room, a wad of cash in his fist. He handed it to Harry, and I heard the *ping ping* of a cash register drawer popping open. Ethan spotted me, a puzzled grin on his face, and he walked over.

"A woman of surprises, Miss Ferber."

"I like this place."

He gazed around the nearly empty room. "You seem to be the only one." He nodded toward Harry. "He take good care of you?"

"The best," I answered.

Uninvited, he sat down opposite me. "Lord, Miss Ferber, Lorena woke me before dawn. Alice called her at five or so. At first I couldn't understand what she was telling me. She's fallen apart. I've never seen her…like that. She's always so composed. I didn't know what to think."

"I'll have to call her."

"She's got us all rattled here. She keeps calling me but then she has nothing to say. You know, Metro is reeling from the news. That's all everyone was talking about at work today. But it's sort of sad…"

"Why's that?"

"They're all afraid news accounts will mention Metro. You know, *Show Boat*. The blacklist."

I made my voice chilly. "Murder has a way of getting in the way of things."

He ignored that but pointed at Tony. "He's out of a job, you know. A new cross for me to bear. The only person surprised was Tony."

My mind was elsewhere, but I said, "Well, I suppose Frank will pull a few strings."

He shook his head vigorously. "No more. Frankie's sick of him. He's told me, Frankie has. No more. 'Let the bastard screw up.' *I'm* sick of him. Maybe a few years ago when he had some talent, when he was skinny and goofy and spouted Jack Benny jokes with a world-weary sarcastic edge, he could get away with it. Now he's just a fool."

"And yet you indulge him."

He squirmed. "You know, I have no choice. I made a promise to my brother Lenny who told me to take care of Tony because he'd never be able to take care of himself. Tony's always been a little too…slow."

"So you feed him money and drink. Lots of drink."

"What choice do I have?" He didn't look happy with my words. "But not drinks. Don't you believe that. That…well, I let him drink *here*, purposely, and Harry and I do our best…I mean, yeah, he gets…plastered. Of course, last night I had trouble saying no, given his moaning over the last stand-up job he'll ever have."

"Well, you can't be a babysitter forever."

He watched me, silent, then turned to gaze toward Tony and Liz, Liz still holding her hand over Tony's. "He'll drink himself to death."

"What a horrible thing to say!"

"I'm pragmatic, Miss Ferber. You know what kind of man I am. I'm being realistic. That's all I can be." He smiled. "But I'm only half serious. I'm hoping he'll marry the lovely Liz Grable, cosmetician to the starry-eyed. I'm hoping he'll straighten out. And the two of them will hole up in her studio apartment and…"

Liz and Tony stirred. Probably sensing they were the subject of our talk, they ambled over to my table. Suddenly it was a party. They pulled up chairs and we sat in a circle. Tony wore a hangdog look of a soul battling a fierce hangover. He said nothing, just nodded at me, a sliver of a smile on his face for a second. Liz glanced at the bartender who shuffled over and poured seltzer into a glass, placing it before Tony. He sipped it slowly, then touched his right temple, as if he had a headache. Which he probably did—and deserved.

"How are you, Miss Ferber?" he asked out of the blue, and I almost missed his words because his voice was so soft, breathy.

I said nothing.

Liz said something about leaving, and Tony looked at her. I found myself staring at him—there was something simple and boyish about the face, bloated through it was. Out of that carnival sequined sports jacket and wearing a simple blue dress shirt and khaki slacks, he looked like an average Joe, the man who pumped your gas. He'd been a handsome man, I could tell, a face that probably charmed and sometimes even dazzled. Dissipated now, florid, spent. A dreaming boy who became a failed man. Listening to Liz, he cocked his head, glanced at me, and I saw wariness there, hesitation. Through slatted eyes, he betrayed a sly regard for the world that made him a figure of fun.

He finished the seltzer.

"Well," I began, stretching out the word.

Tony spoke over my one word. "You know, I'm afraid what's gonna happen to him."

"What?" From me, stupefied. "Who?"

"Frankie. You've heard the rumors. Everyone's talking about it."

"I don't follow you, Tony."

He leaned forward in his seat. "You know that dumb thing Frankie said the other night—that nonsense about killing Max. *Murdering* him in a heartbeat. That bitch Parsons picked up on it and now it's all over town. He *threatened* to kill Max. That can't be good. He's, like, wanted to kill others."

Ethan frowned. "No one takes that stuff seriously, Tony."

Liz grunted. "The police do."

"It seems to me…" I began.

Again, Tony stepped all over my words. "Frankie ain't popular with the cops."

"The police will investigate. He must have an alibi…" My words trailed off. I really didn't care for this conversation. A mistake, my traipsing into this dive.

Tony looked puzzled. "A man like Frankie don't need alibis. His word is his word, Miss Ferber." A child's avowal of faith.

Frustrated, Ethan spoke evenly, looking into my face. "He says he had a fight with Ava and drove out into the desert. Just drove around by himself. All night long. He does that, you know. It cools him down. The emptiness…"

Tony's voice rose. "People are saying he didn't shoot Max himself but, you know, he had someone else do it. I heard that on the radio."

I sipped my wine while planning my words. A few seconds passed. "I find it disturbing," I said in an acrimonious voice, "that we're talking about Frank's sullied reputation and Tony's last job and no one here is talking about Max, a dear man, now murdered. You all knew him for a long time."

Silence at the table. No one looked at me.

"Of course, we're sorry," Ethan said finally, matter-of-factly. "We're not barbarians."

"Really, Miss Ferber," Tony said. His bloodshot eyes clouded over. "That's all we've been talking about." But then he bristled. "You're a little unfair."

"Really?"

Liz crossed her arms and muttered under her breath. She'd dabbed some whitish powder on her face, covered it with rose-tinted blush, and in the dim light, she looked garish, a platinum-blonde geisha girl gone to seed. A smear of red lipstick blotted a front tooth, giving her a jack-o'-lantern look. "Max ruined all of our careers," she said.

"Come on, Liz," Ethan pleaded.

She pouted. "It's true, Ethan. Dammit. You know it. Me and Tony. Tony was a bright, clever comic. *Variety* mentioned him once. Max booked him into fleabag venues."

Ethan held up his hand and said to me, "Tony forgot to show up for work." Then to Liz, "You know that. The drinking. He took Lenny's death…it got to him. And let me remind you that Tony was the one who fired Max."

"There was a reason," Tony blustered. "When Alice married Max…"

Liz barreled on. "What about me? I quit but he'd already really *dropped* me, you know. I could have had bigger parts, but he kept saying this was wrong, that was wrong. He said he took me on as a favor to you two. Baloney!"

Ethan was shaking his head back and forth. "Now's not the time."

"And you too, Ethan. You wanted to be famous. He wouldn't circulate your script. He said it was lame. Remember."

Ethan glanced at me and his eyes twinkled. "'Lame' is a gentle word for my script, Miss Ferber. Like every other person in this town, I came to Hollywood to make my fortune. A passing dream. But it won't be from scenarios, I'm afraid." He smiled. "Real estate, though not this lovely bar." He waved his hand across the dim room. "Numbers for me—not words. And he was right about you, Liz." He drew his lips into a cruel, razor-sharp line. "You have no talent."

She screamed. "How dare you! You…use…Tony. You made him believe all kinds of nonsense. You made him—angry all the time. You, dammit." She stifled a sob.

Tony patted her wrist. "Oh, Christ! Leave her alone, Ethan. Ruin one life at a time, okay? You want to hear my theory about Max, Miss Ferber? I'll tell you. It's something Liz and I talked about earlier. Alice killed him. Just like she killed our brother. She's not that cheerful lady I seen you with here last night. Little miss housewife out with the girls. Lenny was going to divorce her, so she pushed him over a railing. And Max knew it. She shot *him* before she got here. *Planned* it all."

"Ridiculous," I thundered. "For what reason?"

Tony's voice had a metallic tone now, cold and sharp. "Maybe killing husbands has become a habit for her. It gets into the bloodstream, you know. Maybe he got on her nerves. The pinko stuff. She married a Communist. Maybe she didn't like being pointed out as the wife of a card-carrying Moscow boy."

"Shut up, Tony," Ethan said.

"No, I won't."

Liz was talking to the back wall. "Max ruined us all."

"Shut up, Liz," Ethan said.

I stood, tired of the bickering and noise. Enough. "Good night. You've all been delightfully charming."

Ethan scoffed, stood, and touched my elbow. "We all know who killed Max, Miss Ferber."

That surprised me. "Frankly, I don't."

"It wasn't Alice, despite what Tony says. He can't get past Alice who's his bogeyman for all his horrors. Alice is not going to risk murder *twice* in this town. Max was treading dangerous territory these days. That letter he wrote infuriated people. The timing was perfect for throwing gasoline on an existing fire. Timing is everything, Miss Ferber. An actor knows timing. Hollywood is built on timing. Here Max is in the land of *timing*, and he misreads the signals. His timing was off. The America First crowd. The HUAC. The D.A.R. The American Legion. He got hate mail. Death threats. Max was a filthy Communist.

You know who killed him? A patriot, Miss Ferber. Yeah, a misguided, crazy person. But a patriot nevertheless. In some stupid way some lunatic thought he was saving America from Max. Max asked for it."

Chapter Eight

"Ava," I began, and started to cry.

The two of us hung on the line, neither speaking, our mutual grief filling in the spaces.

"I'm a prisoner here," she said, finally. "In my own home. There are photographers camped out in the bushes. The phone keeps ringing. Reporters. Me and Max. Over and over. Reenie hangs up on them."

I could hear someone talking in the background. Reenie, perhaps, a soft, soothing murmur. The sound of her yipping dog Rags.

"I have to be at the studio later today." Ava sounded as if she were talking to herself. "But all I think about is…Max."

"Is Frank there?"

A long pause. "He's been avoiding me. We fought over that scene at the Beachcomber."

"Tony Pannis told me people are suspecting him."

Again, the long silence. "I know, I know. I heard it on the radio. Francis won't talk about it. So all I do is sit here and sob. Poor Max. So…horrid."

"Well, it is," I agreed. "But whoever did this must be caught."

"*Who* would…"

"That remains to be seen, Ava."

"You don't think it was Francis, do you, Edna?"

"You tell *me*, Ava." My voice even, crisp.

"Of course not. I mean …"A deep intake of breath. I could hear her striking a match. "Edna, I need to see you. To see…or to…talk to someone."

"I don't know."

"There's a little coffee shop up the block from you. On Wilshire. The Coffee Pot."

"I've gone by it." I gazed out the window. "Okay, we'll meet there."

"Could I ask Sol to join us? He's called here a number of times. The man is a wreck, Edna. You can feel his pain through the phone line."

"Of course. I'd like to see him."

"He's so…helpless."

I sat waiting in a booth, expecting her to be late. Lateness was a cardinal sin in my book, certainly; but I supposed I could excuse someone who confessed to being an insomniac, who only dozed off at early morning light. And now, especially, having to slip out to avoid the pesky reporters.

A woman entered The Coffee Pot, the country-store bell clanging noisily, and slipped into the booth opposite me. What in the world?

"Edna."

My eyes got wide. The unglamorous Ava Gardner was smiling back at me. "Ava?"

But, of course, it was. Not a trace of makeup on her, not a hint of blush or lipstick or rouge, and yet, unmistakable, that face compelled, drew you in. But I hadn't looked into that face. She was wearing a baggy lime peasant blouse, loose over calf-length pedal pushers, with a pale-green organdy kerchief covering her head, tied under her chin. She wore the most outrageous pair of tortoise-shelled eyeglasses, so matronly I expected her to deal a hand of canasta and kvetch about the agony of her sciatica.

"I'm near-sighted," she told me.

"So this is what you really look like?"

Again, the small laugh. Yet there was no disguising that whiskey voice, so low and rumbling I kept thinking she had a cold. At first she whispered, but then, checking out the empty eatery, began to speak naturally. She debated between pecan waffles or *pain perdu*—"Edna, it's nothing more than French toast with an attitude"—before choosing the waffles. The bored waitress, pencil buried in her messy hairdo and an order pad tucked into a stained apron, paid her no mind. I loved it. A practical woman, I ordered tuna on wheat toast. Coffee with whipped cream.

Ava reached across the table and grasped my hand. For a moment we sat there, silent, though we stared into each other's faces, and she sobbed a little girl's cry: short, raspy breaths, swallowed. Finally she sat back, wiping her eyes with a handkerchief. "I still don't know what to think, Edna."

"None of us do, Ava."

I glanced around the empty eatery at the tacky tablecloths, a blackboard listing specials, a dropped napkin under a nearby table, the waitress chewing gum as she leafed through the newspaper.

We spoke in fits and starts, random chatter about Alice, about Max, about the…horror of it all. "What do you know?" she kept asking, but I knew nothing. She leaned in. "Francis has taken a vow of silence. It's driving me crazy."

"Well, does he have anything to hide?"

That shocked her. "Oh no, Edna. It's just that he keeps stuff inside." A sliver of a smile. "I'm the opposite—I yell and fret and let everyone know my insanity. He's…he broods inside, cool, stewing…it's deadly." A pause. "I don't mean…deadly." She stopped. "I'm not making much sense, am I?"

"Very little, Ava."

She laughed. "You don't let people get away with much, do you?"

"No reason to."

"You haven't seen the best of me, you know. The fights, the bickering…" She slipped her hand across the table and touched mine. "I'm so sorry, Edna. I want you to *like* me."

"Ava, I do like you."

"You do?"

"Of course. Max adored you. That tells me something."

Her eyes filled with tears.

The curious insecurity bothered me…I didn't expect it from a movie star. The love goddess of *A Touch of Venus*. The girl in the bathing suit on the cover of *Photoplay*. Max once told me she'd been on over three hundred fan magazine covers, an ocean of lipstick and eye shadow and sun-tanning lotion. Mechanics in innumerable garages across America checked off the months on calendars that showed her come-hither smile.

What I liked about her was hard to define. For one thing, she was a strong woman who was hell-bent on defining her own life, regardless of public censure. She set the terms. This woman could be hungry for caviar at Romanoff's, yet publicly insist on sticking up for a battered friend. Max. Dear Max. Here was a woman who drank and cursed and slapped lovers, but she refused to be cowed by random and thoughtless authority.

Yes, admittedly not *my* life, my prim and spinsterish life, purposely chosen. Being a spinster, I famously told everyone, was like drowning, a delightful sensation once you ceased to struggle.

Ava's terms were otherwise: men, sex, more men—even scrawny crooners with circus bowties—dancing at the Trocadero, nightlife, cigarettes, coffee, and plenty of booze. Spiked ten-inch heels on the dance floor. Life on *her* terms. Perhaps it was the fist raised against the hypocritical constraints of Metro and Hollywood and Hedda Hopper, the phony and disingenuous morals clause that no authoritarian mogul himself felt compelled to follow, given the stories of sexual peccadillo on the casting couch. A man's world, scripted narrowly for women.

Ava said no! In thunder!

You had to admire that in a fleshpot.

"I'm so sorry for everything."

"Stop saying that, Ava." I made the sign of the cross, or at least I think it was, never having executed the benedictory papal gesture before. "I absolve you of all sin."

"If only it was that easy." She laughed so loudly the waitress glanced over.

"Where's Sol?" I wondered out loud.

She looked toward the front door. "Funny. He's always early. But he seemed so...so broken on the phone. Those sobs that erupt from inside him. Everyone's shattered, Edna. I understand Lorena is distraught, too."

"So the Pannis brothers told me."

"Those foolish guys."

"I made the mistake of stopping at the Paradise for a glass of wine. You know, Ava, they seem more interested in Tony's job loss than grieving for Max."

She tapped her finger on the table. "It's because of Alice. They didn't care one way or the other about Max—it was a business arrangement, rarely social—but when Alice married Max..."

"Tell me about the Pannis brothers."

"I don't care for them."

"I know that. Your likes and dislikes are apparent."

"My mama once told me I was not born to lie."

I arched my eyebrows. "Oddly, my mother told me it was one of the things that I was especially good at—and would make me rich and famous."

"And so it did."

"Yes, indeed."

She sighed. "Actually I used to like Tony—before he became Tiny, if you know what I mean."

"No, I don't."

"Tony was the...softer of the two. A deliberate buffoon, capable of making us all laugh. City-slicker boyish humor. But after Lenny died and Ethan went to the police and called it murder, Tony...shifted. He got sullen, angry, started those sad drinking binges. He never was like that before. I *liked* him. Now he gets on my nerves."

"So sad," I commented. "So Lenny..."

"Lenny is the only important Pannis brother. The dead one. Lenny. There's a photo that Francis keeps in his Palm Springs home of him and Lenny and Lucky Luciano dining together in Havana. The exiled Mafia don. The three men in flowered shirts smoking Cuban cigars."

"So the rumors are true—he was a gangster?"

"Francis has a liking for thugs." The waitress placed the food on the table. Ava sipped her coffee but grimaced. "Dreadful stuff, really." She pushed the coffee cup away. "When the Estes Kefauver committee in Washington started investigating organized crime, Lenny Pannis got…squirrelly, abusive. The FBI was moving in. He began to *hit* Alice. Edna, I'm good friends with Alice. I like her. She's a sweet girl."

"I like her, too. A lot."

"And she was the best girl for Max. She married Lenny back in New Jersey, right out of high school, a simple girl. Lenny was the dashing, flashy boy who wooed the quiet, bookish girl. Then they came here, Lenny spreading his poison, getting into deals with seedy characters. Alice finally wised up. The fights. The beatings. Alice always had bruises on her arms and neck. Francis closed his eyes to it all because he's a skinny little boy who likes to play with the big shots. He likes guns, he likes to hear stories of people getting beat up. He likes playing the tough guy. That's my Francis. Thugs…but from a distance."

"Lenny still has a lot of power over Frank, it seems."

"That's true. Unfortunately." Her eyes got wide, a glint of fear in them. "Francis wants to be in a James Cagney shoot-'em-up crime movie. He loves that scene in *White Heat*, Cagney on top of the oil tanks, yelling, 'Made it, Ma. Top of the world.' The hoodlum and his mommy."

"Everyone out here sees the world through a movie lens."

She shook her head. "I'm drifting. That last night Alice and Lenny had fought. He was drunk. He went to hit her. She ran off the balcony into their house. He stumbled, toppled over the railing. Dead on the pavement. Alice, the widow. Ethan cried murder. He hounded the police. He got Tony all crazy."

"And somehow Max got in the middle of this."

"Well, Max was Tony's agent—back when Tony actually could do a funny stand-up show. So Alice knew…liked Max. Edna, they were meant for each other. Max had been slowing down these last few years, settling, and he needed a decent companion, someone to go to the movies with, someone to make grilled cheese sandwiches with. And Alice, fresh from bruised arms and legs, from shouting matches, from a loveless marriage, needed someone like Max Jeffries. Kind and decent and funny…and, well, by her side." She closed her eyes for a second. "My favorite Gershwin tune, Edna, is 'Someone to Watch Over Me.'" Her eyes got moist.

"And Alice got all the money."

"That's the funny thing. Ethan and Tony, latecomers out here, believed Lenny's stories of colossal wealth. Well, yeah, he flashed a bunch of cash, had that big house in Beverly Hills. A kidney-shaped pool and spiral staircases. He used to point out the spiral staircase like it was the golden path to Mafia heaven. But after the dust settled and debts were paid, and the IRS stepped in with a wink from the FBI, it was not the fortune—the pot at the end of the rainbow—that the brothers believed in."

"They don't accept that fact, do they?"

"I'll tell you a secret, Edna. Ethan *knew* there was no money. He's a moneyman. Lord, he *handled* lots of Lenny's money—so Francis told me. But I don't think he told Tony that. Let the simple brother think he's poor because of Alice. Ethan knows better."

"Ava, I don't understand Frank's friendship with Ethan and Tony. They're hangers-on."

"True, and Francis knows it. He *insists* I like them. He's always dragging them to my house. Yet he gets annoyed with them. It's dumb loyalty to the dead, revered gangster brother."

"It has to be more than that. Why?"

"Lenny."

"Everyone tells me that. It makes no sense."

She leaned in. "Another secret, Edna. Francis will *kill* me if he knows I told you. But back East, Francis was trying to elbow his way into some deal, so he got involved with some local hoods. Money borrowed, fights, even threats against his life. He promised things he shouldn't have—whatever that means. Well, Francis suddenly renewed his old-buddy friendship with Lenny, and Lenny, a real power thug, called off the low-level creeps, paid off Francis' debts, and the two became joined at the blood-brother hip, so to speak."

"So what? Years later…"

"Well, suddenly everyone is out here in happy land, and Francis loses his audience, his record contract. Friends disappear out here faster than loose change in a hole in your pants pocket. Look at poor Max. Loyalty is not a virtue out here. Who stuck with Francis? Lenny way back when—and the brothers. Lenny's long gone and Francis has lonely evenings with me—or, when it's time for fun and games, the boys."

"But it must wear on Frank."

She nodded. "I got to hear all about it. He *liked* them—still does, I suppose. But Tony is on the path to drunkenness."

"And Ethan?"

"He's still waiting for some of the gold dust of Hollywood to land on his shoulders."

I finished my sandwich and tapped my cup. The waitress walked over with a coffee pot. "Ethan struck me as intelligent."

"He is, and sometimes real funny. We find it amazing that he still is on speaking terms with his ex-wife." She arched her back. "Not very Hollywood, that attitude. Lorena's a funny lady, bright. She divorced Ethan but *likes* him. It's like she's afraid to let go of something *important*. I don't get it, but who am I to talk? We end up with men we never plan to, right, Edna? I first thought Francis was arrogant and ego-mad, but one night in Palm Springs the bells and whistles went off in my head. In my case, all it took was a heady dose of his charisma and flattery. I mean, Ethan's too rigid, intolerant of any weakness. All the pencils sharpened, all the sentries lined up." She laughed. "Lorena told me he demanded his socks be ironed."

"And then there's Tony. Or…Tiny."

"Imagine that. Tiny. Both came out here to be rich. Ethan had a feeble scriptwriting course back East and produced *Gone with the Wind Two*, some costume drama he tried to sell to Vivian Leigh. Max scoffed at him, so he fell back on his accounting background. Lenny *demanded* that of him. One thing you'll discover about Ethan is his favorite word. *Failure.* He despises failure, though it's all around him. That's why he can't stand his brother, the current reigning example of failure. His main job these days is stopping Tony from drinking himself to death. Poor Tony—he's such a pitiful drunk." She smiled. "Unlike the rest of us. He keeps asking Francis to use his connections to get him headlined in a good place. Well, these days Francis has no clout. I have it, Ava the vamp. But Tiny won't dare ask me. Francis hugs both boys to his skinny rib cage. End of story."

"And when Alice married Max…"

Ava finished for me. "All hell broke out. They weren't happy with the marriage. Not at all. It had nothing to do with Max. They *liked* Max. But they believed Alice was up to her old tricks one more time. Poor Max, seduced by that evil Alice." She smiled wistfully. "Frankly, it surprised us all, that marriage. *Thrilled* me, I must say. Anything for Max to be happy. Shakespeare's Puck takes a bride."

"They looked good together."

That pleased her. "Of course. Max was *intoxicated* with her."

"I didn't expect to like her—when I heard he had got married. I flew out here expecting, well, I don't know."

Ava tapped her finger on the back of my wrist. "And I bet you expected to dislike me."

A heartbeat. "Yes, the frivolous sulky siren."

She smiled. "I am that."

"But so much more."

"Thank you. You know, when Pop Sidney lobbied for me to play Julie in your *Show Boat*, he fought Mayer, who wanted, well, Judy Garland first…before she fell apart and was shown the door. But Dinah Shore, others. Finally Dore Schary agreed I was perfect. Do you know why? His quote got back to me. He told a disgruntled Dinah: 'Because you're not a whore. Ava is.'"

"My God!"

"Welcome to Hollywood."

"That's unconscionable."

She looked down, trembled, but then her eyes locked with mine. "That brought tears to my eyes. And you wonder why I can't sleep at night—or why I hate it out here. I vowed—I'll show them bastards. Ava Gardner *is* Julie LaVerne. I got her soul inside me. She breathes through me. When I heard that, I decided I can't worry what these foolish men who sign my checks have to say."

"And you, my dear. Your story?"

"Is yet to be written. This chapter—movies—is a prelude."

"To what?"

"Don't know yet. But Francis is part of it. That I know."

"Well…"

She smiled. "You don't like him, Edna. That's all right. It's because he barrels his way through crowds. He can be so *mean* to people. He doesn't stop to understand the…the quality of souls like you. He keeps his goodness hidden, Edna—like his long visits to sick friends in hospitals, days sitting at bedsides. That's Francis, too!" She checked her wristwatch and frowned. "I have a photo shoot this afternoon."

The bell over the front door clanged, and Sol Remnick walked in. He stood there, looking around, unbuttoning his sports jacket and removing his feathered fedora. When he spotted us, he ambled over and half-bowed to me. Ava stood and hugged him, but he seemed to push her away as he slid into a seat, and nodded toward me. He looked broken, this old friend of Max, with a collapsed face, bloodshot and red-rimmed eyes, and a quivering chin. I expected some tears, I expected grief—instead, what I got was sputtered anger. He blurted something out, incomprehensible, then had to start over.

"Sol, what?" Ava pleaded.

He breathed in. "I just had a fight with Larry Calhoun."

Ava turned toward me. "Do you remember…"?

"Of course. We met him at lunch," I broke in. "At the Ambassador. The old friend who warned Max…"

Sol rushed his words. "One of the three musketeers." Said sarcastically, words laced with bitterness.

"What did he want?" Ava asked. "And a fight, Sol? Why?"

"He knocks on my door, this man who avoids me. This is a man who avoided Max, his old friend. I thought he came to talk about Max's death, the two of us grieving, and we did… for a few minutes. How sad, how truly sad, who would do such a thing? Blah blah blah. Then, settling in, he tells me he wants to sell his shares in the property we own. Or for me to make him a loan. And he has the nerve to say—you know, with Max dead, his shares go to both of us. The deal, remember? He needs money real fast—he's being pressured. And I say, such a bad time to discuss this, Larry, Max not in his grave, and he goes, hey, business is business, no?" Sol was sweating, mopping his forehead with a large white handkerchief.

"Why does he need money?" I asked.

Sol smiled. "He told me he had a favorite horse trotting at the track. A *favorite*, mind you."

"I've long ago learned from my family that the ones you favor are invariably the ones who let you down."

Sol said nothing for a bit, his face sagging, his eyes darting, pell-mell, from one corner of the restaurant to the other, unable to focus, settle. Quietly, "He's gotta be in deep to the mob. They're gonna hurt him. Otherwise, he'd never sell his shares away."

The waitress had placed a coffee cup in front of him. When he picked it up, his hand shook. His fingertips were gnawed to the quick, a ragged line of dried blood on a couple of them.

Ava slatted her eyes, threw back her head. "He had some dealings with Lenny Pannis. I remember Francis told me."

"Then," Sol continued, not really listening, "he brings out some papers, says he'll sign everything over to me. Just give him a check. He even quoted an amount. So brazen, hungry. So—*cold*. 'Max has been murdered!' I yelled at him. So he looks at me and says, 'I didn't do it.' Like that ended the matter."

I spoke up. "Where was he that night when Alice called him?"

"You know, I asked him that." Sol tensed up. "It bothered me, him not being home. It bothered me that Alice *called* him, but that was petty of me."

"And what did he say?" Ava asked.

"'Out, I was out.' That's his answer. 'I got a life, you know.' So...cavalier. I wanted to...hit him."

"No." Ava touched his arm. "No."

For the first time Sol smiled thinly. "I realized what a weak man he is—I suppose I always knew it. Max and I both did. Max always made excuses for him—'There's always one friend who weakens the chain.' That's what Max said. But I looked at him and told him no...no sale. No cash from me—even if I had extra, which I don't. I don't care what mobster is breathing down his neck. Let the goons break his legs. Let him get his cash elsewhere." He shook his head. "I'd been waiting for the right moment—even before Max died—to confront him."

"What do you mean?" I asked.

"He betrayed Max. Simple as that. I got this buddy at the *Examiner*, used to act with him in New York. He'd called me about that picture of you and Ava and Max that was in his paper. That nasty attack. He'd heard through word of mouth that Larry was responsible for the tip that led to that photo of you two and Max at lunch."

Ava shrugged. "Sol, I assumed that. When I came in, I saw Larry hiding behind a palm tree, spying on Max and Edna. He was up to no good. He was never someone I liked, you know. An amateur at espionage."

I stared at Ava, impressed.

"So he made a phone call."

"Sort of dastardly," I commented. "To turn in a friend."

"That friendship ended a while back." Angry, he reached for his pack of cigarettes and lit one, the cigarette bobbing in the corner of his mouth. Sol inhaled the smoke, breathed out, and relaxed, his chest swelling. "But the kicker is this—one of the editors at the *Examiner,* it seems, slips him a few bills now and then. A cheesy pay-off."

Ava frowned. "God!"

"My friend found out that he even said *my* name to some folks at the *Examiner* for some cash."

"You?" I exclaimed.

"Some inflammatory letter I signed years back, protesting some half-baked right-wing senator's bill. But we never sent it—it was too over-the-top. But Larry provided a copy to the editor. He's a lousy snitch. You know, he'd kept a copy from the days when we were all close. There's a gold mine of names on that forgotten letter."

"Did Max know?" Ava said.

"I phoned him the day he died."

"What did he say?"

"You know Max. He goes, 'So it surprises you that he's a lowlife? Life turns some people good, turns others bad. A crap shoot.'" Now he laughed out loud. "So Max added, 'Such entertainment we provide folks.' He even imitated Molly Goldberg: 'Yoo hoo, such a lot of *tumul* around me. Oy.'"

Neither Ava nor I laughed. Suddenly it dawned on me that Sol probably had no life outside his popular television persona, the bumbling Cousin Irving. And that scared me.

"Money," I mused out loud. "Had he asked Max for money?"

"Not yet. Max told me he would not—never—give Larry any money. Larry was avoiding Max because of the blacklist nonsense."

Ava took a cigarette from Sol's pack, and he smiled at her. "God, he's the worst of the lot."

"So I called him a snitch to his face. A betrayer. A man who sells his soul for silver coins. A man who turns his back on friends. Turns *in* his friends."

"What did he say?" Ava's fingers trembled as she lit her cigarette.

"He didn't answer for a while. Then he said, 'I tell people what they already know. That's not…snitching.'" Sol's neck was beet red, his lips drawn into a thin line.

"A weasel," I declared.

"You know, Larry got real smug—he knew at that point he wasn't getting cash from me. We all should be worried, he told me. Heads are rolling. His job at Grauman's Egyptian Theatre isn't so secure, I guess. There are problems there. Then he got back on the subject of Max. How Max screwed it up for all of us. That infantile letter to the *Reporter*. Just look at the repercussions. All of us—himself included, an old friend and business partner—are now tainted by it. People may look at him as a fellow traveler, God forbid. I guess he's friends with Desmond Peake, Metro's liaison to the outside world. Babbitt goes to Hollywood. They're both members of America First, that right-wing group. It seems Peake mentioned Larry's old friendship with Max—and Larry took that as a reprimand. Peake's the one who gave Max his walking papers."

"I've yet to meet this Desmond Peake," I said. "Though his messages pile up at the hotel."

Ava shivered. "My Lord, he's attacking Max, a murdered man."

"Then he mentioned *Show Boat* and Ava…and Frank." A nervous chuckle. "He even quoted Hedda Hopper from a recent column. She called Metro 'Metro-Goldwyn-Moscow.' Imagine that!" His voice got ragged. "So Larry said he can't be around people like us. Everyone is going to sink. That isn't all. He had a lot to say about you two."

Ava and I both exclaimed at the same moment, "Us?"

We stared at each other.

"Desmond had already warned Ava to back off Max. But she wouldn't. You know how you are, Ava, hell-bent on doing what you damn well want to do. But he said your career was make or break with *Show Boat*."

Ava whispered, "But I don't care."

"You too, Miss Ferber. He mentioned that you are on the boards for a novel about Texas oil, movie producers vying for rights before publication. Then he said, 'This is the last you'll see of me, Sol.'" He shrugged. "His last words to me: 'If you change your mind about buying my share, call me. And bring a check.'"

Sol was watching my face. "Perhaps, Miss Ferber, you've written your last novel."

We lingered too long in that sad eatery, none of us wanting to leave the others. Ava kept saying she had to go to the studio, but she didn't move. Sol kept saying he'd promised Alice he'd help her arrange the memorial service for Max, two days hence. He lit one cigarette after the other, dawdled with this coffee cup, tilted his head back against the wall. Eyes half-shut, he sat there. And I didn't want to leave them because I felt oddly safe there, Ava across from me, Sol on my right. In the deserted cafe, even the waitress now disappeared back into the kitchen, the tawdry trappings of such a workaday diner—the stained black-and-white linoleum tiles, the cracked leather in the booths, the wispy dust motes illuminated by a shaft of light from outside, even the hiccoughing whirr of an old floor fan that did nothing but circulate the hot sticky air—all of that comforted, peculiarly; this was an American eatery that could be anywhere. Keokuk, Iowa. Kalamazoo, Michigan. The Southside of Chicago. Astoria, Queens, New York. Anywhere. And, for that reason, though perhaps illogical, it was wonderful shelter.

It was getting late. One or two stragglers wandered in. A faint rumble in the air, heat lightning on this hot, hot afternoon. The sun-baked plate-glass front window darkened, the daylight dimmed. "Maybe a shower," Sol mumbled.

"I hope so." Ava glanced at the shadows drifting into the eatery.

Rain, I thought: there were nights back in New York when I sat by my windows overlooking Central Park as thunder and lightning transformed Manhattan. "Rain," I said now.

But people said it never rained in California.

And so we sat there, the three of us, loathe to move, bound by some fierce love for a dead friend, mourning him silently. There we sat, fumbling with our coffee cups—the shabby Yiddish comic, the beautiful movie goddess, and the white-haired novelist who was so far from home—waiting for rain.

Chapter Nine

"What *Show Boat* creator visiting on the coast to add her fire power in support of a local Commie is now planning his funeral?"

I stared at the abrupt, cruel line. Furious, I paced my hotel suite. When I passed an inconvenient mirror, I spied a maddened old woman, her permed white curls in disarray. Worse, it was the face of a woman not used to being stunned—and certainly not bested by lesser forms of humanity.

And Hedda Hopper filled that bottom-feeder niche so perfectly.

Of course, I hadn't read the silly gossip item in the morning paper because, frankly, I valued the English language and, as well, the innate decency of man. I came upon the scurrilous item by chance.

In my rooms all morning, I munched idly on an apple and read the *Los Angeles Times*. No comfort there, to be sure, because a front-page article explored Washington's renewed investigation into Communist influence in Hollywood. In the light of the renewed attention from Congress, *Red Channels*, disingenuously chronicling pinkos on radio and television, was becoming influential. More sad souls would be grilled, ruined, maligned, jailed, ostracized. Max's friends, John Howard Lawson and Doc Trumbo, were headed to prison, appeals denied. Wronged American writers.

So I would have missed Hedda Hopper's snide diatribe had I not wandered out to the Sun Club Pool, dressed in my floral summer dress with a floppy Anne of Green Gables hat on my head. I was intent on sitting quietly under an umbrella. But left behind on a deck chair was the offending column, which I read. Enraged, I carried it back upstairs and read it over and over, fury rising in me like floodtide. When Alice called late in the morning, she asked whether I'd read the column.

"Of course."

Alice spoke angrily, "Max is dead and they won't let him rest in peace. They want to hurt *you* now. You have that new book coming out next year."

"*Giant*. My take on Texas braggadocio."

"Are you afraid?"

"Of Texas? Please. Overgrown boys with their lassoes twisting high in the air."

"Let's hope one of those lassoes doesn't ring your neck."

I touched my ancient but much loved neck, pearl adorned. An ugly image, my fragile body swinging from a cottonwood tree. "I've had bad press before."

"But you haven't been called to defend yourself before the HUAC."

That remark gave me pause. My novels had covered a sweep of American geography—Chicago, Oklahoma, New England, Minnesota, Seattle, elsewhere—and I was praised as a robust chronicler of American life, my fiction a sweet hymn to American ingenuity, resilience, fortitude. I relished my reverential—if occasionally caustic and accusatory—love affair with the Republic… for which I certainly stood.

"I'm not worried," I told her.

A long silence. "Edna, I had the strangest phone call."

"From whom?"

"Larry Calhoun. He said he had a nasty fight with Sol. He said Sol accused him of being a snitch. Of naming names."

I fumed. "Alice, he shouldn't be bothering you at this time. The man has no scruples. What does he want from you?"

"He wanted to know what I've heard."

"About what?"

"I don't know. I gather Sol threatened to expose *him*."

"That makes no sense."

"I told him I didn't want to talk about it."

"The man makes me nervous."

"He makes everybody nervous these days. The older he's gotten the more…distant he's become. Nowadays he's running scared. Max could never understand the change in him." Alice sighed. "Edna, I hung up on him."

"Good for you."

◇◇◇

Early afternoon, back in a deck chair under an umbrella by the Sun Club Pool, I sipped iced tea and sorted through a batch of galleys for *Giant*, zooming in on typos in my epic of Texas oil and cattle and overweening ego. But Texas seemed so far removed from the tin-plated patina of Hollywood life. All that big sky and gushing oil wells and acres of buffalo grass seemed so alien from the plastic palm trees and piped-in Paul Whiteman strings. I missed Manhattan with its black-and-white grittiness, its taxi blare.

Instead, I drifted to the restaurant and ordered a sandwich and coffee. I daydreamed in the nearly empty room, and then spread out my galleys and got to work. Looking up, I suddenly realized that the palm trees lining the room possessed stuffed monkeys, peeking through the polished fronds. Echoes of Don the Beachcomber and that horrible evening. What was with Los Angeles? Did everything have to look like a zoo?

I was placing a mark in the margin when I heard someone grunt. Vaguely familiar and annoying, like a buzzing mosquito in your bedroom. My eye was riveted to a paragraph about some ugly Texas vainglorious boasting. Ten-gallon Stetson ego and ranch-hand swagger. I shivered. Another furor, this novel. Another state I'd risk my life visiting thereafter.

Like that vicious carping when *Cimarron* was published. All of Oklahoma ready to tar and feather me, the intrepid chronicler.

American Beauty. Colonial Connecticut. That book brought out the crazies. What did that Danbury newspaper spout? *How dare a Jew vilify Connecticut?* Nice touch. So much for my First Amendment rights.

My mind sailed to the Hollywood Ten, the blacklist, the dark shadow of accusation, the intolerance. Max, now dead. Murdered.

Something bothered me. Something nagged at me. I needed to do something about it…because, well, I'd come here to support Max. The fact that he was dead simply reinforced my resolve. Now a murderer needed to be identified.

Willy nilly, my mind shot to a ludicrous image: Liz Grable, overfed Oklahoma maiden, spewing lines from *Cimarron* during the legendary land rush. Liz the renegade Sooner, slathered in pancake makeup and hobbling on stiletto heels. What was *her* story? What part did she play in all of this?

The grunting got louder, immediately followed by a boyish titter. Tony and Ethan Pannis were at a table just beyond a bank of English ivy and flowering hibiscus. I put down my galleys when a third voice spoke up. It was Larry Calhoun's. I hadn't realized Max's old friend and business partner—revealed by Sol as a paid informant for the *Examiner*—was friends with the Pannis brothers. Of course, there was no reason why not. After all, they all knew one another—friendships formed in the halcyon days of Hollywood, before war and coldness and backstabbing became the rule of the day.

Tony said little, save for the nervous ripple of laughter—someone uncertain of what was happening at his table. He suffered a brief assault of hiccoughs. Admonishing him to be still, Ethan was clearly irritated, talking in a measured voice. When he spoke, Larry Calhoun seemed tentative, unsure, his voice halting as though he were learning to speak after long silence. The reason was clear: he wasn't happy. Eavesdropping, I leaned so far back in my seat that the waiter eyed me suspiciously and I feared toppling into the hibiscus planter, where, most likely, a stuffed marmoset was waiting to pounce on me. From fragments of chatter, I learned that Larry owned a small three-family rental in the valley, a modest investment from years back, now fallen into disrepair; and Larry was reluctantly deeding it over to Ethan for what he termed "a pittance." This little luncheon was to finalize the deal. Ethan was handing over a check. His voice was ice cold. "You're the one who came to me, so stop whining."

Larry grumbled. "Only because I need cash."

"Who cares?" Tony muttered.

"This has nothing to do with you," Larry sneered. "Ethan, you got to bring Tony everywhere you go?"

"He's my brother."

"He's a zero."

Tony whined, "That ain't nice."

"Boys, boys." Ethan admonished. "Let's keep this civil."

"It's worth more than you…"

Ethan interrupted, icy. "You don't have to sign this. You don't have to take this check from me."

Silence, then, "I got in over my head." A tone of resignation, though mixed with anger.

Tony spoke up again. "Seems to me you still owe my dead brother Lenny some money. Didn't you borrow from him?"

Larry's voice was laced with venom. "That's how I got in trouble. Through *him*. Your cutthroat brother. And it only got worse."

"Who cares?" Tony said again.

Ethan spoke sharply. "Tony, shut up."

"I want nothing more to do with any of you," Larry announced.

Ethan, matter-of-fact, an edge to his voice, "Hey, you can walk away now. You think we want to see *you*? I told you to drop off the papers at the Paradise. My check was there waiting for you. We got sick of waiting for you."

Larry wasn't buying it. "Oh, really? I'm supposed to pick up a check from your resident drunk?"

Tony grumbled, "Screw you, Larry."

Ethan's voice dropped. "Okay, let's all calm down. I'm here with a check. We can wrap this up now."

I decided to be nosy, depositing my galleys into my purse, standing, adjusting the brocade jacket I'd worn and checking my three strands of pearls. I scurried around the hibiscus planter, and feigned surprise. Fancy meeting you *here*. Small world, wouldn't you say? My, my, my. I was just one more Hollywood actress, the redoubtable Parthenia Hawks on the *Cotton Blossom*, intrusive fussbudget accosting some smarmy deckhands.

Everyone looked startled. Larry was frowning.

"May I join you?" I used Magnolia's Southern drawl, syrupy and coy, the aging ingénue.

Clearly the answer was no, but I sat down anyway. Tony reprised his recent battle with hiccoughs, but beamed at me, as though I were an old friend. "Miss Ferber, you do pop up in places."

"The pleasure is all yours, surely."

"A little sarcastic, no?" Larry said.

"I wasn't being sarcastic."

Tony grinned. "You'd make a good insult comedienne."

"I'm more at home being an…insult tragedienne."

"What?" From Larry, annoyed.

Tony laughed. "Miss Ferber, you and I, on the road. The new Burns and Allen."

"Tony. Tiny. Whoever. I don't think the world is ready for our little vaudeville routine."

"I should have met you years ago, Miss Ferber."

"Then we wouldn't be having this friendly conversation now."

He looked perplexed, but Ethan burst out laughing.

"Give up, Tony." He punched his brother on the sleeve.

Tony sat back, looking content, although he had to suppress a new round of hiccoughs. He didn't take his eyes off me, I noticed—that little-boy stare somehow questioning what was happening here. The family pet, long shunned or ordered about, no longer sure when it was okay to wag a happy tail.

Ethan, uncharacteristically effusive, probably because he'd favorably concluded a business deal, signaled for more coffee. The same waiter had served me on the other side of the hibiscus planter and now looked confused, though he nodded when I requested that the skimmed milk for my coffee be whipped first with an eggbeater. "Of course." As I spoke to the young man, Ethan quietly tucked the signed papers into a briefcase and placed it beside his chair, out of sight.

"Are you enjoying Hollywood, Miss Ferber?" Larry asked. A rude and tasteless question, coming from someone who knew I was grieving for Max…indeed, *his* old friend.

"As much as I expected to." I breathed in. "You're aware, Mr. Calhoun, that Max is dead?"

He started, his face reddened, and he reached for a glass of water. Nervous, unable to sit still, twisting a napkin, rocking back and forth, he refused to look at me. Suddenly, while Ethan was in the middle of some blather about the news accounts of Max's death and, to my horror, his astonishment that Hedda Hopper was skewering me in her columns at such a painful time, Larry jumped up, sputtered something about obligations, and nodding toward me, spun around and left us.

"Was it something I said?" I smiled at the brothers.

"A squirrelly guy, that Larry," Ethan mumbled. "Never liked him." He glanced at Tony. "And now I don't have to deal with him in business anymore." A thin smile as he tapped the briefcase at his side.

"How is Lorena?" I addressed Ethan. "I've been meaning to call her. I really like her…"

He broke in. "I like her, too. We like each other."

"And yet you divorced."

He grinned foolishly. "Timing, Miss Ferber. I married Lorena at the wrong time. I was a different person then. Driven, ambitious, gonna set the world on fire. Scriptwriter to the stars. My name up in bright lights. Fame—the empty drug." For some reason he pointed to the ceiling where, I assumed, stuffed monkeys nested. "The cruel reality stunned, frankly. And I lost myself in booze and depression." He glanced at Tony.

"So what happened?"

He looked sheepish. "I got mean with Lorena, a woman who doesn't tolerant meanness. Nor, I discovered, do I. I didn't *like* myself." He looked at Tony. "I come from a family of drinkers. It took every ounce of resolve to…to stop. When Lenny died, I woke up to the emptiness of the life I was leading. But by that time Lorena had unceremoniously waved goodbye. My knowledge came too late. Wisdom sometimes takes a later train."

"But at least you were ready for its arrival." I sipped my coffee slowly.

"Indeed. But, as I say, Lorena was gone from my life."

"Yet you've salvaged a friendship."

"Indeed, we have."

"I don't like it," Tony blurted out. "You can't be friends with your ex-wife."

Ethan snapped, "It's none of your business, Tony."

"She's too opinionated," Tony said. "I don't like women telling me what to do. Liz gets that way, you know."

Ethan grinned. "Only on nights you get drunk."

I had something to say. "When women speak their minds, they are viewed as town gossips. When men blather about their digestive surprises, they consider themselves newly-arrived from the oracle at Delphi."

"Jesus! What?" From Tony.

"It's curious how Frank keeps his old cronies close by," I said slowly.

The remark puzzled Ethan. "Meaning?"

"Loyalty to the past even though I've heard him say the past is dead."

Ethan frowned. "Frankie is afraid of the future."

"Come on, Ethan," Tony pleaded. "Leave Frankie out of this. He's…our best friend."

"What do you mean, Ethan?"

He sat back, breathed in. "Something went off kilter with Frankie's career, so he's stopped thinking about others—like Tony's career. About *our* lives. Things have stalled. The wartime bobby-soxers are buying Guy Mitchell records. He used to sell ten million records a year. Just like that." He snapped his fingers.

"Now Columbia is gonna drop him. Do you know why? He sabotaged his career when he hooked up with Ava."

"I always blamed Max," Tony offered. "He introduced them."

Ethan raised his eyebrows. "Nonsense. That's just not true. Max had nothing to do with Frankie. For God's sake, Tony. The man is dead."

"I don't care."

"Yeah, sure. That small-time agent nobody heard of until he became a pinko poster boy. I don't know where you…"

"You don't like Ava?" I broke in.

Ethan shrugged. "She's all right. A fighter."

"I used to think she *liked* me," Tony said. "I made her laugh. But she's too much a hellcat. A crooner's supposed to have a girl, you know, like…"

"Like his wife Nancy," Ethan went on.

"Ah, the fireside Madonna," I said.

"You know, Frankie is a womanizer, plain and simple. But he's not a man to divorce the mother of his three kids. Think about it. His Nancy is a beautiful woman herself, a hometown bride, good Italian Catholic girl, homemade tomato sauce you can weep over—well, you got a girl on the side, that's okay. Next week you go back to Nancy. Another girl, some nightclub tramp. Always back to Nancy, who sits there piling up pasta in front of you. You eat so much you can't leave the house. That's marriage in Hoboken." Ethan laughed now, a long rumbling chuckle. "Ava comes along and changes the rules. She says… you have to *divorce* her."

"The nuns in New Jersey are praying for Nancy." Tony was dropping sugar cubes into his cup of coffee and stirring with his finger.

"It's true," Ethan added. "Catholics don't divorce."

Tony stammered loudly, "Ava made him go crazy. That's the problem. With her looks and that temper, she…" He trailed off.

"You know," I concluded, "Frank is a big boy. And from what I've seen of him these past few days, he likes to call the shots. He does just what he wants to do."

Tony sipped his coffee but sloshed some on the table. Ethan frowned and blotted the spill with his napkin. "Be careful, Tony."

Tony ignored him. "He got a weakness, Miss Ferber. Beautiful women. I mean, when he came to Hollywood he made a list of the gorgeous actresses in town and taped it to his dressing room mirror. Lana Turner. Marlene Dietrich. And he's checked them off, one by one…"

Ethan slammed his hand into Tony's shoulder. "Don't tell Miss Ferber that. She'll think little of him."

"I couldn't think less of him than I already do."

Ethan eyed me suspiciously. "We're loyal to Frankie. No matter his…his weaknesses. He's only human. Frankie and Lenny were blood brothers. A bond to the grave."

"Is his career really over?"

Tony started to sputter, but Ethan got reflective. "Let me tell you a story, Miss Ferber." A hint of sarcasm laced his drawn-out words. "I know you like stories. You make your living at it, no?"

"And a good one, I assure you."

"I had to be in New York earlier this year. Some work at the Metro offices in Times Square. Frankie happened to be playing a date there. He'd performed somewhere in the city to a half-empty house, which made him depressed as all get out. So one night I went with him out to Hoboken, some rinky-dink piss-water joint where he sang as a favor to some local hood. Well, that night he had no voice, scratchy, off-key. Nothing comes out. A blank. The audience booed and hissed and drove him off the stage."

Tony interrupted. "Nobody got class there."

Ethan squinted his eyes. "In Hoboken? Anyway, Frankie, he's down in the dumps. So that night, back in the city, the two of us are walking through Times Square. A cold March night, snow showers, nippy. Suddenly there's crowds of screaming, hysterical girls, a wild scene, these girls pushing against a police barricade. Dumbfounded, we stood there. I looked at Frankie and he looked at me. 'What the hell?' he asked. And then we looked up at the marquee and you know what it said?"

I shook my head.

"Eddie Fisher. It said Eddie goddamn Fisher. Some new headliner on the block. Fresh-scrubbed, brand-new. I'd never heard of him."

"And Frank?"

"Frankie got drunk and smashed his fist through a hotel wall. I had to call a doctor."

"It's because of Ava," Tony stammered. "They want that small-town boy who's wholesome in the tux and bow tie, the boy next store, married to the good Catholic girl. Not a slut who breaks up marriages."

I rolled my tongue into the corner of my mouth. "Ava is a plain, simple girl right off the farm. At heart."

"A Jezebel," Tony thundered. "I used to *like* her. That was when she liked *me*."

"Shut up, Tony," Ethan said.

"It's a shame you missed my act at Poncho's in the Valley, Miss Ferber. My stand-up show. I was damn good."

Ethan was frowning. "I doubt that Miss Ferber would be entertained by your brand of humor."

Tony bristled. "*Everyone* liked me." He peered into my face. "Miss Ferber, I was real good at insults—real funny. People came back for more. I tell a dumb joke, the audience heckles me, and I insult them. Pick people out. You should have seen me."

"Tiny, in my social circle I'm the one who delivers the insults. It's never the other way around."

Chapter Ten

Desmond Peake stood outside the MGM town car like a ramrod sentry, heels together, arms locked at his side, mirrored sunglasses shielding his eyes. A black double-breasted suit and a shirt so laundry-day white it dazzled. He reminded me of a Prussian extra in an old von Stroheim silent movie—some robotic underling. I feared he'd salute me as I hurried toward the door opened by the Negro chauffeur.

Mr. Peake greeted me with a facile nod, muttered my name, and ushered me into the back seat where he handed me a sheaf of typed sheets, including a publicity release for *Show Boat*. Silent, mechanical. The well-oiled manikin.

He'd called last night to confirm that I'd be at the scheduled private showing of *Show Boat*. "So long as I'm back by four in the afternoon. Max's memorial service."

He'd grumbled and didn't answer.

"I'm Desmond Peake," he announced now. "Metro liaison."

"I know."

A tall string bean of a man, all joint and angle, pale worm-white skin, splotchy with patches of sickly red. Large, flinty gray eyes, magnified behind enormous black-framed eyeglasses which replaced the sunglasses as he slid into the seat next to me. A thin Clark Gable mustache incongruously plastered to his weak upper lip gave his Ichabod Crane physiognomy a rarefied comic touch. But there was nothing funny about Desmond

Peake. Officious, Metro's gatekeeper for scandal and misdeed. Or so Max had warned me.

"He's the studio's favorite interference man, a passionless henchman, a founding member of America First, a watchdog group of right-wing fanatics dedicated to policing Hollywood. He lives and breathes Metro. In fact, when he walked me out of the studio and confiscated my I.D., he did so without speaking more than a few words, a sardonic smile on his face." He'd chuckled. "You'll enjoy his company, Edna."

As the Lincoln town car buzzed down Wilshire Boulevard, sped across white concrete pavement, everything pasty yellow under an early-morning sun, even the ragged palm trees seemed props from a desert melodrama. Unnatural city, imagined, temporary, built up to be torn down. Everyone seemed to change one's mind a moment later in L.A.

In New York folks believed they got things right the first time. I liked that in a city.

The town car slid out of downtown, headed out to Culver City, Metro's hundred-acre sprawling world of soundstages, cottages, sandstone buildings, commissaries, imposing walls and gates, fantasy backdrops, a self-contained world of wondrous and gripping story-telling.

"Mr. Peale," I began, "have you seen *Show Boat*?"

"No."

"Then you don't know if it's good or bad."

"It's good."

I smiled. "Are you certain?"

"Metro makes musicals. The best. And MGM has more stars than there are in heaven." A mechanical wind-up toy, though one in need of oil.

"I've heard that phrase before."

"I didn't make it up."

"Max Jeffries was my good friend."

"I know."

"You knew him, right? His name has been taken off the movie. And then someone murdered him."

Silence for a time, Desmond examining the cut of a particular fingernail, absorbed in the expensive manicure. The corners of his mouth twitched, though he turned his head away.

I cleared my throat. "How well did you know Max?"

A heartbeat passed, awkward. Then that granite head swiveled, his tongue rolling across his lower lip. "Not well."

"What did you think of his being blacklisted by Metro?"

Another pause. "I think 'blacklist' is a harsh and unnecessary word. Too extreme. There is no blacklist in Hollywood."

Annoyance laced my words. "What would you call it?"

Desmond clicked his tongue. "I wouldn't call it anything. It's not my job."

"Knowing Max, his touch is all over this new *Show Boat*."

"That may be."

"And yet he was barred from showing his face in Culver City. By you."

"Not my decision, Miss Ferber." He gazed out the window, trying to close off further talk.

I wouldn't have it. "When a man does work, he should receive credit for that job. His legacy now, his last movie. A man who touched every movie version of *Show Boat*."

He didn't answer. Then, a surprising anger in his tone, he faced me. "You don't understand the climate out here."

"Meaning?"

"Moscow has tentacles that reach out and grab and…"

"Nonsense. Max was a good American."

"Good Americans can be duped, manipulated, deceived. Soviet police agents, firebrands."

"Max wrote one letter…"

"Look, Miss Ferber." He sucked in his breath. "You may not believe this, but I always respected Max Jeffries. But Metro has a product to protect. Pinko affiliations hurt not only Metro but…America. God rest his soul, but Max showed himself to be a troublemaker…"

I cut him off, furious now. "Hogwash, young man. A lot of blather and rumor and innuendo. It's laughable."

"Max had become a tool for evil." A dry cough.

I echoed his own words, "Good MGM folks can be duped, manipulated, and deceived."

He turned away, his shoulders hunched against the door as if he were trying to escape. I noticed a conspicuous vein in his right temple throbbed. The manicured fingers tapped on his pants leg, a hailstorm drum beat.

◇◇◇

Arrived at Culver City, cruising through back lots of African jungles, New York tenements, artificial lakes, Alpine castles, medieval kingdoms, and all-American small towns, the town car seemed purposely maneuvered through unnecessary by-paths, a circuitous route that suggested the range and power of the massive company. Acres of diamonds, fields of gold, subdivisions of platinum.

A message was being delivered to me, small cog that I was in its world.

Desmond Peake spoke not at all until the chauffeur pulled up in front of a building. Smiling thinly, he escorted me to a projection room in Sound Stage Four, seated me third row center—"Are we on Broadway?" I quipped to his stony face—and then excused himself. I sat alone in that shadowy room. No popcorn? No juju beads? Was I an exile in paradise? Not that I expected to be greeted by Louis B. Mayer, for I was given to understand that he'd been squeezed out of the organization, though he was an early advocate of *Show Boat* and of Ava Gardner herself. Perhaps Dore Schary, the new head honcho, would greet me. But no bigwig appeared. I didn't hold my breath. I understood that I was a trespasser in an alien landscape.

Of course, I'd already registered my disapproval at Max's cruel removal from the credits, messages met with silence. After all, having flown across the country to lend Max support and having publicly trumpeted my disillusion with this *Show Boat* remake, I fully expected to sit alone at this courtesy screening for the originator of the money-bags product, the unwed mother of

Show Boat who now wasn't on speaking terms with her wayward and flamboyant offspring. So be it.

The lights in the room flickered, on and off, a hidden projector behind me groaned, hiccoughed, whirred, and then the lights popped back on. I heard a door open, a rustling in the aisle and, to my surprise but utter delight, Ava Gardner slid into a seat next to me. She leaned over and smelled like fresh oranges. A quick, friendly hug—yes, I'd come to expect those spontaneous hugs—and vastly appealing at the moment. Dressed in a floral sundress with baggy sleeves and turquoise beads that hugged her neck, her feet encased in jewel-covered strip sandals, she looked ready for a beach party, cocktails on a deck overlooking the Pacific in Malibu. I grinned back at her.

"Bastards," she muttered. "They told me the wrong time. On purpose, I assume." She laughed, a whiskey growl. "Lucky I have spies in this house of illusion."

"But why?"

"You're tied to Max."

"Pinko high tide in Hollywood?"

Ava leaned in. "I wanted to be here with you today." Her cigarette voice got low, confiding. "Edna, I'm nervous about what you'll think of me in the movie."

"Why? For heaven's sake."

"Because I'm given crappy parts at Metro. I'm a face and legs and bosom. Cheesecake you don't get at Little John's Steak House. If I see disapproval in your face…" She breathed in. "It was Max who suggested to the director that I'd be good as Julie. Pop Sidney had worked with me before and liked me. I expected Lena Horne to get the role. She lobbied for it, but she's also suspect these days, hints of being pinko. And she's a Negro. Don't forget that. Black on the outside, pinko inside. She's a friend of mine, so she understands the politics—she's been around the block. God, Edna, she *looks* the part of Julie. The mulatto."

"Why not her?"

"They'd have trouble distributing the film down South. But she sings the Negro songs like Julie should sing."

"I can't wait to hear your version."

"You won't, I'm afraid. My rendition of 'Can't Stop Lovin' Dat Man' is *good*. It is. But they're using Annette Warren's high-pitched soprano, dubbed in. They don't *believe* in me." She snarled, "They're bastards."

A hum, a click, a man's voice yelling something inarticulate, and the lights dimmed. The credits rolled in glorious Technicolor, a wash of vibrant color that pleased me. Ava and I grew silent, though she was leaning so that her shoulder brushed mine. A delight, this wayward daughter comforting a mother who is about to be abundantly disappointed. Magnolia Ravenal at the side of her carping matriarch, Parthenia Hawks. The ingénue and the puritanical mother.

What thrilled, of course, was the music, especially William Winfield's basso rendition of "Ol' Man River." Paul Robeson in 1936 had been brooding, elegiac, gripping, and I confessed to liking that moment in the movie. How could I not? This version was more hopeful, exuberant. Both caused the hair to rise on the back of my neck. Kern's elegant yet sing-along score haunted me, carried me off. Prepared as I was to dislike the movie, I found I couldn't: its sheer sweep and color and range held me. It was a big budget extravaganza, no holds barred melodrama. This movie was why they invented a place called Hollywood.

Not that it lacked faults, to be sure—after all, they'd abandoned Oscar Hammerstein's pithy, intense libretto for some pay-through-the-nose hack's turgid dialogue. And, of course, they brutalized the last part of the story. The charming cad Gaylord Ravenal had wooed the lovely Magnolia, an onstage romance that became love—and then marriage. My line in my book: "Their make believe adventures as they lived them on the stage became real." But real life paled, ultimately, when the bounder deserted her.

In this oh-so-happy version Ravenal returns to the boat when they are both young and vital, with daughter Kim still a young child. They warble "Make Believe" as hymn to their blissful reunion, the showboat sailing down the Mississippi into the new and glorious day for all. That was what they called a Hollywood ending.

What truly amazed, though, was Ava as Julie, the half-black, half-white doomed beauty. This new version paradoxically played down the racial underpinnings of my novel and the stage hit, but then, ironically, framed the entire movie around Julie LaVerne, Ava's presence dictating the narrative. Julie and Steve, the married performers, are turned into the sheriff for the crime of miscegenation. In a dramatic move Steve takes out his switchblade and slashes her finger and drinks her blood. It's a thrilling moment, staggering melodrama. When the sheriff arrives to arrest them, Steve insists he has Negro blood. After all, one drop of Negro blood makes a soul a Negro in the Old South. So they're not arrested, but cruelly exiled, the beginning of Julie's downward path of destruction. Brothels and honky-tonks and alleys. That scene was at the heart of my *Show Boat*. That scene said something important about America.

In this new movie Steve uses a pin to prick her finger—and it's out of camera shot. Someone not conversant with my book or the stage version might wonder what in the world was happening, this cryptic mixing of blood. Let's not offend any viewer. God forbid. Please. How bizarre: a Victorian sensibility to phony propriety in a shell-shocked age that just went through cataclysmic war and holocaust and nuclear annihilation. Please.

But…Julie. Ava. Ava Gardner. A luminous presence, stagger-ing. A beautiful woman in person, even sitting next to me with almost no makeup on, but someone who, captured magnificently on that huge celluloid screen, mesmerized. Her movements, fluid and sulky, demanded your full attention. Kathryn Grayson was pretty and sweet as the girl next door, if next door was traveling on a lumbering showboat. Rebecca of Sunnybrook Farm. Pol-lyanna. The ingénue was the wholesome lass from an operetta. Ava Gardner could never be that girl next door. No, she was the dark of the moon; she was a total eclipse of the sun. You could not take your eyes off her. It helped that I was sitting next to her, experiencing some sort of *doppelganger* moment. She was an actress, surely. I'd not expected that. Helen Morgan, an earlier Julie on Broadway, sat atop an upright piano in a Chicago dive, singing the torch song "Bill." Just my Bill. Just plain Bill. The ache in your heart when you love so much…Ava moved around the piano, seductively, forlornly. You *watched* her.

It was Ava's movie. Howard Keel and Kathryn Grayson could warble, but Julie's exile and decline defined the movie. You wait, anxious, until she reappears on the screen. When she and Steve leave the showboat, a scene filmed in murky darkness with the ponderous strains of "Ol' Man River" rising solemnly behind them, you have the movie's rawest moment. Suddenly, startlingly, I thought of Max, expelled from Metro and Hollywood. Like Julie, a soul dispossessed of life. Exiles from the garden of earthly delights.

Then Ava ends the movie, standing on the shadowy wharf as the showboat drifts down river, Gaylord and Magnolia reunited through her intervention, Julie blowing that final kiss to them and her life on that boat, her only safe haven. She is left now to end her life a drunk and a whore.

I was breathless. Tears blurred my vision.

Silence.

Ava spoke into the darkness. "Damn, I'm good."

I laughed. "You are…Julie."

She looked into my face, a moment of doubt there, surprising me. A little girl's voice. "Thank you, Edna."

She started crying, and the two of us sat there sobbing like high-school girls in a malt shop swooning over some matinee idol. Within seconds, catching our breaths, we giggled.

"You're a treasure, Edna," Ava whispered.

The moment was shattered when Desmond Peake slinked in behind us. "The car is ready to take you back to the Ambassador, Miss Ferber."

"Desmond, Desmond." Ava pointed a finger into his chest. "You're not a good host. Edna and I will have coffee in the commissary first. I'll drive her back." Ava reached out to touch his cheek, and for the first time I saw Desmond tremble. A slight twist of his head suggested that he could also collapse under Ava's innocent flirtation. A moment I relished, though short-lived, for he pulled himself together, backed up, gripped the back of a seat, and spoke in a gravelly voice. "All right."

He walked with us to the commissary. At one point Ava stopped to talk to someone, an assistant director who'd called out to her, and she told me she'd catch up. Desmond and I moved ahead.

"Miss Ferber," he began in a hurried voice, "I feel I need to *warn* you."

The word startled. "Warn?"

"The company you keep."

"You mean Ava Gardner?"

"You know what I mean."

"Actually, I don't."

That gave him pause. His fingers played with the lapel of the suit jacket. "Reputation is everything."

"You're wrong, sir. Reputation is often the threat that petty folks use to manipulate others into behaving their way."

"I don't understand."

"Of course you do. You're an intelligent man. Don't worry about others' reputations, Mr. Peake. Worry about your own."

"I'm in charge of Metro's reputation."

I stopped walking and faced him. "Then you're clearly failing at your job, given the reports circulating in the gossip sheets. I seem to recall Walter Winchell reporting that at Metro…"

He cut me off. "Hanging out with Commie sympathizers… well, Metro needs to clean house."

I grimaced. "Then your expulsion of Max Jeffries must have helped."

"He endangered my job. *He* did."

Now this was a sudden burst of truth, an unexpected revelation.

He walked away as Ava rushed up. "What did you say to Desmond? He doesn't look happy."

"He warned me to be careful."

Ava glanced down the hallway. "He wants the world to be at attention."

In the commissary, sipping coffee, we chatted about the movie. People walking by watched her, warily, admiringly, joyously, and she nodded and smiled at them.

"I never come here," she admitted. She waved at someone. "You know, Louis B. Mayer is a real bastard. But like most cruel people, he has a sentimental streak. He demanded homemade apple pie served here, and the chicken consommé is his own mother's Old Country recipe. It's delicious." She lit a cigarette and sat back. "Ignore Desmond, Edna."

"I already have."

She took a sip of coffee, put down the cup too hard. The saucer rattled, as coffee sloshed onto the table. "You know, Francis is getting a little nervous. I guess they're getting to him. I mean, he's telling folks the only organization he's joined is the Knights of Columbus. He's been named as sympathetic by *Red Channels*, America First claims he's a front for Communists, and Hedda Hopper continues her snide remarks. You want to hear something bizarre? Hedda actually addressed a column just to *us*. 'Ava and Frank: Behave Yourselves.' Bold headlines. She mentioned that Francis has been investigated by the FBI for Mafia activities, along with Lenny Pannis. Blood oaths and codes of silence and *amici nostri*. Well, Francis didn't care about that. But now this 'pinko' label has thrown him off balance. He's told me to back off."

"Back off?"

"He wants me to stay away from Max's memorial this afternoon." She raised her eyebrows. "Of course, Desmond Peake warned me not to be there, too. But Francis is running scared."

"You're in a frightening place, Ava."

She rolled over my words. "His career is stagnant. No more screaming bobby-soxers fainting in the aisles, girls running into barber shops to grab snippets of his hair, a slip in record sales, MGM not renewing his contract. He's angry, sullen, a pouting little boy."

"But you love him to death."

She winked. "But I love him to death." She leaned in, confiding. "I'm pushing folks at Columbia to give him the part of Angelo Maglio in *From Here to Eternity*. He wants it desperately, but we don't talk about it. It will save his career, push him back on top. He has it in him. But he's telling everyone the mob is pushing for him—his buddy Joey Something-or-the-Other, a cousin of Al Capone—because he doesn't want people to know a dumb broad—his lovely words—has that kind of control over his life."

"And you allow this, Ava?"

She breathed in. "I'm not painting a good picture of him, I'm afraid. That's so wrong of me, Edna. There *is* a good side to him, a decent side. He can be funny and charming…"

"So, I gather, was Mussolini."

Ava roared. "Oh my God, I have to tell him that."

"Please don't, Ava."

"It doesn't matter. He's already told me he's not fond of you."

"Good, then we meet on the same playing field."

As we strolled into the hallway, she stopped and placed her fingertips on my shoulder. A woman a half-foot taller than I, she dipped her head into my neck. "Edna, I'm worried about Sol Remnick."

"I know. I could see it in your face when we had lunch. He's so…shattered."

"He used to be one of the funniest men around. He could crack me up, have me and Max and Alice rolling on the floor. He plays that lovable schmeil Irving on *The Goldbergs*, of course, but I swear Gertrude Berg had to base Cousin Irving on Sol himself. She had to. He *is* that character already."

"He's just so…sad, Ava. I sensed it. It's as though he's lost his heart. Even before Max died."

"That's my point." Ava drew her lips into a thin line, a red gash on her face. "People like Desmond and his America First group have a mission to destroy people like Max and Sol. Now, with Max gone, he's a…shambles. He lives in a world where people cross the street to avoid him." Her face took on a bittersweet look, haunting. Now she was Julie in the creeping shadows, watching as the showboat chugged away, and with it…her hope for a life.

"And Sol?" I found myself choking up.

"The rumor is that he's on the chopping block."

Chapter Eleven

Alice chose an abandoned art deco movie theater in West Hollywood for the memorial service for Max, somewhat faded from its 1920s heyday, the splashy red, green, and black tiles and arches peeling or washed out. It looked charming to me, the kind of venue Max would have chosen, its vaulted interior filled with resounding echoes of vaudeville acts and one-reel silent pictures. I could imagine a piano player punctuating those tense moments up on the jerky screen as the mustachioed villain harassed the menaced whimpering virgin.

With an excited Max, Alice said she'd recently seen *The Squaw Man* there, a creaky, grainy print of the legendary first Hollywood movie ever made, back when L.A. was rolling acres of avocado and orange farms and the locals were none too friendly to the fancy New York actors suddenly invading their sunny landscape with megaphones and tin lizzies. "Max used to bring people here to look at the deco trappings."

On the day of his service, a breezy Thursday afternoon, the sky loomed a dull gray, a clammy mist lifting slowly as we sat in cars in front of the theater. Three cars, with Alice, Lorena, and me in the front one, Lorena's clunky Buick. The sun hovered high above the red-tile roof of a pink stucco building at the corner, suspended there, tantalizingly, fogged over by a dense yellow haze. "In Hollywood," Alice noted, "movie funerals never take place in sunshine."

Three or four reporters and photographers were stationed at the curb, leaning against cars, smoking cigarettes, gabbing, and joking. One snapped a photograph of me. I snorted at him, and he tittered. They kept looking up and down the street. If they were waiting for Ava Gardner and Frank Sinatra, they'd wait in vain.

Inside, as we gathered in the lobby, the Reverend Smithson appeared from a side door and looked for the crowd that wasn't there. A Unitarian minister, he'd known Max for years. They'd served on a committee together—to save a deco movie palace on Hollywood Boulevard from the wrecking ball, and now and then they played cards. The two men liked each other, Alice told us. When they played cards, they chatted about the news of the day and inevitably, as the night went on, they abandoned their card playing and simply talked and talked about old movies, about Francis X. Bushman, about Cecil B. DeMille. All night long. Neither one ever cared who won a card game.

We waited, fidgeting. The echoey lobby seemed too vast for such a smattering of souls, maybe ten, no more. Alice, Sol, Lorena, me. A couple of old men in rumpled suits, one of whom Alice whispered was H. C. Porter, who'd directed *The Time of Your Life* with James Cagney. "I wouldn't have expected him," she told me. No one else. Space between us, uncomfortable.

At the last minute the front door opened and Desmond Peake hurried in. For a moment, startled, he stood in the entrance and surveyed us all with a jaundiced, squinty stare, oddly accusatory. All conversation halted. Alice let out a raspy gulp and turned to me, a helpless expression on her face. Standing on my left, Sol Remnick bristled and looked ready to approach the Metro rep.

"No," I whispered to him, a hand on his elbow.

"Mr. Peake," I raised my voice, "I'm surprised you're here."

Looking at Alice, Desmond stammered into the awful silence, "I came to pay my respects."

No one believed that. I certainly didn't. Of course, I'd been expecting the brazen reporters to sneak in among us, masquerading as anonymous keeners, though the minister had purposely spoken to the few gathered on the sidewalk and forbade it.

Desmond stood close to me, this telephone pole of a man, and bent into my neck. "I'm here because Metro assigned me... suggested I..."

"You're checking to see whether the troops have obeyed orders." I waved my hand across the small space. "Anyone under a Metro contract here?" I smiled cruelly. "Besides you?"

I turned my back on him, facing the others who were staring at him.

To my stiff back he muttered, "I got a job to do."

I swung around to face him, my words even and chilly. "I've heard those words before. And in the not-so-distant past. You've heard of the Nazis?"

Desmond's face blanched as he shuffled past me, grazing Sol's shoulder, headed into the theater. Everyone was looking at me, but Lorena, her face hidden by a black contour veil, moved to my side. "Good for you, Edna."

"I was hoping Ava would come," I murmured.

"I spoke to Ethan last night..."

I broke in, testy, "And where is he? And Tony?"

"I didn't expect them to come. Max...Alice...you know."

"A sad commentary, no?" I stopped. "I interrupted you, Lorena. You were saying?"

"Just that Ethan told me that Ava was ordered not to show up today. She *wanted* to. Orders from the top brass, loud and clear. Dore Schary, he thought. They can't afford one more embarrassing photo in the papers. Her careless abandon—God, how she loves to thumb her nose at Metro!—can cause real harm, and if she showed up here, with that gaggle of photographers outside ready to pounce..."

Sol had neared and was now peering into my face. Lorena smiled sadly at him and then drifted away, standing at Alice's side. "Yes, Sol?"

For a moment he said nothing as he stared into my face. A short man, we saw eye to eye; and what I saw now disturbed me, for here was a man's craggy face ravaged by grief. I started, so intense was the anguish there, the bleak loss. Trembling, his hands flapping like wild birds against his sides, he'd clearly dressed in a fog. A button was undone on his shirt. There was a dried smear of shaving cream on his lower cheek, a dime-sized spot of pale white. That vagrant spot, stuck there, seemed such a violation, such a token of his absolute sorrow, that I did something I'd never done before. "Give me your handkerchief, Sol."

He squinted, confused, but extracted a large white linen cloth from a pants pocket and handed it to me. I took it and rubbed the spot on his cheek, wordlessly, quickly. He realized what I was doing, and for a moment a silly smile surfaced, the inveterate comic's sense of absurdity, Cousin Irving cavorting with Molly Goldberg on a television soundstage. "Even at my age, go figure, people got to dress me."

"You all right, Sol?"

"No." Serious again, the words fierce. "Max's death is beyond the pale, Miss Ferber. I'm awake all night long. I keep saying to myself, what could I have done? Did I...was I in some way responsible—all those talks we had about the blacklist, my encouraging him to send that letter." Then, as though he just had a revelation, "No, that had nothing to do with this." A wash of tears leaked out of his eyes, ran into the wrinkles of his cheeks. He reached for the handkerchief and, realizing I'd just used it, he smiled and said, "Perhaps I should keep it out."

"You were ready to attack Desmond Peake."

His lips drew into a razor-thin line. "That bastard. How dare he come here? God, he walked Max out of the Metro gates and to his car. Like Max was a misbehaving child in school."

"Mr. Peake told me he was only doing his job."

Sol grunted. "The job you do sometimes is a snapshot of your own character."

"Yes, the butler who takes on the airs of the master of the house."

Sol lowered his voice. "He's a top dog in America First. Him...and that traitor Larry."

"I know about them, Sol. Boys with their vendettas and intolerance."

Suddenly, a shift in his tone, the voice gravelly, halting. "Max was my last friend, Miss Ferber."

What could I say to that? Could this talented man, this popular television comic adored by millions—I assumed so, though I had no idea, never having heard of Cousin Irving before—lead so solitary a life? A man who spent his lonely nights in an apartment somewhere in this sprawled-out city? Or back in New York, lost in some small walk-up as he readied for the Monday night broadcast at NBC?

"I'm so sorry," I said.

"They will never find his murderer," he suddenly announced.

That startled. "Why? For heaven's sake, Sol."

"Because the cops don't really care."

"Of course, they do."

"You have more faith in authority than I do, Miss Ferber."

"What else is there that we have, Sol?"

The others were filing into the theater, so I nudged Sol. Yet he stood there, eyes brighter now, determined. "They think it's some obsessed patriotic fanatic. You know, all those death threats Max got. Some America First zealot, armed with a gun and a head filled with delusions. Why should the cops care? One more Red sympathizer bites the dust." He took my arm and we walked toward the open doors of the theater. "Or," he added, "it was Frank Sinatra or one of his goons." A sickly smile. "I guess the cops could believe that scenario."

"You don't really believe that, Sol?"

He stopped and I crashed into his side. "No, I don't. Frank is a blowhard. I don't like that man, but I think he's a scared little boy playing in the big leagues with the tough guys. He'll always be a loudmouth boy performing for the bullies in the class. Not a bad person, Miss Ferber, and sometimes I think deep down he's a *good* person at heart, but he'll always be a scared, bad *boy*."

I breathed in. "So who killed Max?"

We were the only two standing in the aisles now, and I pointed toward seats up front. Sol deliberated. "Everyone is wrong in thinking it had to do with the blacklist. With the infernal letter.

Those phony patriots with their Bibles tucked up against their firearms, posters of George Washington and Abe Lincoln taped to their walls." He lifted his arms and spread them out.

"Then who?" I persisted.

"Those cowards don't kill. You know why? The blacklist is their most powerful weapon. They want the Commies to be alive. To *stay* alive. They don't want people like Max Jeffries or Doc Trumbo or Ring Lardner Junior—any of the Hollywood Ten and the others—to die. They believe in public humiliation. They want us out of jobs, imprisoned, begging, impoverished, suffering. They want to see our children starving. Beg for crumbs. That's the American way. Death is too simple for them. No, Max's death had nothing to do with being blacklisted. Someone wanted him dead for another reason."

In a low voice, "God, what?"

"Find out, Miss Ferber. You find out."

I nodded. Yes, I thought, I will find out. I had no choice: my mind catalogued and sorted through the folks I'd met out here, watching, watching, the faces tugging at the edges of my days.

He blinked wildly. "Be the irritant that produces the surprisingly important black pearl."

I nodded again. Yes.

Already the organ music swelled from the side of the room, a lugubrious hymn that sounded like a liturgical rendering of an old Irving Berlin show tune. Then, to my horror, I realized it was. Sol and I rushed to our seats, joining the others huddled together down front. Desmond Peake sat alone a dozen seats back on the side, the solitary Greek chorus, hopefully mute.

At the microphone Reverend Smithson spoke in a dreary monotone, an informal greeting and a brief remembrance of trying to cheat Max at rummy, and Max letting him. A curious beginning, I thought, especially coming out of a clergyman's mouth. *I cheated at cards and he let me.*

Few trappings of religion here, to be sure, though the Reverend Smithson did read a passage from Ecclesiastes—*to every thing there is a season*—and the Twenty-Third Psalm. The Lord is my Shepherd.

Finally, he signaled the organist who played a morbid medley of music Max had composed or orchestrated, a rolling hodge-podge that sounded painfully labored.

The organist was an old woman who wore an incongruous straw sun hat, her ample body bursting out of a black dress that probably had been bought off the rack a good three decades earlier. As she assaulted the hapless keys and stops, I thought I detected the strangulated strains of "Mis'ry Comin' Round," that mournful dirge from *Show Boat*, the haunting Negro chorus that augurs the exit of Julie and Steve from the *Cotton Blos*som and the downward spiral of Magnolia and Gaylord Ravenal. A dark lament, and, played here, appropriate.

Then, her body trembling, Alice approached the stage and talked briefly about Max's love of theater and movies, and his deep love of his friends. She read a letter she'd received from George S. Kaufman celebrating Max. I thrilled to hear my old New York friend's loving words. Finally, her voice a whisper, she stopped and walked back to her seat.

No one moved.

I stood and moved in front of that imposing and unnecessary microphone. I told stories. The oft-repeated tale of our first meeting at the *Show Boat* tryout in Washington D.C. The two of us in a New York deli sending back the split pea soup over and over because it was too cold. Max tickling a howling Fanny Brice in Times Square. Then he tickled me. I recounted his years of involvement with the various incarnations of *Show Boat*, his particular fondness for Paul Robeson's rendition of "Ol' Man River," and quoted him: "It always makes me sob, that memory." He'd learned to make crêpes Suzette for Ava because it was her favorite dessert. He had a childlike love of root beer. His joy at marrying Alice.

I ended with: "Sometimes Max and I didn't see each other for years, though we always wrote long, chatty letters, his humor livelier than mine. But, as with any true friend, it didn't matter the distance of miles or time, the long silences—I felt Max was always right next to me." I sat down, and Alice nodded at me.

Beside me, Sol squirmed. He stood now, though I could see he was nervous. Hesitantly, shaking, he walked to the front. For a while he said nothing, this stump of a man in the over-sized suit. Near me, Lorena rustled in her seat. Then, in a tinny voice that was nearly a stage whisper, he began, and immediately he found his wonderful power.

"Max used to say that I was the funniest man he'd ever met in his life. That wasn't true. He was. Yes, I did the stand-up routines, the radio skits, the vaudeville *shtick*, but Max would sometimes look at me, after I'd blathered some nonsense, and you could see the funny in his eyes, in the twitching of his lips, the way he tilted his head. One time, years back, he was working on a score and had a bout of insomnia. So he went to a doctor for sleeping pills." Sol imitated Max in a Yiddisher voice: "'So doctor, some pills to sleep, yes?' When I saw him I said, 'For God's sake, Maxie bubbe, sleeping pills? What for?' With a shrug of his shoulders he says, 'Because I keep waking up in the middle of our conversations.'" Sol chuckled. We joined in.

But then Sol shifted his eyes. Another long silence, his head bent to the side as though listening to some inner voice, his hand rubbing the side of his jaw, his body trembling. He looked out over the few of us. "He shouldn't have died like *that*."

We all tensed up, waiting. Alice sucked in her breath, a rasp that made everyone look her way.

"You know, Max helped hundreds of careers, but that's not important. What was important was that he was a friend to hundreds, and they turned their backs on him. Such a good, good man, a mensch, let me tell you. So where are they?" He stopped, pointed around the nearly empty chamber. For some reason, probably nerves, the aged organist inadvertently touched a key of the organ and the discordant note, powerful as a gunshot, made us jump. Sol glanced at her but then went on. "There's something wrong here today. Small-minded people, narrow and mean-spirited people...they use innuendo...they say they speak for America…but…they…" He trailed off, helpless, now weeping.

Lorena looked at me, despairing.

Then he gazed at us. No, he looked at the vast number of unoccupied seats, the ghosts of Max's friends and acquaintances oddly there—at least to him. "Old friends," he muttered. Then, almost incoherent, "The three musketeers." And I knew—I supposed we all did at that moment—he was talking about the absence of Larry Calhoun.

Sol's voice became thunderous now. "Belly-crawlers," he yelled out. "Turning in their friends for a few pieces of silver. Judas." He faltered and let out a teary gasp. "The Talmud says… the man who turns in his brother, the one who betrays…" Then, loudly: "*Akhal Kurtza.*" Hebrew, I assumed. "The man who ravishes the flesh of a brother…gnaws on the marrow of his brother…"

It was an awful moment, raw as dripping blood. Sol, confused now, stood there, unable to move. Quietly, in an act of utter beauty, Alice went to him, wrapped an arm about his waist, and led the weeping man back to his seat.

Dizzy, spent, I bent over in the seat, my eyes closed.

Nothing happened. Reverend Smithson sat on the side, the lost Lamb of God himself.

The creak of a stage door at the side, behind a tattered curtain.

Ava Gardner walked out of the back shadows. A collective intake of breath, as I turned to glance at Desmond Peake, sitting behind us. A stony face, though the knuckles gripping the back of the seat in front of him were white and tight.

Ava, the forbidden congregant.

Her eyes downcast, she stood silently before that microphone. Dressed in a simple black dress, with decorous black ruffles at the neck, elbow-length black cotton gloves, a single strand of pearls around her neck, a black scarf draped on her head like a mantilla, she looked the modest mourner, though that would be impossible for her: she stunned us, this woman. She glanced at the Reverend Smithson, who smiled at her and nodded.

She cleared her throat. Immediately the organist hit some keys. Ava glanced her way, shook her head, and said in a throaty voice, "No. But thank you."

Then, a cappella, she sang a slow, bluesy version of "Can't Help Lovin' Dat Man," Julie's haunting lament from *Show Boat.* A perfect voice, compelling, thrilling. It was the doomed mulatto's hymn to a loved one, the inevitability of a passion that takes over one's life. *Fish gotta swim and birds gotta fly...* and, for one woman, for both Ava and for Julie, there could only be one man till they died. A lament for a lover, true, but now, transmogrified by Ava's dirge-like piano-bar rendering, it was reinvented as a testament to her love for her friend Max.

And just like that it was over. She stopped, backed up, and disappeared into the back room. We sat there, all of us a little drunk with the moment. I started crying, big sloppy tears that rose unexpectedly, and I couldn't stop. This was for Max, this special moment. It was, I told myself, a melodramatic moment from a nineteenth-century showboat revue, some climactic sweep of tears and drama. *Tempest and Sunshine. The Parson's Bride.* The hero and heroine on the stage of the *Cotton Blossom,* a chorus swelling behind them, as the heroine emoted before a clamoring audience. This was the wondrous melodrama that made life on a showboat so important to the river towns and hamlets along the Mississippi River. It was right, it was sublime. It was theater, yes, and sentimental; but it was the life we all wanted to believe in, that moment when we feel so exquisitely alive and true and good.

Everyone wept.

Well, not everyone.

I turned to look back at Desmond Peake. I stopped sobbing. A ridiculous smile was plastered on his long, gaunt face. Rattled, I had no idea what it meant. Was he pleased that he'd caught the rebellious Ava in some Metro violation, the insubordinate actress playing fast and loose with her contract? Or was he pleased that she'd done the right thing? Or...or was Desmond more than the simplistic troglodyte or villain—let's hiss and boo the showboat heavy—that I'd easily categorized?

With echoes of Ava's bravado performance ringing in my ears, I stood to leave the room. But Desmond had gone before me. I wondered now: what manner of man was this Desmond Peake?

Chapter Twelve

I'd been jotting notes on a yellow pad, concise biographies of the folks who'd touched or, frankly, bruised Max in his final days. Sooner or later, I knew, some kernel of discovery—what did Sol call it? a "black pearl"?—would assert itself. And then I'd know. A pot of tea and an untouched watercress sandwich on the table. When Alice called, she spoke so rapidly that at first I had no idea what she wanted, though her strangled voice alarmed me, her words running together.

"Slow down, Alice," I pleaded. "For God's sake, what?"

"I can't reach Sol."

"What happened?"

A deep breath, a whistling sound from the back of her throat. "I was sitting here going through some letters when Sol called me." Her voice broke. "He wasn't making much sense, Edna. He rattled on and on and I kept saying, What? What? Those gagging sounds, senseless."

"Tell me. Did anything happen?"

"I don't know. He said he needed to go for a ride. Out of the city. I heard that clearly. 'My head hurts.' I heard that. 'I gotta drive around.'" Alice's voice rose. "Why does everyone out here have to drive around so much? Everybody is always driving out into the desert or up into the hills. Driving, driving."

That made little sense to me, yet I let it go. People had their own ways of dealing with the junk that fell on them. In New York when I was rattled—though I rarely allowed myself such a weakness, considering it a frailty best given to some of my heroines—or when I was getting ready to do battle with someone, a more common occurrence given the bumbling souls I encountered in my workaday world—well, I *walked*. Up Park Avenue, over to Lexington, back home, down and over, one mile, sometimes two. Early morning. Late afternoon. In rain and snow, faithful to my regimen. It cleared the soul and calmed the digestion. It made people…bearable. People shuffled out of my barreling way, instinctively aware of the termagant in their hapless path. Back in my penthouse, purged and spent, I'd stare down at the tops of trees in Central Park below me and feel back in control.

Here, in this godless paradise, this land of vulgarity, people drove into the desert, often in darkest night when lizards slithered under a chalk moon, when night creatures bayed and hissed. Not for me. I'd take the helter-skelter barbarism of Manhattan any day. A city with gusto.

"Well," I said now, "let him get whatever it is out of his system."

"You don't understand, Edna. Sol is falling apart."

I waited. "Do you want me to stop in, Alice?"

A pleading in her voice, tremulous. "Will you, Edna?"

"Of course."

By the time the taxi dropped me off in front of her bungalow, Alice had put on a pot of coffee. Her expression grim, she placed a cup before me, sat down opposite me, and quietly slid a copy of *Variety* across the table. "This arrived minutes ago."

I glanced at the trade magazine. "What are you trying to tell me, Alice?"

She started to drink some coffee, but stopped, replaced the cup on the saucer. "It's the first thing I spotted. I don't know why, but I knew I had to look inside." She took the magazine and flipped it open. Her fingers tapped on a small news item. "Sol never told me. Yes, he mentioned rumors of trouble, but maybe he didn't know it until today."

"What?" I demanded.

"General Foods, you know, Sanka coffee, the sponsor of *The Goldbergs*, has dropped the show from its listings. Because, supposedly, some actors are Communists. Or, maybe, they have a tinge of pinko coloring their marked-up scripts. The veteran character actor Philip Loeb is out, the man who plays Molly's husband Jake and…and…"

"Sol," I mumbled.

"Sol," she echoed. "He's not these things, you know. All right, he's joined some leftist groups. He's signed petitions. We all have. All of the good folks in Hollywood have. Katherine Hepburn. Groucho Marx. Judy Garland." She stopped. "Sol is a man who despises Communists, Edna. God, his family fled Russia to find freedom in America." She fell back on the sofa, her hands fluttering.

"That explains his bizarre phone call to you."

"Well, he's out of a job. *Variety* says Philip Loeb has left. Now Sol has to go. He saw this coming, you know. So many times Sol talked to Max about it. He said Gertrude Berg was worried— she'd been warned. General Foods warned her. Him, some others. Philip Loeb is fine gentleman, funny. Sol, the primetime comic as Commie? Who's gonna turn on their Admiral televisions and watch him crack Cousin Irving jokes?"

"Could he have known already? I mean—if it's in *Variety* today?"

"Who knows? He's away from New York for the summer. Maybe he was hoping…Maybe the black and white of it hit him. Maybe…I don't know."

"What's left for him?"

Exasperation in her voice. "Nothing. No work. He has a studio on Hollywood Boulevard for the summer. He's got a tiny room in New York on Fifth Avenue most of the year when he has to be there. So little money saved—I know that. Thank God his parents are dead, and recently—he took care of them. They hardly spoke English, he told me, laughing about it; but they turned on the television he bought them to laugh at Cousin Irving, their pride and joy. And"—almost a smile—"he told me they didn't get any of the jokes but they laughed like crazy. Cousin Irving, their boy, the Yiddisher bumbler with the wise-crack and the good heart." Alice sobbed and, for some reason, picked up a pen and drew a large circle around the article in *Variety*.

"He has to come back home."

"His phone call to me scared me, so I kept calling back. I don't know what to do with myself, Edna. I bang around the house like a crazy lady. I worry about Sol, but my mind sails to…Max. Max is everywhere. I can *smell* him here when I touch a book. It's as if he just handed it to me. A piece of paper. A kitchen plate reminds me. I look at his side of the bed and I'm afraid I'll forget the way he slept, the way he sighed in his sleep, the way he curled his fingers around the pillow. And now I'm alone here. I can't get back to the quiet life I loved."

"Alice." I didn't know what to say.

She tilted back her head, a longing gesture. "I married Lenny when I was a girl, a foolish girl, and he kept me away from his world of syndicates and showgirls and mobsters and men who knocked on the doors late at night with wads of cash. I hid in my kitchen. After a while, though, I felt on edge, like any minute I was going to be slapped awake. A cop knocking on the door. Some goon with a pistol. An empty-headed showgirl showing me his love letters. When he died, I was *glad*." She smiled. "I didn't kill him, but I was glad." She paused. "Edna, I will confess something to you."

Dear Lord, I thought: No. When people confess things to me, invariably I have sleepless nights and need a late-night run to the drugstore for bicarbonate of soda. Emotional confessions only give pain to the listener.

"Of course, Alice. Tell me." I closed my eyes.

"That night we fought out on the balcony. I was sitting out there when he came home. He was drunk, nearly tottering over the railing. Something had gone wrong with some deal, I guess. The FBI was breathing down his neck. I don't know. He slapped me. I wanted him to fall, Edna. When I rushed back inside, he screamed, 'Get back out here, you whore,' and I slammed the glass door as he rushed at me, fist raised. He ran into it, reeling, then staggered back and toppled over the railing. I watched him fall."

There was nothing I could say. The clock on the mantel was too loud now, the minute hand barely moving.

She stared into my face. "He was dead. And Max was the one who allowed me to *breathe* again, to look out a window and see *nothing* and enjoy that *nothing* so much. He filled up my life with…a good *nothing*. You know what I mean, Edna? The nothing that is peace and serenity and…" She stopped. "My God, Edna, I can't stop talking."

"It's all right." I patted her wrist. "Of course, it's all right."

She pointed to the workroom. "I'm afraid of that room."

I peered through the open door at a desk covered with folders and books and accordion files. Leaning against it were tall wobbly stacks of papers and newspapers and cardboard boxes. The Hollywood agent as hoarder of every scrap of the industry, as though when he closed his office downtown he simply emptied that world into this small, impossible space.

"Tell me about Max's agency," I said suddenly. Tell me, and maybe I can begin to understand what happened.

"Why?"

"I'm curious. You know, he never discussed his clients with me. We talked musical scores, openings, closings, tryouts. The nitty gritty work of an agent—he said it was too tedious for conversation with friends."

She smiled. "That sounds like Max. He'd tap dance to a Gold-diggers routine, but forget to file his tax return." She glanced at the room. "I had some money squirreled away from Lenny's accounts after he died—not the fortune his brothers still dream of and blame me for—so we did all right."

I smiled. "So you're not as rich as the Pannis brothers insist?"

"The government took nearly everything when the dust cleared." She waved her hand around the room. "Look where we're living, Edna. Lenny Pannis had a huge home in Beverly

Hills, right near Pickfair. He was into lavish spending, vulgar clothes, flashy jewelry. He treated his little brothers like princelings, feeding them dreams and bits of cash. They got besotted with the idea of wealth. 'We're all family,' he told them. 'If I'm filthy rich, you will be, too.' Only Tony bought that line."

"Not Ethan?"

"Tony is the romantic. Ethan counts the pennies in his loafers. What happened is that the IRS tapped into this account, that one. The house. The pool. The cars." She grinned. "That damn spiral staircase. Gone, all of it. And I said thank God."

"Talk to me some more about the agency, Alice."

She looked at me, puzzled, then considered her words carefully. "Well, let's see. Many small fish, you know. People you've never heard of. Juggling acts for television, ventriloquist acts for Ed Sullivan or Milton Berle. No big acts. He didn't want that kind of responsibility. The performers were all like the ones you've met, Edna. Tony or Tiny, whatever he calls himself. At one time a fresh comic with some promise. I went to a couple of his shows—with Max. Early on. He had an innocence that warred with a slightly sardonic tongue. Very funny. I mean, Max always insisted Tony didn't understand *how* his humor worked—it just did. But ruined now by drink and gluttony. After Lenny died, he forgot who he was. And Ethan reinvented him as an insult comic."

"Ethan?"

"Ethan got tired of having him hang around, moody and bitter. 'Go on stage with that attitude.' So…the reinvention of the failed comic…comical no more."

"I'm interested in Liz Grable. How does she fit into all this?"

"Tony's sometime girlfriend. Liz Grable was a favor, bit parts, but she got to be a nuisance. She was a pest, knocking on our door because his office is here now. Calling all hours of the night. Tony fed her the idea that she was an undiscovered talent, some sort of chubby Clara Bow with a cutesy giggle and an intense stare. A couple parts, and then Max couldn't place her."

"So Max had to deal with these…small-time egos…"

"He even read Ethan's script when he first got here from New Jersey. Max told me it was painfully sophomoric, stale. Ethan thought that Hollywood was waiting for him to show up. He already had a spot on his mantel for the Oscar for Best Screenplay. Ethan was drinking then, filled with hubris by way of Lenny. Lorena told me he was angry that he failed at something, but then, you know, she said he read parts to her—they used to act out skits together—and they ended up laughing about it."

"I remember their impromptu moment from *Othello*."

"How they amused themselves, I guess." She shrugged. "Those were the kind of clients Max had. He supplied the extras in *Sunset Boulevard*, for example. The one-line actors. Small fry, people needed in this vast dream factory out here, bit players never destined to shine up the night sky."

"Yet he represented Sol and not Larry."

She nodded. "With his looks, Larry thought he had a chance for big time, so he got a bigger name agent. Max didn't *want* to deal with him—he knew Larry would burn out. Directors always ended up hating Larry. Sol turned out to be his really important client, I suppose, who stayed with Max out of loyalty. Sol was small-time before *The Goldbergs*. Sol piddled around with bits on radio, played some old vaudeville dates, lots of grade B movies out here. Gertrude Berg had seen him at the Yiddish theater on Second Avenue, loved him, and talked to him—and Cousin Irving was born. A success story."

I needed to move around…to grapple with the questions that buzzed in my head. I stepped toward the workroom, stopped in the entrance. "May I go in?"

"Of course." She looked uncertain, though.

Inside I glanced at Max's stack of clippings on the blacklist, a chronicle of his fall from grace, on cronies like John Howard Lawson and Doc Trumbo. A pile of old scripts, one for Trumbo's *Kitty Foyle*, inscribed to Max with affection. An open loose-leaf notebook, with Max's scribbled notations, lines drawn, marginal flourishes. It seemed madness, this room. Yet, standing there, my fingers rifling through the mess, I felt that here, perhaps, might be some clue to Max's murder. I ached to tackle the stacks of papers, to delve into them.

There had to be something here. But what? What madman—a Commie hater, a disgruntled lounge singer, a failed music man, a two-bit actress—wreaked vengeance on the quiet man? Who harbored a hatred so keen it led to murder? Suddenly it seemed impossible—the stakes were too small, too petty, too parochial. The bit player who possessed a huge and terrible anger. Most likely not. How could we possibly ever know? But I *had* to know. The ghost of Max tapped me on the shoulder.

Who knocked on Max's front door that night as Lorena, Alice, and I sat in the Paradise Bar & Grill? Max said…come in…follow me to the workroom…Who?

Suddenly, jarring us, there was a quick rapping on the front door, and Alice jumped up. "Thank God. Finally. He's here."

"Sol?" I stepped back into the living room and closed the workroom door behind me.

But she was followed back into the living room not by Sol Remnick but by a sheepish Larry Calhoun, who seemed annoyed that I was there, staring back at him, an admittedly unfriendly expression on my face. Feathered fedora in hand, he was dressed in iron-pressed white linen slacks over tasseled oxblood loafers, a pale yellow cotton shirt under a white linen summer sports jacket, and, with that bronzed face, with the shock of iron-gray matinee idol hair, he looked very much the famous star he never, unfortunately, became. "I'm sorry…to come here," he mumbled. "I'm sorry," he began again, looking from Alice to me.

"No, no. Sit down, Larry."

He sat on the sofa. "I didn't know where to go." A strained voice, hollow, wispy. "Sol called me out of the blue and told me about *The Goldbergs*. You heard?"

We nodded. "Yes. *Variety*."

He glanced at the magazine on the coffee table. "I couldn't make out what he was saying at first, so crazy he was. I wondered why he was calling *me* because we stopped being friends a while ago. He doesn't *like* me. He thought I was the one who…" A deep ragged breath. "But he started to *accuse* me, Alice. On the phone. Horrible things. He blamed me for everything. I didn't do this to anybody. I'm not a…an informer, a stoolie. I mean, people *ask* me something, and I tell them. But I would never turn against Max or Sol or…"

He went on and on, a steady stream of seedy defense that ultimately rang false and callow.

"He thought you sold out his friends for cash," I said, bluntly. "Named names." I spoke evenly, each dramatic syllable steely, cold.

He looked at me, eyes wide. He wouldn't answer.

"Well?" Alice probed.

"If someone treats you to a few drinks or…"

"Why are you here, Larry?" Alice sounded fierce now.

Larry smiled weakly, a simpering look on his face. I shuddered.

"I want to reach Sol. I'm worried. He mentioned Max…and you. And I thought he'd be here. He talked of coming here. I don't want him telling people I'm a snitch for money. God knows, I don't want my name in the press. You know, linked with the HUAC and the Hollywood Ten. Lord, that's trouble enough. My job. I would never betray Max."

"You've been trying to raise money," I began.

He glanced at me but spoke over my shoulder. "Foolish gambling debts. A weakness I got, I admit. For a long time now. I got involved, some years back, with that creep Lenny Pannis and recently others and…well, never mind about it now. You can't get out of their hold. All I know is I was trying to do it the *right* way, selling my shares, my property, to Sol and others. I need quick cash. I'm in trouble. I knew Max would refuse me, but Sol might listen to me."

"No, he wouldn't," Alice said sharply.

"What was I going to do?" Helpless, palms out.

I smiled. "Obviously not sleep well at night."

He crushed his fedora between his fingers and reached for his pack of cigarettes. "Alice, I didn't come to the memorial service because I felt I didn't belong there. I *wanted* to. Max was my friend, but you know the way things have been lately. And I heard what Sol said at the service—how he was probably talking about me, that Yiddish stuff, eating a man's flesh…I was told that. That's why I want to see Sol now. On the phone he blamed me outright. He was sobbing and sobbing, talking about Max dying, about Cousin Irving and…" He breathed in. "I have no secrets, Alice."

"Everyone in Hollywood has secrets." For a second she closed her eyes.

A strange line, I thought.

"I'm a member of America First, good people, and Sol always condemned us. *Blamed* us. He attacked Desmond Peake for being a member."

"So you are close friends with Desmond?" I asked.

"We talk at meetings. He knew I was Max's friend, so he kept warning me. Stay away. He told me about walking Max out of Metro."

Silence, no one ready to say anything, Larry fumbling with the squashed fedora.

"Why are you here, Larry?" Alice asked again, her voice icy.

"I told you." He sucked in his breath. "Sol said he'd be here. I think he did. Alice, when I talked to you on the phone, you hung up on me. I need to ask you something. Sol said something about evidence that I betrayed people. Some papers. I don't know. With Max being murdered and all…well, I thought that I…" His voice was suddenly loud. "Do you know anything about that, Alice?"

She shook her head.

"Why would Max have it?" I asked.

"Sol said Max had written another letter, this time with my name in it. Naming *me* as a pinko." He drove his fist into the fedora. "Years back, I signed all kinds of petitions. Me, Sol, and Max. Local politics. Innocent stuff then. But now, through the distorted lens of Washington and even the gossip queens, well, it could look bad for me."

Alice scoffed. "Sounds to me like Sol was trying to get under your skin, Larry. Max didn't write another letter. I'd know." She frowned. "Just the one that seemed to work its evil magic."

"Are you sure?"

I was angry now. "Mr. Calhoun, don't you think that this visit is in poor taste? Self-serving, granted, survival of the unfit. Your failed acting career probably resulted from your lack of timing, which everyone tells me is a necessary skill for an actor. Your being here is proof that you didn't have a chance in hell that…"

He stood, plopped that crumpled hat on his head. It slipped to the side, giving him a vaguely raffish look, the handsome man gone off on a lark. "Yes, it was a mistake coming here." He viewed me with appropriate venom, which oddly pleased me. It was the reaction I wanted. Alice seemed inordinately delighted with my harangue.

The phone was ringing. No one moved to get it. It stopped.

He was fumbling with his pack of cigarettes. "I'm sorry, Alice. I mean it when I say I miss Max. In the early days he and I and Sol were, well, we traveled together, one man, a bond…"

The phone rang again. Absently, Alice lifted the receiver.

Larry was backing away, half-bowing, jittery, while I cast a baleful eye on the shallow man. He avoided eye contact with me.

At that moment Alice screamed and dropped the phone.

Larry jumped, spun around, kneed a coffee table. The pack of Camels sailed into the air.

"What, Alice, what?" I rushed to her.

She sank to her knees, swayed, covered her face with her hands, and trembled. The phone chord dangled over her, the receiver swinging back and forth.

I touched her shoulder. "What is it, Alice?"

She stared up at me, her face awash now in tears. "It's Sol. He's dead."

I heard a gasp and looked at Larry, a stunned look on his face. Crazily, he took off the battered fedora and then put it back on his head. It was a mindless gesture, the hat lopsided, situated now on the crown of his head so that he looked the vaudeville slapstick comic, the goofy one, the one who didn't duck when the two-by-four swung around.

"Tell me," I yelled.

But she couldn't. Leaning over her shoulders, I reached for the receiver. For a moment I could hear nothing, then a faraway voice started to say something. "Hello?"

"Oh my God, Edna. It's you. It's Lorena."

"Tell me."

Her voice shook. "I'm calling from Paramount. At work. Somebody called me here. Somebody from NBC that I'm friendly with. Harry Levy, a man...never mind. I don't know what I'm saying, Edna. Sol's dead. Harry just heard it from a reporter." She sucked in her breath. "Edna, he hanged himself."

I looked down at Alice, bunched up on the floor. She was looking up at me, doe-eyed, pitiful, as though I'd tell her she'd misheard the awful news.

"My God," I whispered. "My God."

"He hanged himself," Lorena repeated.

"Edna." Alice struggled to stand and touched my shoulder. "Tell me what happened."

But I was listening to Lorena. "Edna, he left a note. They found it in his room. He hanged himself with a cord, but he left the door open. The landlady found him."

"What did it say?" Fatigue in my voice, a dead tone, low.

She drew in her breath. "Something about America being a place that has forgotten how to love the people who love it."

"Thank you, Lorena." I replaced the receiver back in the cradle.

"Max. Sol." Alice rocked back and forth on her heels.

Then, suddenly, she stopped moving and took a step toward Larry.

"Alice, I'm sor..."

She put out her hand, traffic-cop style, into his face. "Sol is dead, Larry."

Quickly. "I heard. It's so horrible."

"He hanged himself."

"I'm sorry."

"Stop," she yelled. "I don't want to hear your phony sympathy now. He's dead. Max. Sol."

"I'm sorry."

"Stop," she screamed again. Then a strange smile covered her face, her eyes wild with panic. "The three musketeers are no more. Max and Sol. And Larry is left to pick up the pieces. If I remember correctly, if anything happened to one, the other two got the property they shared. The investments, small as they were. The blood-brother bond you all swore to." She gave out a harsh, gritty laugh. "Guess what, Larry? You're suddenly a man with a lot of money."

Chapter Thirteen

Ava had promised me a Southern fried chicken dinner. She called to remind me, her voice a rumbling whisper on the phone. "I told you I'm a damned good cook, at least of chicken." She paused. "I know you're feeling down about Sol. I heard it was a quiet funeral."

I didn't answer. I'd been lying on my bed, eyes closed, the radio playing Tony Bennett's "Cold, Cold Heart" over and over, the DJ intoxicated with the song.

That afternoon, haunted, I hailed a taxi and sailed into the hills, an aimless ramble that let me ponder the sprawling, ungainly city spread before me. The cabbie, at first confused by my vagueness, kept quiet after a while, simply nodding at my directions, probably believing a maddened lady was in the back seat. But no: the spacious landscape allowed me to think, making me more determined than ever.

"Don't be alone tonight, Edna. Tonight at my place. Just you and me. No one else. I promise. Cozy, relaxed." A pause during which I heard her sighing deeply. "No one talks to me about poor Sol, Edna. I don't know anything but what I read in the papers, and that's drivel. A photo of Gertrude Berg weeping. Max…and now Sol. I need someone to talk to me about it. Francis avoids the subject."

"Just the two of us?"

"I promise. I'll come get you. Tonight."

I didn't know what to answer. The splash and tumult of Sol's sudden death laced all my brief conversations with Alice and Lorena. Worse, I'd spotted Desmond Peake lingering in the lobby of the Ambassador earlier, then having a drink in the cocktail lounge; but when I approached him, he made a rapid exit, nearly colliding with a woman with too many shopping bags. My nerves frayed, my disposition sour—and my suitcase already opened in my room, a few items dropped in—I didn't want to stay in the suite listening to the radio all night. Every song—now I was subjected to Tony Bennett's "Because of You"—reminded me of loss.

"Yes," I told Ava. "Yes."

We sat in a long sunroom filled with plants, clinging vines twisting around posts and inching over the window sills, pots of red geraniums and lavender phlox, a gone-to-mayhem spider plant, its shoots dangling over a wicker table covered with movie magazines. Issues of *Modern Screen* and *Flirt* and *Titter* with Ava on the cover. "I don't know why I can't stop buying magazines about myself," she confided. A lived-in room, welcoming. Wide wicker chairs with overstuffed floral cushions. The late day sun peaked through the simple white-cotton dimity curtains, but the room was refreshingly cool.

She sat opposite me, her feet bare and cozily tucked under her legs as she reclined on the chair. "The tobacco field girl at home. Artie Shaw had a fit when I sat like this. Or walked barefoot in the house." She grimaced. "Or, in fact, when I opened my ignorant mouth in front of his friends. John Steinbeck, I remember, kept saying, 'I want to hear her voice, Artie. She has a great voice.' Like I was a wind-up toy they bought at a fair. William Saroyan wrote a limerick about me after I did *The Killers*. The girl silhouetted against a chiaroscuro moon."

"You look happy sitting like that."

She looked surprised. "And I don't look happy other times, Edna?"

"Not *so* happy, I suppose. Out in Hollywood"—I pointed nonsensically out the sunlit windows—"you look…modeled. You know, stylized."

She grinned. "That's Ava Gardner out there. The girl who is nervous when the cameras roll. Acting is…well…embarrassing for me, you know. Here is…Avah Gardner." She pronounced her name with a Southern twang, the vowels exaggerated and harsh.

She served iced tea, heady with wild mint she insisted had taken over her back yard. The glass had beads of water on it, cold to the touch. "Good."

"Sol." Ava's sudden mention of the dead actor was stark, abrupt. "Tell me what you know."

I told her about the funeral. "How close were you to him?"

"Through Max, of course. He'd visit here with Max. We met for lunch when he was back from New York. He lent me jazz records. He was a private man who got nervous around me. He'd stammer and bumble, and that made me tease him horribly." Her eyes got moist. "But a man who caused no trouble for anyone, a decent guy who liked to make people laugh. Since the blacklist nonsense, he never laughed again. He took it so hard, Edna."

We sat with our tea and watched the sky darken, the leaves of the ice bushes brushing against the windows, rustling in the slight evening breeze. "My sister Bappie was very fond of him. After her marriage fell apart, she was footloose, scattered. Some summers back, when he was out here, they found each other, not romantically, I mean, but like two wandering souls who bump into each other in the night. They'd go to the movies, plays, stuff like that. Then she met a new guy and they drifted apart. Sol, being Sol, didn't resent it, though I think he was lonely much of the time. I know he spent more and more time with Max. And then Max and Alice."

"Another life shot down."

Ava stood and peered out the window. "Remember back at The Coffee Pot with Sol? How we waited for the rain that never came? Sometimes I pray for rain at night, especially lately. You know, that drumming on the roof, on the windowpanes. When I was little, I slept under the eaves of the attic, the rain drumming *ping ping ping* all night long, and I'd drift into a blissful sleep." She turned to face me. "Nothing has ever been that good, Edna. The rain riled the flies trapped under the shingles, and they'd buzz around me. *Ping ping ping*. You know, I can't sleep out here in this land of perpetual sunlight. I stay awake all night long." She tapped the windowpane. "Sometimes when the breeze starts up at night I stand in the dark and wait for rain." She smiled wistfully. "Help me with dinner, Edna."

I hadn't planned on constructing my own meal that evening, but, led by Ava's rhythmic direction, I found myself bustling about her kitchen, shrouded in one of her full-length aprons with so many ruffles I feared I'd become one of the Floradora girls in a vaudeville song-and-dance routine.

"Now drop the pieces in that flour mixture there, Edna, because it's filled with special spices my mama told me about. *Secret* spices." Then: "Edna, you need to let the butter melt *first*, otherwise…"

The two of us moved in curious syncopation.

Slowly, wonderfully, thrillingly, the meal took shape: chicken sizzling and popping in the hot oil, potatoes mashed and garnished with parsley, green peas—"I grew them myself, but no one will believe me"—gleaming in salted water, a loaf of sourdough bread rising in the oven. Aromas flooded the room, the inviting tang of bubbling yeast, of crispy chicken skin, of peas slathered with butter, a conflicting war of tantalizing smells. Dizzying, the sum of it, but totally satisfying.

There I was, dressed in my fine black silk dress with the filigreed lace collar, covered now from neck to knee with Ava's own apron, my hands caked with flour, my eyes watery from the boiling water and the diced pearl onions.

"Edna, too much salt. What are you thinking?" She moved me aside and tasted with a spoon. She nodded: yes. Yes. And yes. Yes, indeed, I thought. I was flabbergasted by it all, and rapturously intoxicated with her.

By the time we sat at the kitchen table, side by side—"Not in the dining room, for heaven's sake, we're friends"—I found myself smiling with a kind of mindless delirium: I'd rarely had so satisfying an evening as this.

The sex goddess Ava Gardner—and me, the aging novelist, the world's finickiest eater, culinary martinet. Delightful, marvelous. I ate everything on my plate and Ava sat back, her eyes twinkling, and watched me. "Good Lord, Edna. You have the appetite of a fifteen-year-old boy."

Darkness had fallen outside now, lights switched on. A coziness here, safe haven.

Of course, it couldn't last. Ava started talking about Frank's moodiness lately. "He sulks now. Everything gets him down. His career, Max, Columbia Records." The wrong conversational turn because, as my old Negro housekeeper liked to say, we talked him up. She made him appear on her doorstep. A car stopped on the gravel driveway as Ava rushed to the window. "I told him *not* tonight and he promised me." For a second she shut her eyes, biting her lower lip. "Damn him."

I stood next to her as we watched the occupants tumble out of the flashy car. "Damn *them*."

Frank and the Pannis brothers stormed in, resentful that I was there, my arms folded over my chest as though I were a threatening schoolmarm, my cheeks sucked in—my most practiced look of disapproval.

"Christ, I forgot," Frank said. "I'm sorry, angel. I *did* forget."

She looked ready to slap him.

"Tell her," Tony bellowed.

"Tell me what?"

"Calm down, boys," Frank muttered. "Both of you are making way too much out of this." But the news obviously bothered Frank himself because his reassuring words were yelled out, rushed. When he looked at Ava, his face seemed to collapse, the blue eyes downcast and troubled, his chin bobbing up and down. Frank suffered out loud, I realized, the public groaner. Taking care of him when he had the flu would be a battlefield assignment. "All right, all right." Anger in his tone. "The bastards. I should have expected this."

Ava walked up to him and placed an arm around his waist. "Tell me, darling."

Tony blurted out. "The cops took him in, Ava. Frank Sinatra, the hottest singer on the planet. They took him downtown. They questioned him like a street thug. Frankie boy. Where's the respect…"

Ethan was burning. "Shut up, Tony."

Frank eyed him. "I can do my own talking, Tiny." Said with white-hot anger, his words punched the stage name. *Tiny.* Dismissal, mockery, the fat slob in the schoolyard made fun of one more time by the class lover.

Tony shot him a look, not a happy one. He looked ready to cry.

Ethan nudged Tony into a chair but I noticed he didn't seem pleased with Frank's treatment of his brother. Frank was oblivious, his arm around Ava's waist, his face nuzzled in her neck. "Baby, the way things are in this damn town."

Ava tightened her hold on him. "I don't know what's going on, Francis." Loud, insistent. "Tell me now."

Frank glanced at me, a look that communicated his desire that I be elsewhere, preferably out of town: the ancient dowager back among her lavender and old lace, her white curls under a Mother Hubbard bonnet. "Yes," I said, "tell us."

"Max's murder." The two words hung in the air, ominous. "Can you believe it?"

Tony joined in. "Just because they can't *solve* it and can't pick up the nut out there who's popping off the Commies in town…"

Ethan poked his finger into Tony's side. "Could you let Frankie tell…"

Frank rushed his words. "They never talked to me about that incident when I threatened Max at dinner, that stupid squabble, the shoving. Yeah, Louella Parsons and the gossip sheets had a field day, but that's nonsense for the lame-brained knucklehead readers in Hollywood. Yeah, I had my publicist talk to someone at the precinct—and nothing happened. I never thought the cops would pay any mind to it. But I guess there's been a few pushy calls to the police, you know, folks who can't stand me, resent me, and today they made me go downtown."

Tony sputtered. "We drove him there."

"They wanted to know my alibi. My *alibi*? Jesus Christ! I got none. I was in the desert all night."

Ethan was matter-of-fact. "The matter should end now. Finished. Your word is good."

No one paid him any mind.

"The police have a job to do," I offered.

Ethan pursed his brow and eyed me. "Frankie doesn't lie."

Frank let go of Ava, dropping into a chair, his elbows on his knees, his hands cradling his head. "I guess I lost it a little down there. I played the wise guy at the precinct."

"Oh, Francis, no."

"I told one cop who pushed me around—'You'll get a belt in your stupid mouth.' I don't like cops."

"So now what?" From Ava.

"I gotta make a statement. Go back with my lawyer tomorrow." He looked at me now, hurt in his eyes, disbelief. "They might charge me with murder."

"I think that's premature," I began.

But Tony roared over my words. "Christ Almighty."

"I didn't kill Max, Ava."

"I know you didn't."

Frank eyed Ava. "You and me, baby. They don't like us. The hillbilly and the guinea."

No one spoke for a while. Finally, Ethan broke the dead silence. "We need to identify the murderer."

We all stared at him, flabbergasted.

Ava smiled. "And just how do we do that, Ethan?"

"I mean, offer the police possibilities."

Again she said, "How? Do you have a list?"

He ignored her, staring directly into Frank's face. "It seems to me a simple scenario. Sol Remnick killed Max. Then, remorseful, he hung himself."

Clamor in the small room: Ava gasping, Tony choking, Frank whistling. Except for me, sitting there in stunned, dreadful silence, as cold as a meat locker. I was surrounded by dinghies, I thought suddenly, all loosed from their moorings.

Ava stammered, "Are you out of your mind, Ethan? Do you really believe that preposterous story?"

A long pause. "Well, no, of course not. But it *works*. We plan a story, make believe it's true, and at least it gets the police thinking…maybe, maybe."

I flared up, the hair on the back of my neck bristling. "Have you people all lost your minds out here? Is that all you can do? You fashion clever storyboards for real life, like you're sketching out the next scene of a Metro thriller? Do you hear yourself, Ethan? You're talking about peoples' lives here."

He looked at me with cool deliberation, eyes shiny. "They're both dead, Miss Ferber. Let them solve a situation that implicates…Frank."

Ava covered her face with her hands, muttering, "Why do I put up with this?"

Tony bubbled over, excited, rolling in his seat. "Maybe Sol did kill Max. Maybe Max screwed up his career, too. He killed himself because…"

I stood, raised myself to my full five-foot height, and my voice cut through the blather in the room. "Enough. You're maddened…all of you. Frank"—I cast him a steely eye—"do you agree to something so absurd and deleterious?"

He waited a long time. Finally, he sputtered, "No, of course not. I'm not crazy… I may be a lot of things but…not crazy. It's nonsense." Another pause, a heartbeat. "Sol loved Max."

It was, I thought, a simply beautiful statement, and took me by surprise.

Ethan broke in. "People kill folks they love."

Frank held up his hand. "Come on, gang. No."

Ava snarled, "Why don't you turn in Sophie Barnes? You always made fun of her, the crazy secretary with the hots for Max. Maybe she got tired of her pain, her loneliness, and… and she shot him. Remember Harry said she stormed out of the Paradise Bar in a fury, sending the candles flying. In a rage. Maybe she killed Max because…" She stopped.

"She *did* run out of the restaurant. We saw her." Tony glanced at his brother.

Ava screamed, "Francis, stop them. Now. The police are doing their job, just as Edna said. You know that. Nobody is going to arrest you. You're allowing these fools to enflame you. Come off it."

Frank nodded at us. "Let's get out of here. Screw this!" He pointed at the brothers—*bang bang*, as though he had a gun—and turned away. The brothers leaned into each other, their voices overlapping, doubtless formulating other outlandish suspects: perhaps the headwaiter at Chasens'…or Greta Garbo… or…Lana Turner. Why not? Eleanor Roosevelt, sneaking into town…I imagined their scrambled minds teeming with such absurdities.

"I think Alice did it," Tony blurted out. "Before she left for the Paradise."

"No," I said. "Remember Lorena called from the bar and spoke to Max. He was alone. Someone knocked on his door. He hung up. Alice was on the way to the restaurant."

"I don't care," Tony said. "She snuck back in."

His words suddenly made me wonder about that knock on the door. Who did arrive that night? Sophie before she joined the party at the Paradise Bar? A mysterious woman, this Sophie Barnes. Blighted love, anger, passion, a volatile temperament.

"How do we know Lorena's even telling the truth?" Tony added. "Maybe *she* was there first. Maybe. You see how she's weeping for Max, Frankie. Like she's out of control. She was always so friendly with him. Maybe an affair…maybe he turned on her…" He was counting off the reasons on his fingers, the none-too-bright schoolboy trying to do sums.

Ethan glared at his brother. "Leave my wife out of this."

"She ain't your wife anymore."

Ethan raised his voice. "You heard me, Tony. Lorena isn't part of this. She spoke to Max, and she then told you to call him. I was *there*. You mean she's making that up about the job he'd get you?"

Suddenly, Tony crumbled, his eyes tearing up. Looking at Frank, he blubbered, "Liz told me to get out—now that I lost that job at Poncho's. She's *leaving* me, Frankie. I thought that if I can get another job, she'll...you know...take me back." He faced his brother. "I promised her I won't drink. I got nowhere to go."

Ethan softened. "Tony, I told you. She won't leave you. She *won't.*"

Tony smiled at him. "She used your favorite word, Ethan. *Failure*. I'm a failure. She called us both failures. Me and you, Ethan."

"Me?"

"You ain't got your dreams, she said. Nobody does...except some. She wants to be rich and famous and I'm a...a burden."

"She called me a failure?" Ethan looked stunned.

"Because you came out here to make millions, and you took that job in accounting at Metro."

Ethan was furious. "I will be rich. Someday. Why else come out here?"

His eyes narrowed, Frank mimicked him. "I want to be rich, too, boys." His voice became mocking. "Why else come out here?"

Why else come out here?

It was brutal imitation of Ethan's whiny declaration, and Ethan glared at him. I expected him to say something but he watched, eyes slatted. "How can I become rich when I got to support Tony? Lenny left us *nothing.*"

Frank sang in a silly singsong voice: "I wanna be rich. I wanna be rich. Listen to the two of you. Your brother Lenny knew the game. He had smarts. That's what Lenny had that both of you don't. He built a fortune out of grit and sweat. That man understood honor and loyalty. I wouldn't be alive if he hadn't stepped in. They were gonna take me out. You two are pale imitations of that pal of mine."

"All right, Francis. Enough." Ava was blinking wildly.

Tony sagged into his chair, moody, hunched over. Looking up at Frank, he moaned, "You're rich, Frankie." At Ava. "You're rich, Ava." At me. "Even *she's* rich. *Show Boat* fills her pockets with gold. She doesn't even have to work anymore." He turned back to his brother. "We're the only two poor people in this room, Ethan. You and me." He started sobbing and wiped away tears with the backs of his hands.

"Oh, Christ," Ethan muttered. "Stop it, Tony."

"Are they smarter than me? Frankie? Ava? Her?"

Her had already answered that question some time ago, but decided now silence was preferable. Why articulate the obvious? Let them rattle on, I thought, these destructive hangers-on.

Ethan snickered. "Actually they *are*, Tony."

"No, they ain't. Mr. Adam and Miss Ava. You told me Frankie was just plain lucky. Luck is the game in this town."

Ethan squirmed. "Not everyone is lucky, Tony."

"You deserve to be rich, Ethan."

"Okay, enough, Tony." He stared at Frank, nervous.

I broke into the brotherly keening. "Who gains from Max's being murdered?"

My startling outburst, intentionally off the subject, silenced the brothers' inane bickering. All eyes landed on me.

Sitting up, Tony started to say Alice's name, but Ethan reached out and touched his sleeve. "Not now. Haven't we embarrassed ourselves enough tonight?"

Ava whispered to Frank. "Get them out of here."

Frank smiled. "Did you hear them, though? They don't think much of my brain, Ava. I'm just a lucky so-and-so…"

Ethan pleaded, "Don't listen to him, Frankie."

Tony looked helpless. "Do you really think Max found me a job? Lorena said she talked to him."

His shoulders stiff, Ethan walked to the door. "Maybe Lorena lied, Tony. Maybe she made the whole damn thing up. We'll never know, will we? Maybe Lorena was trying to make Max look good. Good old Max, unselfish Max, no-hard-feelings Max."

"But Lorena did speak to Max that night," I added.

Ethan frowned. "But who knows what that conversation was about? The only part I heard was when she asked for Alice."

Tony burbled, "I need a job."

Ethan turned the doorknob. "Good luck." He focused on Frank. "We need a lift back to civilization, Frankie." He waited until Tony was at his side. "We're going back to New Jersey. I've had it out here. Lenny is dead. He was murdered, too. It's too dangerous out here in Hollywood land. God knows when one of us"—His hand swept the room—"will face the barrel of a gun. Little Alice-sit-by-the-fire did *him* in. It's you and me, Tony. Back home. People come to Hollywood to die. I'm not ready for that."

◇◇◇

Ava and I sat alone in the quiet room, sipping iced tea and eating slabs of chocolate cake. Frank had driven the brothers away, begrudgingly, annoyed with them. We'd watched him careen out of the driveway, nearly clipping some bushes. I surmised the ride back would consist of silence, and a whole lot of groveling.

"I keep failing at my promises to you, Edna," Ava finally said.

"Not true." I smiled at her. "You came through with the magnificent fried chicken."

"Which, you remember, you had to fry yourself."

I breathed in. "Listen to me, Ava. These things happen, and I suppose they happen more with volatile people. You and Frank are a train wreck, but there's nothing that can be done about that. You have to play that love game out. You have no choice, toppling chairs in restaurants, knocking over drinks, screaming at each other. And everyone watches. Neither of you is ready to jump off that speeding train."

She leaned over and poured me more tea as I gazed out the window into the pitch-blackness: no moonlight, no stars.

Quietly, "I know."

"I don't like it out here," I said.

"Who does?"

"But you stay here. I can leave. New York may be a lot of things, but there's a gritty, hard-nosed reality about it. New York tells me the truth. New York slaps you awake every day of your life. Out here in the constant sunshine with wide boulevards and sparkling cars, well, people come to believe they can reinvent themselves, their failed lives. That's always been the promise of the West, of course—new beginnings, second chances, new blood pulsating through the anemic body. And, I suppose, it can be true. But not for L.A., not this oasis that looks to Hollywood for answers. Make it up and see if it flies. If it doesn't, make something else up. A culture of sandboxes with children restacking the blocks that keep falling down."

Ava had been staring at me, mouth open. "God, Edna. Stay away from the Chamber of Commerce. They'll crucify you. Tar and feather you and ride you out of town on a rail." She started giggling.

"And it would be filmed for a scene in some celluloid epic."

She looked to the ceiling. "But I wanted to come out here."

"It's your career."

"I know, I know. I make my money here. Lots of it. Tons of it. But most don't. A Tony Pannis. Liz Grable who waits for that talent scout every time someone walks into the soda parlor where she waits and waits, perched on a stool. We keep lying to them."

"Otherwise there'd be only desert and orange groves. L.A. circa 1900."

She sipped her tea. "Sometimes I dream of going back home. I wanted to be an actress—I wanted to shine in *Show Boat*, get fantastic reviews—but I don't *want* it. You know what I mean? Francis doesn't believe me. For him it's everything. Hoboken is grubby and horrid…and over. L.A. is…is the flashy Cadillac convertible, the big house in Palm Springs, and the screaming girls. I dream of North Carolina because no one bothered me there. Yes, I like the fame, I guess, but I feel *owned* here. Eaten alive."

"You are so good in *Show Boat*."

A wide grin. "Keep telling me that. I don't *like* myself most of the time."

I sipped my tea. "What do you want, Ava?"

"I don't know. Right now, I want Francis. But I also know that he's...Hollywood. Exciting. He's L.A. He's Palm Springs. He's beautiful at the moment but he's temporary. Everything out here—even people—are rented for the short term. Ironically he's probably the love of my life. Paradox, no?" She chuckled. "I learned *that* word from Artie Shaw. He described *me* that way."

"Well, you are."

"Everyone is."

"True. But some more than others."

She drew her bare feet up under her legs, snuggled into the cushions. "I will always make movies. I'm supposed to." She struck a pose. "'The most beautiful woman in the world.'" Said with a bittersweet wistfulness. "But I want to live in Europe. Spain, probably. When I was there, I felt...comfortable. Everything is old and they like it that way." Now she grinned. "And the bullfighters wear such tight pants, Edna."

I ignored that. "Does Frank know about this dream of yours?"

"I've told him, but he's not one to listen. He thinks Hollywood is paradise on earth. El Dorado. The seven cities of Cibola, acres of gold all contained in one big movie contract. You know, he's so...soft a man, Edna. He's afraid he'll break."

"He reminds me of a mischievous little boy."

"Exactly." Her eyes got merry. "It must be illegal to go to bed with a little boy in Hollywood." She laughed outright, long, full.

My mind wandered. "Ava, I go back home in days and Max's murderer is still at large."

Ava leaned into me and smiled. "But you're doing something about it, no?"

Startled, "How do you know?"

"I see the way you look at folks, Edna. You know, I've watched you at the cocktail party and at dinners and the public melees that Francis and I stage for Hedda Hopper and her ilk. This is a puzzle you're working on. You got a bag of pieces and you're shaking it."

I nodded. "I owe this to Max."

"You know all the players in this little costume drama."

"How do you know it wasn't a stranger?"

"Of course not. This was a deliberate killing...and *personal.* Somebody had something *against* Max. Some vendetta. No Commie nonsense. That was a convenient excuse, used by someone. Think about it, Edna. Someone took advantage of the moment to kill poor Max." She locked eyes with me. "We agree about that, don't we, Edna?"

"I know that."

"It's about timing here. Timing."

I sat back. Everybody in Hollywood talked about timing. The glib catchphrase covered a multitude of sinning. The players. Who gained by Max's death? I asked that question over and over. What satisfaction did someone have in seeing him dead?

Ava got reflective. "The night he died, Edna. Think about it."

Yes, I thought: the night he died. Where were all the people? I counted them in my head. Who?

"You know the answer, Edna. I suspect you know most things before they happen." She smiled.

"Tiki voodoo, Ava?"

"What?"

"Nothing." I pointed a finger at her. "There's always black magic in paradise."

Chapter Fourteen

"Miss Ferber." A scratchy voice, grating. For some reason Desmond Peake glanced over my shoulder, toward the doorway. "Miss Ferber."

I looked behind me. "Are you seeing double, Mr. Peake? Perhaps a visit to the eye specialist…"

He glared at me and the pencil in his hand snapped into two. "What I need to say, well…needs saying."

He made no sense, of course, but I let it pass. Desmond Peake, Metro's troubleshooter, had reached me at my hotel, insisting I visit Culver City for a short luncheon. When I said no, he announced that the studio car was already in the Ambassador parking lot, waiting. "It's important."

"I doubt that."

"Why would you say that?" Real concern in his voice.

"Because such words usually introduce topics that don't live up to the promise."

He blathered for a bit and I almost felt sorry for him, so I consented.

Delivered by a taciturn chauffeur to Culver City, then sequestered in a private room, I dined quietly with Desmond Peake, though he wolfed down his pot roast with such alacrity I feared we were being timed in some competition no one had told me about.

"Tell me why you've summoned me here, Mr. Peake."

He swallowed and wiped his mouth with a napkin. "You must be joking, ma'am. Four words. Max Jeffries. *Show Boat*. No, make that five words. Murder. Let me add two other words. Hedda Hopper. Very chilling words."

"I'm aware of the meaning of all of them, sir."

"Put them together and they spell trouble."

"For whom?"

"Look around you, Miss Ferber. For Metro. Even after Max… died, Hedda Hopper persists in referring to you and *Show Boat* in her columns. Her last comments were beyond the pale."

"I agree with you. Max was already removed from Metro some time ago. By you, I believe. And most unfairly, to be sure. He was uncredited for his work on *Show Boat*. None of that was acceptable to me…so why now…"

"You don't seem to grasp the situation, Miss Ferber. Millions of dollars are at stake here. Reputations. *Show Boat* is to be premiered in two days. Today's *Examiner* published another photo of you and Max and Ava Gardner from that infamous lunch you all had. This time with Ava sticking out her tongue. And then Louella Parsons' blow-by-blow account of the melee at Don the Beachcomber. My God, Miss Ferber. Max did himself in."

"And?"

"And you're not listening to the message."

Desmond Peake folded and unfolded the napkin in his lap. He was so tall and lanky, with such a long graceless neck on a head that seemed to bob as he spoke, that even sitting opposite me, five-foot little me, he loomed over me. Disconcerting, that image, for I had to look up at him though we were both seated.

"I'm going back to New York," I announced. "I came here for Max and someone killed him."

He placed his napkin on the table. "I'm happy you'll be returning to New York. I know you were invited to the premiere at the Egyptian Theatre but…"

"I've already refused."

The air went out of him. "I know. Wisely."

"But I could change my mind."

He narrowed his eyes. "But you won't, will you? That's why I invited you here today...to talk. You're a sensible woman. I sense that about you. Hasn't your name been in the scandal sheets too often lately? With Max, with Ava, even a casual mention of you with Alice Jeffries at the Paradise Bar the night Max died—and none of it favorable. You're so...visible in Hollywood these days while publicly shunning our premiere based on *your* novel. People wonder why you're *still* here. It's only natural. So people expect you to be there. *Show Boat* doesn't need that. Dore Schary is nervous." He grunted. "The only one not nervous is Ava Gardner."

"She loved Max, you know."

"Max Jeffries is dead. So will be her career if she isn't careful." The napkin slipped off the table onto the floor. He glanced at it but didn't retrieve it. I assumed it was too far to travel.

"Aren't you concerned that Max was murdered?"

He didn't answer, but shuffled to his feet. "I'm glad you're leaving L.A., Miss Ferber. And I'm glad you'll be absent from the premiere." An anemic smile, forced. "It makes my job a lot easier. I'm glad we have this...understanding."

Outside, standing with him as we waited for the car he summoned, I heard my name called. Ava Gardner rushed up, swaddled in a terry cloth robe, a scarf around her head, cold cream slathered on her cheeks. "My spies reported in," she whispered. "I had to escape from makeup. No one told me you were here."

Desmond bristled but stepped into the street, frantically waving to an approaching town car, probably hoping it would bump me onto an unused soundstage.

Ava whispered again, "I'll call you later. We need to talk. Me and Francis and you. I'll call. Don't make plans. Please. I'll reserve a private room at the Brown Derby."

As Desmond Peake rushed back, out of breath, grasping my elbows, she winked at him and disappeared through a doorway.

He spoke through clenched teeth. "If *she* won't listen to me, perhaps you will."

I sank into the back seat. "This has been delightful, Mr. Peake. As always, you show a girl a good time."

◇◇◇

Back at my hotel, lying on my bed with my eyes shut, the telephone jarred me. As I lifted the receiver to my ear, Ava was already in mid-sentence, a rush of words that ran together. "That ass, Desmond. When will men learn that there are certain women you do *not* warn? Edna, I couldn't talk to you at Metro. Desmond chased me around until I slammed a door in his face. He's so afraid the premiere will be one publicity nightmare." She waited a second. "Edna, we'll pick you up at eight tonight, if you're free. Please be! We need to talk. Just the three of us." I could hear her deep intake of a cigarette, a slight raspy cough. "That is, if you *want* to. I'm being pushy here, Edna."

"Talk about what?"

"Francis."

"Has something happened?"

"This morning a New York columnist named Lee Mortimer from the *Mirror*, some cheap tabloid, actually accused Francis of murder. In black and white. It's causing a fire storm."

"It's just a rumor, Ava. We've already discussed it…"

Her voice rose. "The wire services have picked it up. Soon it'll be…true."

A heartbeat. "Could he be the killer, Ava?"

For a moment I thought she was laughing, but it was a jagged cigarette cough. "I wouldn't put it past him, but…no."

"I wondered."

"Tonight, Edna. Please. You can ask him yourself."

"Ava, I'm not his favorite person. Would I risk an ashtray hurled at my ancient head?"

"I'll make him behave."

"You haven't in the past."

"Please, Edna."

"All right, but he must be kept on a leash. There are times I think I might like him, but I wouldn't put my hand into his cage."

"Edna, really. Sometimes you talk like a gossip columnist."
She hung up the phone.

"Well," I talked out loud to myself, "there was no need to
insult me."

◇◇◇

Ava told me we'd be entering the Brown Derby through a side
door, slipping in unseen. I'd been to the famed eatery before and
never liked the unhealthy mix of noisy tourists, second-rate film
stars, and obsequious waiters. As Frank, Ava, and I approached
the landmark I mocked its garish exterior: that Stan Laurel derby
perched atop a building already fashioned after a derby. I was
sitting in the rear seat of Frank's Cadillac convertible and had
insisted he put the top up. I was in no mood for a breezy joyride.

Frank turned back to me and laughed. "Edna, people travel
across America to eat this expensive food."

To which I replied, "Must we be part of that mindless herd?"

Inside the eatery, snuggled into a small room where we could
still hear the hum of diners nearby, I noticed the décor was
merely a hiccough of the larger room: the worn red banquettes,
the glittery crystal chandeliers, walls covered with caricatures of
the famous and not-so-famous-anymore celebrities.

When we were alone, Ava reached over and grasped my
hand. "I can't believe you're leaving so soon, Edna. I've come
to rely on you."

"You'll have to visit me in New York, Ava."

She nodded. "Of course. You know, I'm still afraid to stop
in to see Alice. Whenever I turn around, there's a photographer
lurking nearby."

Frank sat with his hands resting on the table, his eyes focused
on Ava. He spoke quietly. "I've told her not to go."

Ava narrowed her eyes. "I'll do what I want, Francis." But
she pulled back. "I don't want cameras flashing around Alice.
She has enough to deal with." She shuddered and said, strangely,
"Max is not supposed to be dead."

We stopped talking as a waiter knocked, entered, bowed
deeply to us as he was walking in. I thought of movie scenes

in which the royal factotum salaamed his way before the king, then backed out, apologizing, groveling. No eye contact. Well, this bronzed young man didn't approach that caricature but he did warrant an Oscar nomination for servile flattery. Each menu was dispensed quickly but with a flourish. "Miss Gardner." A Prussian bow. "Mr. Sinatra." A similar bow. Then a short, barely perceptible pause. "Madam…" A pause, then, "Ah, Miss… Ferber." Well trained and briefed. I like that in a man.

But the only one he looked at was Ava Gardner.

And I didn't blame him. Tonight she was dressed in a strapless ivory and gold silk cocktail dress, with a cut-jade silver necklace. Quite striking, indeed. My simple black dress with the three strands of pearls and the modest onyx brooch made no statement at all that registered on Hollywood's glitter meter.

Ava was in a mood to reminisce about Max, and she shared some stories I'd not heard before: how he appeared as an extra in the background in *Jungle Book* in 1942, dragged in for a crowd scene at the last moment by director Zoltan Korda, a reluctant Max who looked very unhappy holding a basket cradled against his chest. He'd worked on the soundtrack for the Kipling adaptation. She recalled being with Max in a Montgomery Ward in Fresno where the saleslady kept saying, "You don't look like Ava Gardner." Late one night Max appeared at her Nichols Canyon home because he dreamed she was in trouble and she wasn't answering her phone.

Another time he showed up at Ava and her sister Bappie's apartment, surprising Ava on her Christmas Eve birthday with an autographed photograph of Clark Gable, Ava's long-time hero. This was long before she was famous, of course—when she was a fifty-dollar-a-week starlet living in a cheap hotel, the Hollywood Wilcox. Max had personally knocked on Gable's dressing room door. The joke, realized later, was that Gable, in a hurry, had signed the photo "To Eva," which Max didn't realize until back in his office. Ava, of course, cherished the error.

"Bappie and I grilled hamburgers, played rummy, and listened to the radio. I was in bed by nine because I had to catch three buses out to Culver City." Her eyes got moist. "Max warned me about Hollywood, especially the old lechers like Mayer who groped the girls, even little girls like Judy Garland. He told me—just *slap* them. They only understand violence."

Frank said nothing the entire time Ava rambled on, a monologue punctuated now and then by my occasional interjection. Obviously she needed to do this…this beautiful ramble, heartfelt, and finally, her eyes closed, she stopped, slumped in her seat.

Frank poured from the bottle of champagne the waiter delivered and seemed to be waiting for something to happen. At last, Ava smiled thinly at me, a wistful smile, and sipped her drink. We ordered Cobb salads because that's what you ordered there, in the eatery where it was first created.

As we ate, I noticed Ava got more and more agitated, picking up her fork, putting it down, leaning forward toward me, drawing back, jittery. "What, Ava?"

She shook her head and her eyes got dreamy.

"Something is going on," I insisted.

When I looked at Frank, he was sitting back in his seat, arms wrapped around his chest, rocking his body. He didn't take his eyes off her. What he doubtless saw was what I was seeing now: that beautiful face trembling.

Finally Frank looked at me. "Ava is going nuts over Lee Mortimer's column in the *Mirror*. The tide seems to be turning against me."

"But there's no proof," I protested.

She shook her head vigorously. "Does it matter out here?" She swung around and looked into his emotionless face. "Francis did not *kill* Max." A deep intake of breath. "He didn't *murder* my friend." She reached for a cigarette and lit it with a shaking hand. I wondered why Frank didn't light it for her, the gentlemanly gesture. But he seemed frozen in that chair, save for the maddening tapping of an index finger against his chest.

"They're rumors, Ava."

"This afternoon at Metro, in my dressing room after I saw you, I was leafing through a pile of clippings Publicity sent over, like ads for Lustre Creme Shampoo." A fuzzy grin. "'Ava Gardner of *Show Boat* uses Lux soap.' Really insipid stuff. It piles up. Fan magazine hype—'Trying to De-Glamorize Ava Gardner, Hollywood's Toughest Job.' Nonsense like that. They send it over, and I file it all away. But under that pile someone had maliciously slipped Mortimer's vicious column." She shook her head back and forth. "And someone scribbled on it: 'Frankie Boy is a killer, you witch.'"

Frank said nothing, just picked at his salad.

"Lord," I said. "Such mean-spirited folks."

"I don't like where this is heading. I always felt *safe* in my dressing room."

"Ignore it, Ava."

Frantic, "I can't."

"You can't stop people from being vile or sneaky."

Her eyes got wide, saucer-like, moons in that stunning face. "I didn't ask for any of this." She paused. "But what if the rumors don't stop...poor Francis."

Frank made a grunting sound, unpleasant.

Ava touched his sleeve but he didn't move. It was as if he wanted to be invisible, away from there, perhaps out in the night desert, driving, driving.

It now struck me that Frank had said little during Ava's lament for a lost Max, as well as her frenzied recounting of the circulating rumors. Just that one sentence. He sat there, leaning forward to sip his champagne, and watched, quietly, sullenly. A curious passivity, as though this had nothing to do with him.

I looked at Frank. "Well, you did threaten to kill him."

Casually, "I threaten to kill a lot of people. Mostly photographers. And I did knock Lee Mortimer around at Ciro's one night. Since then, he's always had it in for me."

"Perhaps you should stop, Frank."

"People bring out the worst in me. They make me mean." He chuckled and reached for his drink.

Ava hurriedly said, "Francis, be serious. This *is* serious."

"I didn't kill him. I had nothing against Max. End of story."

"But the world"—she actually pointed at the closed door, beyond which we could hear the murmur of voices—"thinks differently, Francis." Now she turned to me. "Mortimer talked about underworld gangland shootings. Lenny Pannis and his goons."

"My brother."

"A thug."

Frank bristled. "Hey, you're talking about me as though I'm not here. I happen to like them. They're brothers."

"Thugs," she thundered.

Frank sat up, his face red, his voice booming. "Screw you, darling."

It was, frankly, a horrendous moment, the pathetic curse flying across the room like a sudden slap, so abrupt that I jumped and toppled over an empty champagne glass. It crashed to the floor and shattered.

Ava searched my face. "Francis won't *do* anything."

"Can it, Ava. Christ Almighty. I thought we'd agreed to shut up about it."

"All I'm saying is…"

He yelled, "I know what you're saying." His foot pounded the floor.

"I told you I talked to Dore Schary. Metro wants a meeting with you. Maybe they'll take you back."

Frank looked at me, disgusted. "I wanna get out of here."

Ava pleaded. "Edna, I love a man who wants to see his whole life fall apart."

Frank fumed. He tried to light a cigarette but his hand shook. The match and cigarette dropped to the table.

"Perhaps now is not the place to…" I began.

"Help us, Edna."

Frank stood up abruptly. "I don't need help. Ava. Old maids need boy scouts to help them across the wide boulevards of L.A. I'm not a boy scout."

Ava stammered, "Francis, how dare you!"

Frank avoided looking at me.

"Ava," I said brightly, "why are you so sure Frank did not kill Max?"

"Tell her, Francis." Ava looked up at Frank who was shuffling from one foot to the other.

Frank moved toward the closed door. "I wonder why I let you talk me into these evenings, Ava."

Ava stood, grabbed at the sleeve of his sports jacket. He twisted out of her grip, and sputtered, "Christ, Ava! Leave me some dignity."

"You didn't do it, did you, Francis? I called you that night, but you weren't home. You told me you'd be back in Palm Springs."

"I told you already, Ava. I've told everybody. I went for a ride out into the desert. By myself. I do that a lot. With broads like you, a guy has to get away sometimes."

The look on Ava's face startled me. Perhaps I expected a belligerent yet hopeful trust in what he was saying to her—a trust that a man who lied to her so many times would not, this time around, lie again. She wanted some black-and-white resolution to this dilemma...to convince herself that her instincts were on target.

But what I saw in that beautiful face now was confusion, doubt, and with it an abundance of pain. Conflicted, torn, she glanced back at me, as though I held an answer for her. Though I immediately regretted it, I closed up my face and stared, steely-eyed, at a helpless Ava.

Now Ava whispered at Frank, who had his back to her. I could see his neck muscles tighten, swell. "Your bodyguard said you left in a fit. You were angry."

He swung back to face her. A vein on his left temple throbbed, his eyes so dark now they could be black instead of that deep-sea blue. "You interrogated Angie? You questioned him?"

Ava slumped back in the chair. "We were talking."

"Christ."

Frank opened the door and kicked it back against the wall. From where I sat I could see the upturned heads of a few diners, suddenly startled by the movement. "Another pleasant evening,

Ava," he sneered. "Miss Ferber, a real delight." He sailed through and slammed the door behind him.

I tried to smile at her. "That went well."

Ava stared at the slammed door. When she reached for a cigarette, her hand shook so much she had to give up.

Chapter Fifteen

Ava's words. *You know the answer, Edna*. Ava's panicked response to the accusations against Frank. Ava's declaration that…that night held the answers we all sought. That night, and the assembled cast of this sad drama. I couldn't escape thinking about her words. In the middle of the night, suddenly awake and sitting up in bed, I played with her words. The night of the murder. Put the pieces together, Edna. Block out the scene. Stage the performance. Place the characters. Lift the curtain. Roll the cameras. Lights, camera…inaction.

Lorena Marr seemed surprised to hear my voice on the phone. "Edna, my word. Has something happened?"

"No, Lorena, I haven't spoken to you since Sol's funeral."

There was hesitation in her voice. "I know. I've been in hiding. Ethan called me early yesterday morning and told me Frank was mad at Tony. I guess Tony mouthed off at Ava's house."

"Yes, not pretty."

"It's amazing how Ethan checks in with me now more than when we were married."

"What did he say?"

"Just that Tony made a fool of himself."

"He did that, certainly, but I don't think he knows how to behave anymore. He's wading in quicksand." I waited a second. "He hates Frank, doesn't he?"

Long silence, the dead space of a phone conversation. "Why do you say that?"

"Because it's obvious. He resents Frank's success the way a poor family member hates the crumbs a wealthy relative tosses his way."

"No one wants to face that."

"I do." I waited. "And Ethan himself was not the picture of decorum that night."

Surprise in her voice, a chuckle. "He didn't share *that* information with me."

"Doubtless."

Lorena spoke matter-of-factly. "Ethan keeps his emotions hidden." I could hear her lighting a cigarette, the striking of a match. "Ethan is troubled, I guess, because Frank was ice cold on the ride back into town."

"Well, they said some unflattering things to him." Now I warmed up. "I gather Ethan refers to them as Adam and Ava. The lost souls of paradise."

"He doesn't mean anything by that. Ethan is hard to read sometimes."

"You make excuses for him, Lorena. Patient Griselda, home waiting for her man."

"That's not fair, Edna. We *were* in love."

"Past tense?"

A pause as she changed her mind. "I'm lying to you, Edna. It does mean something. With Frank losing favor these days, he's shoving the boys aside, particularly Tony. He's…impatient. It's hard to *like* Tony, loyalty to Hoboken notwithstanding. Some of us remember the quiet, funny guy—before Lenny died. I suppose Tony *does* resent Frank's stupendous success, even though he's been riding his coat tails freely."

"I sensed that." I waited a second. "What about Ethan? How does he view Frank?"

"Well," Lorena breathed in slowly, and I could hear the intake of a cigarette, "lately he's told me he doesn't like Frank's mockery of Tony."

"But that's so much sport these days. The lost drunk. Tony's out of control and you're all watching him as though he's a scene in a movie you don't care for."

"You know, Edna, out here in gaga land, everyone is surprised when they realize they haven't become rich and famous over night."

"That's Ethan?"

"A little bit. Back when. But I was thinking more of Tony."

"Sometimes I think that he's never so drunk as he acts. Even smashed, he's watching everyone."

A long silence. "God, Edna. I don't think so. He gets hammered and passes out."

"True, but at the Paradise, under Ethan's watch. But I sense a bit of the actor in him. A bad one, yes, but I detect cleverness in him. Acting the fall-down drunk allows him to get away with things. Oh, poor Tony, the sad drunk on Saturday night. Poor Liz, putting up with him. Poor Ethan, the guardian angel. Well, what can you expect from a drunk?"

Again, the hesitation. "Well, maybe."

"Ethan mentioned that he and Tony are headed back to New Jersey."

Now she laughed out loud. "Ethan has been threatening to do that for a while. He claims to be sick of L.A., that he is saving Tony from a drunk tank and death. God, back in Hoboken he'd disappear into a package store and never come out. But L.A. is in Ethan's blood. Go to the movies with him sometime—he's like a little kid, all revved up, almost giddy. 'They make movies *here!*' he once chirped at me. Imagine!"

There was a rush of voices behind her. "You're busy." But I added, hurriedly, "I called for a reason. Do you have Liz Grable's phone number?"

"Yeah, why?"

"I'd like to talk to her."

A long pause. "Liz?"

I stammered. "I told her we'd have a talk."

"Really?"

My request puzzled Lorena, though she gave me Liz's number as well as that of her hair salon.

"Call me, Edna. Before you leave."

"We'll talk, Lorena. I promise."

"No, no," she insisted. "Call me. Do you know how rare it is in L.A. to talk to someone who listens to you?"

When Liz Grable was called to the phone in the hair salon, she began talking immediately, her voice loud, angry. "You were supposed to call this morning, Tony. I want my goddamn key."

I broke in. "Miss Grable, I'm afraid…it's Edna Ferber calling."

Silence, heavy breathing. In the background women's high-pitched voices, a lazy voice on the radio. Finally, Liz spoke into the receiver, her words clipped, wary. "Miss Ferber? What do you want?"

"We haven't spoken…"

"I'm at work. I'm busy." She repeated, "What do you want?"

Good question, I reflected: what *did* I want? Ava's comments had me mulling over the circumstances of the murder, prodding me to dwell on the night of the murder and the people—the players—involved. Who was where that fateful night? And, of course, missing from the equation was Liz Grable. Tony admitted to calling her from the Paradise Bar & Grill, but claimed she wasn't at home.

"I was wondering if you'd join me for lunch."

She didn't answer at first. Someone nearby called her name. "What?"

I repeated my invitation. "I thought it would be nice…"

Bluntly, her mouth too close to the receiver. "Why?"

"Liz, we barely had time to talk at Ava's when we met."

She gave out a false tinny laugh. "I wonder why." Her voice had a whiny, hollow tone, as annoying as grit in your eye, and it baffled me that she believed she could be an actress. Perhaps in silent pictures, one more fledgling actress tied to the railroad tracks with the locomotive barreling down at her. *The Maiden's Mistake; or, How Lizzie Caught the Train.*

A deep breath. "I'm curious about something."

"Like what?"

"Your…perspective on the murder."

"Max?"

"Yes."

A heartbeat. A whisper. "I have nothing to say."

"A short conversation."

"Oh, I don't think so." A slight, phony laugh.

"People don't let you talk, Liz," I began. "Tony and Ethan dominate, and Frank…well…"

"Is a bastard," she finished for me.

"It's unfair to you, Liz."

"You said it."

"That's why I thought…well, you must have ideas. You've been around…"

"Well, yeah, but I don't know."

Exhausting, this disingenuous probing on my part. Liz, the unfriendly witness—to use that sickening and destructive phrase so happily employed by the HUAC in Washington. *Are you now or have you ever been…?*

"I'd like to hear you."

"I don't think so."

I shifted gears, so blatant a move I expected her to slam down the phone. "We started talking about *Cimarron* that night. You mentioned my heroine Sabra Cravat, the land rush, your family settling there. The Sooners. Your family in Oklahoma."

The abrupt shift in my words startled, but I had little time for the diplomatic niceties of journalistic interviews. The train was coming down the track. Excitedly, Liz told me, "My grandpa was late for the land grab then, so we missed out, but he had some wild stories."

"I wish he'd been someone I'd interviewed when I was there."

She *tsk*ed. "Too bad. Yeah, but you'd have to talk to the dead." She considered her line funny because she chuckled.

"That's a problem I have when I research the past."

"A killer, no?" Another sigh. She covered the receiver and her muffled voice addressed someone nearby. She came back on the line. "All right, Miss Ferber, I can get out of here early afternoon. Say one o'clock?"

I agreed to meet her at Jack's Luncheonette two blocks over on Hollywood. "One o'clock," I stressed.

"I know how to tell time."

When the taxi dropped me off at Jack's, she was already standing in the doorway. Nervously, she shook my hand, a quick, blustery gesture, and then mumbled something about almost changing her mind. As the waitress seated us. Liz told me over her shoulder, "I'm not one to talk about people, you know."

"Neither am I, Liz."

She eyed me suspiciously. "Hey, you make living talking about people."

I grinned. "But they're not real. I make them up."

"I wouldn't be too happy seeing myself in one of your books."

"Why not?"

She tilted her head and rubbed an ear. She held up the menu in front of her face, shielding her mouth. "I'm the dumb blonde who's got dreams that get her nowhere. That picture is all over the movie screen now, that kind of broad, and it ain't the real me. I ain't daffy."

I made eye contact with her. "You shouldn't let other folks tell you what you are, Liz. That's a secret most women don't know. Invent yourself, and stick with it."

She scoffed. "Yeah, sure. Nobody believes that I got a brain. I mean, Tony thinks *he's* smarter than me."

I assumed my Magnolia Ravenal Southern-belle voice. "Get out of here!"

For the first time she laughed out loud. I joined her.

We ordered sandwiches and coffee. "I like your dress," she said. "It goes great with your white hair."

She sat back, relaxed. The waitress filled water glasses and Liz frowned at her retreating back. "A girl that skinny should never wear her hair like that."

I hadn't noticed. "Tell me something, Liz." I put down my glass. "You were the one who knocked on Max's door the night he died, right?"

The question, hurled so brutally at her, stunned her.

She'd been sipping water, a gingerly movement she'd obviously appropriated from some Jean Harlow movie, but my words made her sputter. Water dribbled down the side of the glass, and she wiped her mouth with the back of her hand. Her eyes darkened, scared. For a second, she reached up to check on her puffed platinum hairdo, as though she feared it had collapsed like a surprised soufflé.

"How did you know?" she whispered.

"A guess, and not a very clever one, Liz. Someone visited Max that evening. You didn't answer when Tony called you from the Paradise, which surprised him. No witness has come forward to the police, so far as I know, and, frankly, you're one of the few players unaccounted for that evening. I had the feeling that Tony was suspicious when you weren't home. As I say, a guess."

She grinned. "A good one."

"Tell me."

"Nothing really to tell, though I don't want anyone to know. I mean, like Max got killed right after that visit. So I can't go to the police…"

I cut her off. "Of course, you can. You have to."

She shook her head. "God, no. They'll think I…"

"Tell me what you know. Liz."

She sat back, folded her arms across her chest, glanced around the crowded room. She leaned in and seemed to be weighing her words, time for intimate confession. "I'm sick of it all, Miss Ferber. I'm sick of Tony. Of Ethan. Of Frank. All of them. I stayed too long at the fair, as they say."

"What do you mean?"

"I've *had* it. You gotta know that I told Tony he had to get out of my place now that he's lost that dumb job in the valley. Yeah, quite the job! A measly few dollars a week, lost on the ride back home. Drinks and poker. I mean, I sort of love the slob— I mean the *old* Tony who made me laugh, who bought me cheap trinkets on Sunset, who promised me the moon." She sighed. "Before everything fell apart. The drinking. You know, I won't allow *that* in my apartment. I don't even wanna be around him then—like that night at Ava's when we showed up there with Frank and Ava was having that cocktail party. I told them I didn't wanna go. I know how those nights end, for God's sake."

"So he drinks at the Paradise."

"Yeah, that sleazy gin mill." She bit the corner of a nail. Red enamel flecked off. "You know, I started thinking about *my* life. *My* career. I was dumb enough to believe that Tony had some influence—with Frank and Ava. But they're in their own pretty little worlds. Frank's *mean* to me. Ava is sweet but only looking at Frank. Ethan thought I'd be good for Tony—he *pushed* the relationship on me, paid for everything. He planned it like a military operation. He didn't know how to handle Tony—once Tony became this…you know, different guy. Get Tony out of his hair once and for all. But Ethan's a jerk, too. 'Are you going out looking like that?' 'Why would someone your size wear a dress like that?' That's how he talks to me. I know style, Miss Ferber. I got a chinchilla fall jacket with a velveteen collar. High style. Look at Ethan. Mr. Neat Freak…ooh ooh ooh, I got me a button loose. Help me! Ooh ooh, somebody scuffed my shoe." She paused, out of breath.

"Don't let people be mean to you, Liz."

She nodded, eyes wide. "Anyway, I decided to back off, cut my losses, you know. Especially now. It's annoying how one day you wake up and there it is slamming you in the face: time is going by, lickety-split, and I'm wasting it with a bunch of creeps. Tony is the dirt road to nowhere. I'd thought I'd get *parts* by now."

"You got Max as your agent through Tony, right?"

She rolled her eyeballs and grunted. "That's funny. I had this here agent—at least he had a *card* that said that—when I met Tony. Ethan introduced us. Max was Tony's agent. Tony started out okay, a decent stand-up comic making fun of himself. Real likeable. He ain't as stupid as…well, he lets on like he is. It made for a funny act onstage. But he got fat and drank and started wearing those sequined tuxedo jackets with wide lapels with bells and whistles all over them, and he practiced insulting old ladies in the grocery store. Real clever, no?"

The waitress placed our sandwiches on the table, poured coffee, so Liz stopped talking, watching her intently, waiting until she moved away. She spoke in a theatrical whisper. "Waitresses hear too much, Miss Ferber. They're phonies. I don't want to end up in the gossip sheets."

"I wouldn't worry about that."

She squinted at me. "I am with *you*. You're famous."

"Not in this restaurant."

"Well, anyway, Max said some nasty things to me. I started hating him."

I bristled. "Max could never be unkind."

"Try going into business with him, lady." She rolled her tongue out suddenly, like an anxious frog. "Lord, I shouldn't speak bad of the dead, right?"

I shrugged. "I do it all the time. The dead are wonderful targets."

Now her tongue rolled over her lower lip, the frog having captured the unsuspecting fly. "Not surprising to me. You got you some mouth." She looked smug, happy with her put down.

"Go on, Liz. In a war of words, I…well, never mind."

She leaned across the table, her pale gray eyes becoming dark marbles. "I just lied to you, Miss Ferber. Max wasn't that bad. I mean, I used to get mad because he couldn't find me no work. But then Max married Alice, and all hell broke out. World War Three. I mean, Tony went ballistic. Ethan couldn't speak in complete sentences. I only met this holier-than-thou Lenny one time, but he was a grease ball, flashy suits and women and doling out those dollar bills to the dizzy boys. But suddenly everything had to change. Tony quit Max. So I did. It was a dumb move because it left me with nothing. But at the time I thought—well, Tony says Frank Sinatra is going to get him gigs. Why not me, too?"

"Was Ava around then?"

"Yeah, Ava was in the picture then. The first time we met she was real nice, which surprised the hell out of me. When Frank made fun of me, she rubbed my shoulder, like we were old girlfriends. I mean, you'd think she'd be a bitch." She smirked. "*I* would if I was her. With *that* face. I used to be friends with a crew guy at Metro. He said she was common people. She'd eat lunch with the crew, not in her dressing room. So I thought, well, she'd help me. I wasn't *allowed* to ask her. Ethan warned me—don't you dare ask for a favor. Frank'll go nuts."

"Tell me about Frank."

"What's to tell?" Liz took a compact from her purse and checked her face. "Excuse me a sec, Miss Ferber." She found a tube of lipstick and dabbed at her lower lip, then rolled her tongue over her lips. Satisfied, she sat back.

The waitress dropped dessert menus with us, and Liz deliberated with rapt concentration, her fingers pointing from one to the other, unable to decide. "The cheesecake," she told the waitress. "You know, a big slice." She checked her wristwatch. "I gotta watch the time, Miss Ferber."

"Frank," I repeated.

"A smug bastard. Treats me like I was a streetwalker. But then he treats all women that way, even his beloved Ava. He *likes* that about her. He's got a voice and all, but so what?"

"I know. It's amazing how the world makes excuses for people with talent or genius. The poor slob who plods along at his job is roundly upbraided for a minor mistake, while Einstein can routinely and carelessly spill his coffee on you and we'd find it harmless, if not an amusing lapse. A charming idiosyncrasy perhaps."

Wide-eyed now. "What?"

"Do you think that he could *kill* anyone?"

The question stopped her cold. A giggle escaped her throat. She pointed a finger at me, a gun, while she mouthed the words: *bang bang.* "Anyone could. *You* could." She gave me a creepy smile. "You probably have, Miss Ferber."

I grinned. "I've been tempted."

She laughed. "Ain't that the truth." She lit a cigarette as the waitress placed a slab of cheesecake before her. "One of Frank's goons might. Have you seen them? They're like…buildings. But I don't know…"

"Yes, I've met one. He was very polite."

She grumbled. "Under orders probably not to kill you just yet."

I clicked my tongue. "Thank you, dear. A comforting thought."

"Frank is real sick of Tony these days." She dug into the cheesecake.

"I noticed that."

"After a while a leech starts getting on your nerves. Ask *me* about it. Tony *lives* with me—not for much longer, though. Anyway, Frank's had it up to here, and Tony knows it now. That's why they're yammering about moving back to old New Jersey again, life among the goombahs. It ain't gonna happen. Ethan thinks he can make Frankie boy beg them to stay here. Lot of good it'll do him. But Frank's a savvy L.A. customer, no? It don't work. But, you know, it's not only Tony. Frank's had it with Ethan, too."

"What do you mean?"

"Ethan used to see Frank as a God. Frankie this, Frankie that. He got on my one remaining nerve, let me tell you. Again, you know, the coattails to a world of money and cars and Palm Springs homes and Malibu and la-di-dah stuff. But Frank looks at Ethan as Tony's zookeeper, small fry Metro hack that he is. It finally dawned on Ethan. Suddenly Frank's colors are fading away. There's Ethan, grinning that empty smile of his—alone. He's got a brain that scares me—like a machine chugging along. He said something smart-ass after that ride home from Ava's. Frank dropped both of them at my apartment—*dumped* them at my place. Tony said Frank treated them like trash in the car. Ethan said, 'Frankie isn't worth my little finger.' Wow! Then he said, 'Someday somebody is gonna plug him. Whoever did Max in got the wrong slob!' Wow!"

"An angry man."

"Tell me about it. Inside my apartment Ethan started in on that 'failure' crap—how he despised failure. Failure is an awful word, he said. All around him is failure. My God, he's a bore. He pointed at Tony. Then at *me*, would you believe? The bastard. Then, at a picture of Frank Tony pinned to the goddamn wall. The biggest failure of all, Frank is. He's glad that Frank is slipping, out of a contract at Metro, you know. 'I still got my job at Metro,' he said. 'And my real estate.' And Tony, to the slob's credit, yelled back at him, "Yeah, but you just got enough to pay the tax on the Paradise bar."

"How did Ethan take that?"

"He walked out, headed downstairs to get a cab." Liz glanced down at her watch, and jumped. "For chrissake."

"So you decided…Max…your visit."

"I decided, what the hell, retrace my steps."

"Max?"

"Exactly."

"Why didn't you call him?" I asked. "Instead you went to see him."

She deliberated. "When we parted company, well, I had a few harsh words to say to the man. I ain't a woman to mince words. I told him I hated him, that we all hated him. You know, over the top dramatics." She preened. "I *am* an actress. So I figured he'd hang up on me." Her eyes suddenly got moist. "I didn't hate him, Miss Ferber. I *liked* him. I thought that he would see me standing there, all pretty in my new dress and my hair done nice like it is now, platinum and shiny, and he'd give me a break."

"And did he?"

Gingerly, she patted her hair with her fingertips. "You know, Miss Ferber, I got something nobody else has. Nobody believes that, Max didn't. But I got something. I watch movies and I think, yeah, I could do that. I'm perfect for this part or that one. I know I'm not Ava Gardner, but who the hell is? She comes along, a nobody, some cotton-picking gal from the backwoods, but God gave her that shape, those green eyes, that dimple. Christ! I swear when she looks at you, you sort of melt. But there's something else there in those eyes…like a speck of gold dust. If you got the eyes, you make it out here. Look at my eyes. Gray, no? Drab. But I can make them sparkle."

"Liz, tell me about going to see Max."

She waited a while before answering. "Are you going to the police?"

"I think you should. You didn't kill him."

"Oh God, no. Will they think I did it?"

"I can't speak for the police, but probably not."

"Are you sure?"

"I'm not sure, but honesty is best, Liz. Sooner or later, they'll know and knock on your door. They will, Liz. Rest assured. It's better if you tell them yourself."

She debated that, but I could see her rejecting the idea.

"I don't know. I can never *decide* anything." She waved a forkful of cheesecake at me.

"Throwing Tony out is a decisive act."

A wide, pleasant grin, her head tossed back. "Maybe you're right. Thank you for that."

"What did Max say when he answered the door?"

She had a faraway look in her eyes, as though she now reconstructed the scene. "I could hear him talking on the phone to someone. He yelled, 'Just a minute.' When he opened the door, he smiled at me. Well, I started to cry, Miss Ferber. I guess I'd been hungry for someone to smile at me. Tony grumbles all the time. Ethan frowns. Frank snaps. Christ, what do you gotta do to get a smile out of somebody these days? Anyway, he steps back inside, motions me in, and I tell him, 'Can we talk, Max? I made a mistake.' Direct as I could be. I could see he didn't know what to think of that, but that was all right."

"You went inside?"

She shook her head. "No, because I noticed his bandaged jaw. I'd heard that Frank knocked him down, but seeing that small man...battered like that...well, I asked him how he was. He was all groggy from painkillers, and he said he was going to sleep. Alice was out with you and Lorena, but come in. So I backed off. I said, 'But will you call me, Max?'"

Liz started sobbing now, and globs of makeup bunched in the corners of her eyes and mouth, splotches of caked rouge. "'Yeah,' he said, 'don't worry. There's always tomorrow.'"

She dabbed at her face with the cloth napkin, but that only seemed to make it worse. Her face looked ravaged and pocked.

"And so you left?"

"Yes. 'Go to sleep,' I said. He reached out and shook my hand. A gentleman, that Max. I stood on his doorstep and realized I was shaking." She grimaced. "So now I'm back to bad-mouthing him 'cause I got to when I'm with the boys. I hate myself when I say nasty things about him."

"Yes, I've heard you."

"I ain't proud of myself, Miss Ferber. I do what I gotta do."

"You have to tell this to the police."

A sigh. "I know."

Watching her now, this woman who believed excess defined her—the skyward platinum hair and the garish lipstick, the brilliant spangled blouse, and the chunky rhinestone earrings and necklace—I felt sorry for her. Probably in her early forties, she most likely wrestled with late-night reveries about fame on the screen, though she felt, to the marrow, that life was somehow a dirty trick. The shadowy mirror she peered into in the bathroom at four in the morning told her a story she'd rather not hear, and so each day she renewed her dream with a grim resolve that you had to applaud. A cheap dream, this sad romantic, but it was hers. And, therefore, I supposed, wonderful.

"You went home?"

She shook her head. "No. Seeing Max really made me…fierce. I headed home but I was going nuts, so I drove around for a while. I even stopped for a hamburger and sat there almost crying. It got late but I decided to tell Tony what I'd done. So I drove to the Paradise bar because I knew he and Ethan would be there in that damn booth. Tony wasn't working so he'd be drinking all night."

"What did he say?"

She lifted her eyes, a gesture of disgust. "He was slumped in that booth. Drunk, staring at a wall, in a stupor. I doubt if he even saw me in the doorway. I didn't bother to go in. I changed my mind. Why bother?" She reached for her purse and searched for the compact again. "I'd have to repeat the conversation the next morning anyway."

"So you went home?"

"Yeah. Cried myself to sleep."

Chapter Sixteen

I woke with a start: the face of Max's murderer flashed before me. A suspicion, yes, but I felt it to the core of my being. Only one person, without a doubt. I lay there, trembling, as Ava's provocative words spun around in my head. Those casual words—how she dwelled on that last evening of Max's life and the whereabouts of the featured players in this Hollywood dark movie. The Hollywood script we both were living.

Dressed, refreshed with two cups of coffee and orange juice, I phoned Ava, afraid I'd be waking her after a night of insomnia. But she answered on the second ring, her voice hurried. For a second I heard disapproval. "Ah, Edna, good morning."

"Ava, I'm sorry to call so early. You were expecting another call?"

I heard her lighting a cigarette, the striking of a match. "Francis was supposed to be here. We're going to Metro today. I have work to do and he has to talk to one of Dore Schary's minions about his canceled contract." She seemed out of focus, as though she'd pulled the phone away from her ear. "A desperate attempt. He's not happy."

"Is he ever happy?"

She laughed. "Edna, of course. But it's never when you're around."

"Well, thank you."

She rushed her words. "No, no, that's not what I mean. Lately, he's…"

"I know," I broke in, impatient. "Ava, something you said the other night got me thinking about Max's murder."

A nervous titter. "My God. What?"

"I know something, Ava."

Suddenly I could hear her start to sob in quick, choked gulps. "I don't know if I want to hear this, Edna."

I had little patience, so my words were sharp. "Of course, you do." I breathed in and went on. "Ava, this is between you and me. No one else. Listen to me. Here's what I think happened." And methodically, as though checking off a to-do list, I spelled out my reasoning. Ava didn't say anything, though now and then I could hear her sighing or clearing her throat. When I was finished, I waited, pensive, listening to the eerie silence. "Say something, Ava."

She hesitated. "You have no proof, Edna."

"No, I don't."

"What can you do?"

"Do you have any ideas?"

Another hesitation. "Check Max's files. His letters." She clicked her tongue. "His papers. I always joked that he kept a tell-all diary, but I don't know. He did jot things down. Maybe..."

"I'll call Alice." I was ready to hang up.

"Call me, Edna. I'll be at Metro all day. I'll wait for your call."

"I may want to see you there. Late today."

"I'll leave word at security." The striking of another a match. Another intake of smoke. "Edna, be careful. Murder." As I started to replace the receiver, I could hear her voice quivering. "Please be careful. This story already has an unhappy ending."

When I told Alice what I wanted, she immediately invited me to her home. I didn't mention my suspicions, and strangely she didn't probe. "I can't go into that room yet," she confided. "I will eventually." Then her voice dropped, melancholic. "It doesn't seem to have anything to do with the Max that I want to remember."

Sitting with Alice in her living room, I had no desire for pleasantries, though I nodded and smiled. Instead, my mind was riveted to that workroom behind the closed door. Ava's words and my wide-awake suspicions. Max's murderer was out there, cocky perhaps, confident, because the L.A. police had no substantial leads. Yesterday a back-page mention in the *Times* noted that the police were stymied. Neighbors spotted nothing unusual, and no one had come forward with information. Nothing. A blank page. I suspected the authorities were beginning to chalk the cruel murder up to a political killing, perhaps a random, maddened one, the embittered public rhetoric on Communism fueling some fringe fanatic's dubious quest to purify America from unsavory elements. My mind sailed to America First, the group Desmond Peake belonged to—and Larry Calhoun.

Alice detected my edginess, so our socializing ended abruptly when she stood, pointed to the door of the workroom, and said, "Whatever you want, Edna. Please feel free." She waved toward the door. "Max's world."

"Alice, did Max keep a diary?"

"Just a journal in which he jotted down things." She smiled. "Ava always joked about Max's secret diary, a treasure trove of inner sanctum gossip that Hedda Hopper would kill to get her hands on. He always laughed about it."

"I suppose the police have gone through the room more than once?"

"Yes, three times, in fact, before they unsealed it. I know they leafed through the journal because one of them mentioned it. But what could they find? Business receipts, appointments, innocent stuff."

"Did they take anything away?"

She shook her head. "A list of his clients. Addresses, phone numbers. Mainly *former* clients, of course." A pause. "I never got it back."

"Do you know who was interviewed?"

Again, she shook her head. "I mean, I guess they spoke to Frank Sinatra—because of that stupid threat. Ava told me that.

I think Sophie Barnes because she worked for him. They talked to the folks at the Paradise. Harry the bartender. Ethan and Tony, I think. I'm not sure. Lorena, I know. Mainly because I was there that night. Checking in on me." She shuddered and smiled sadly. "I'm still suspect number one, I suppose."

"Do you believe Frank would kill Max?"

"Of course not. Frank threatens to kill someone any time he's out drinking. It's the way he is." She paused. "Edna, Frank has never said a mean word to me. Not one. Even though Lenny and Tony and Ethan constantly badmouthed me."

"A knight in shining armor?" Sarcasm in my tone.

She smiled. "In some way, yes."

She left me alone in the small, cluttered room that hadn't been dusted since the murder. I'd walked into the room the last time I was at the bungalow, observing the clippings piled on the desk, the sloppy mess of scripts, the accordion files. Nothing had been moved. Max's desk and chair and file cabinets still bore the faint patina of fingerprint residue. At first, daunted by the messy piles of papers, sagging cardboard boxes stacked in corners, accordion files bunched in heaps, I had no idea what to do. My cursory look-over last time had told me nothing, but that was idle curiosity. Now, focused, I tried to reason out my calculated moves. Had the police actually spent time sifting through all of this? I doubted that. A week's work here, hours of drudgery. The death of a Commie might not warrant such fastidious attention by the sheriffs in town.

I sat at Max's desk and stifled a sob as I touched the desk mat and his favorite fountain pen. Notoriously he'd always gnawed on the tip of the stem, a nervous habit I now found endearing. A desk calendar was filled with notations, deadlines, scribbles. I checked the dates listed. Another tug at my heart as I observed a dark line drawn through all the days of my visit, with nothing else scheduled. One word: "Edna."

But I got busy. One drawer held nothing but receipts bound by elastic bands. Another held trade magazines, issues of the *Hollywood Reporter* and *Variety*; another was jam-packed with abandoned scripts and headshots. The desktop was cluttered with clippings relating to the blacklist, his most recent and passionate obsession. A few jottings in the margins, but mostly dotted with angry commentary: "Ridiculous!" "Impossible!" "C'mon now!" "Oh, really?"

I could hear Max intoning these fevered exclamations as he annotated the clippings. But no name was highlighted, other than those of his friends…and his own.

But I stopped looking through this pile because I believed, to the depth of my soul, that the blacklist, while playing a crucial role in this horrid murder, was tangential to finding the murderer.

In a file cabinet I located the manila folder containing a list of his clients, a carbon copy of what the police confiscated, but was startled to realize how few clients were active during his last year. An alphabetical stack of clients' folders. I glanced at Sol Remnick's file, which contained a headshot of the dead comic actor. An early photo. Sol onstage in New York, looking like the sad sack he played, though a younger version. Another in a minor role in some Hollywood movie, dressed as a businessman with briefcase—a debonair and fashionable gentleman. Sol the bit player in grade B movies.

Tony's file had a notation that the sad comic had called to terminate his contract. Max had scribbled, "A fool." Liz Grable's termination was a day later. Max's notation was bittersweet. "Tony got to her. Poor Liz, going off in every direction but the one she needs to find." I liked that. I searched for Ethan's file, but there was none. Of course, he was not an actor. There would be no headshot. His one script had been rejected by Max—and Hollywood. So brief a moment in entertainment that he didn't warrant a manila folder.

Nothing was clicking—nothing. But inside his desk, in the center drawer, I located his journal. It was not a diary, true, despite Ava's gentle teasing, but a thoughtful man's random jottings on the course of his day, reminders of conversations, obligations, even some notations on the folks who trooped through his office. Small paragraphs about people whose names meant nothing now—this one stopped in, that one phoned, others demanded meetings. A multitude of anonymous souls, forgotten. Dead end comments: "Fired for the third time." "Called to say hello…moving to Kansas." "Hates the part." On and on. Carelessly dated, with whole months slipping by before another dated entry. I stopped when I came upon a two-page summary of a talk he had with Sol about Frank Sinatra. I read comments about Ava, and, as expected, they glowed with the friendship.

There was also a paragraph about Liz and Tony, both sitting in that room with him, both berating him for his inattention to their piddling careers. Sad, wistful reflection, Max ruing the day he ever got involved with both of them. "Oh well," he concluded, "you do a favor for someone and it can come back to give you pain. Or acid indigestion." Echoes of Max's soft humor.

Give you pain. I repeated the words to myself.

Give you murder, I thought.

And then I found what I wanted. A scribbled account on one page, Max's summing up of a brief but troubling talk he'd endured. A spitfire exchange, Max acknowledging that he'd lost his temper. I smiled at that: if I jotted in my own journal the times I flew off the handle, usually for trivial matters best ignored, the collected volumes would outnumber the entire Encyclopedia Britannica. Battles royale, Edna Ferber style. High dudgeon, my only gear shift.

Max had responded to a cheap yet vicious accusation, and he wasn't happy with his own anger. That didn't matter to me. What did was the fury hurled at him. Not death threats, nor some intractable ultimatum, not even a cruel personal jibe. Nothing the police would latch onto as motive for murder. But the dreadful words, illuminated as they were on that yellow page, especially filtered through my early-morning suspicion, told me that my hunch was on target.

I slammed shut the journal and sat there, my fingers intertwined, my knuckles white. Yes, I thought. Yes.

Alice watched me as I walked into the living room where she sat, tense, her face rigid. "Edna, did you find anything?"

"We'll see," I muttered.

Alice stood. "You *did*, Edna. I can tell."

"We'll see," I repeated. "I have to go, Alice." My mind was elsewhere. "Could you call me a taxi?"

While we waited, standing in the doorway, she touched my shoulder. "Edna."

I looked at her and attempted a smile. "I'll call you, Alice. I promise."

"Edna, I'm worried now. You seem so…determined."

"Alice, I know what I'm doing."

As I stepped outside, walking the pathway toward the approaching taxicab, I started to tremble. The projectionist was running the last reel of a sad movie, and I was now the unwitting protagonist.

◇◇◇

The taxi scrambled to an abrupt stop in front of Hair Today on Hollywood Boulevard, and I lurched forward, banging my shoulder. "Am I to believe the state of California actually gave you a license?" I asked. The cabbie was obviously a movieland hopeful, a sandy-haired fresh-scrubbed lad with hooded hazel eyes and a pile of headshots on his passenger seat. When he thanked me for the meager tip, I heard a Midwestern twang. Iowa, I thought, or Kansas. Flat and nasal, reminding me of an enamel pan dragged across a sidewalk. Welcome to Hollywood.

Hair Today was a glitzy salon with black-and-green art deco stenciling on the plate-glass windows. An overly large neon sign announced the preposterous name and, though it was broad daylight, still blinked and hummed, the red letters popping on and off. Inside, I spotted a row of bubble-head helmets, under which women idly browsed through movie magazines.

Liz Grable stopped what she was doing, a comb in one hand, scissors in the other. She froze, ignoring the remarks her client was making, and nodded toward me. A woman in a frilly blue blouse with a name tag sewn on approached me and asked whether I had an appointment, but I was already moving past her. Liz, mumbling to another woman to finish up the disgruntled customer, walked toward me, a slow-motion walk, the comb and scissors held before her like weapons. Two western gunslingers pacing each other at high noon.

"What happened?" A voice hollow, strained.

"May I talk to you a moment, Liz?"

She spun around and bumped into a small table, which teetered. "I'm working."

"A minute of your time."

"I don't know…"

"It has to be now." I raised my voice.

She looked over her shoulder as a catlike squeak escaped from her throat. "Follow me." She yelled to the woman up front. "I'm on a break."

"You're not on a break, Liz. Not until…"

Liz cut her off. "I'm on a break now."

I followed her into a back room, a tiny space where cardboard boxes were stacked to the ceiling, shelves lined with hair products. For a moment I was overcome with the heady scent of lotions, cloying tropical fragrances. A face buried in a bouquet of gardenias. Fainting time at the funeral parlor. But near the back door there was a small table with two folding chairs, empty coffee cups bunched and stacked together in the center. Liz motioned for me to sit down.

"What?" she said, breathless.

"I need your help."

"Tony…" she faltered.

"I want you to tell me what you remember about the night you went to see Max at his home."

She looked puzzled. "I already *did*. I told you everything."

"Yes, indeed. But I didn't get to ask you the right questions."

"Miss Ferber, please. I don't want any trouble. Last night I threw Tony out of my place and he was…"

"That's a good move, Liz. I applaud that. You need to start making the right decisions for your own life. But I have to insist now—tell me about that night. Every little detail."

She looked helpless. "I don't know…"

Hotly, "Of course you do. Now start at the beginning. What time did you go to Max's?"

She started to cry. "I can't help you. I can't think…"

"You can, Liz. Stop crying and talk to me. Let's create the scene. You were sick of Tony, you wanted to get back into Max's good graces, and you decided to see him. What time?"

She thought about it. "Early. I don't know. It was light out." She brightened. "Max said Alice had just left—gone to see you and Lorena at the Paradise. Just left."

"Good. Now imagine everything you did—*saw* that night." Slowly, methodically, prodded by me, Liz reconstructed the events of that awful night. Step by step, her voice tentative but then assuming confidence, Liz told me her story, but this time, prompted by me, she added details she'd previously omitted. I could tell, as she stammered through her memory, she had no idea the impact of what she was telling me. She paused after each sentence, trying to weigh its significance herself, but she was thinking only of one person: Tony.

She told me what I wanted to hear. "Thank you, Liz." I stood.

"It doesn't matter, Miss Ferber. I mean, I don't got nothing to do with anybody any more." She stood, smoothed her dress. "I got to get back to work." A moment's hesitation. "This is about Tony, isn't it?" She waited, her lower lip trembling.

"Thank you, Liz. You've been a big help."

"Tell me, please."

"There's nothing to tell you yet," I insisted. "I'm just asking people some questions."

A flash of fire in her eyes, the words spat out. "I don't believe you, Miss Ferber."

No one was home at Sophie Barnes' shabby apartment complex on Santa Monica Boulevard in the flats, a third-floor walk-up over a hardware store and a green grocer. I'd taken the address from Max's files. I expected her to be sitting at home, quiet in a small apartment, listening to *Mary Noble, Backstage Wife* on the radio. No one answered the doorbell upstairs and I tottered back down to the lobby. My eyes scanned the rows of mailboxes. I turned to face a tiny sunburnt man holding a broom and dust-pan, a glint in his eye, amused at something, rocking on his heels.

"You seem a happy man," I observed.

He chuckled. "You got some look on your face, lady."

"Which communicates what?" I began to push past him.

"It says how dare Sophie not be at home."

That gave me pause. "How do you know I'm here to see her?"

"Well, the other four apartments got lost souls inside them, including the one across the hall from Miss Sophie's. Young folks from Nebraska or Ohio who work in diners and department stores, strutting around like they already are up there in the movies, and at night they prowl the streets hoping for dreams to come true."

"And Sophie has no dreams?"

He didn't answer, tucking the broom and dustpan into a small closet under a stairwell. As he straightened his body, he rubbed his lower back, groaned, stretched. "Getting old, ma'am." He glanced up the empty staircase. "She's got little old ladies complaining about them flights of stairs."

"No other visitors?"

"No one as I can see."

"I thought she'd be at home."

"Well, ma'am, some folks gotta have themselves a job."

That surprised me. I just assumed Sophie, leaving Max's employment in a huff, had resigned herself to a life lived with early suppers and genteel canasta and Arthur Godfrey.

"And who are you?"

"The superintendent." He nodded toward a closed door. "That's my apartment right there. The wife is probably pinned against the door eavesdropping on us now. She's got less of a life than me." He chortled, his head bouncing up and down.

"Can you tell me where she works?"

Sophie, he volunteered, worked part-time a couple days a week in a real estate office around the corner. "Pays the rent," the man muttered. "Barely." Leading me outside, he pointed me in the right direction, though when I glanced back, he was still standing on the sidewalk, that same bemused look on his face.

The real estate office was a cubbyhole occupying the corner of a flat-roofed stucco building, the anteroom the size of a closet, where Sophie Barnes now sat leafing through a movie magazine—*Movieland*, I could see from the doorway. There was an office behind it, the door shut, a brass plate announcing Private. She scarcely looked up when I walked in, engrossed in her fan magazine, and she mumbled something about Mr. Janssen being gone for the day. Then, recognizing my face, she sucked in her breath and dropped the magazine on the top of others. *Photoplay, Modern Screen*. "Miss Ferber."

"Hello, Sophie." I moved closer and smiled. "You recognize me? We spoke on the phone years ago and…"

Abruptly, glancing back at the closed door, "I know you. You were at the Paradise with Alice and Lorena that night. Someone pointed you out to me."

"That's right. You were there with friends."

"Yes, I was." Brusque, unfriendly.

"Is something the matter, Sophie?"

She shuffled the movie magazines on her desk, and then neatened the pile slowly. Her fingertips drummed on the top one. Betty Grable smiled at the camera, leaning against a white pillar.

"I don't want to be bothered." She looked away.

"I'm here for Max."

At the mention of his name, she flinched, and her right hand flew to her cheek. "Max." She said his name softly. "He's dead."

"Sophie, someone murdered him."

Her eyes got wet, and she rubbed them with the backs of her hands. Her words were whispered. "Who would do that to Max?"

I slid into a chair in front of her desk. "I have some ideas, Sophie." I waited patiently. Her eyes were hard, but there was something else there now: curiosity.

"What do you want from me?" Her fingers drummed Betty Grable's face.

"I think you can help me."

She gasped, threw back her head. Red blotches on her neck. A hand gripped the edge of the desk. When she looked back at me, her eyes betrayed fear. "I warned him." She swallowed her words.

"How?"

"He was playing with fire. That support of those men. Max talked a blue streak about politics, but he just…talked. I'd know if he was a Communist. I knew *all* his business."

Flat out, "Of course, he wasn't a Communist."

"I know. He wasn't. But he *had* to get involved in that brouhaha, him and Sol yammering all day long. So angry at the way the country was going. And now he's dead." She blinked wildly. "And…Sol."

"Why did you leave him, Sophie?"

A long silence. She fiddled with the copy of *Movieland*. She held a pencil in one hand and idly doodled on the cover, black lines drawn across Betty Grable's pristine and glossy complexion. Finally, nervous, she picked up all the magazines and dropped them into a drawer. She smiled thinly. "Mr. Janssen gets angry when I read them. He says they're trashy. But when he's out of the office…" She flipped her hands in the air, a devil-may-care gesture. "I spent a lifetime with Max and with movie stars." She chuckled. "That is, people who *wanted* to be movie stars. So it sort of got into my blood. It's a bad habit to break." She rolled her eyes.

"There are worse habits, Sophie."

She nodded. "Now I set up appointments for newcomers to L.A. to look at cheap apartments. Not quite the same thing, is it?" She stared into my face. "With Max, I felt a heartbeat away from the world of the movies."

She lapsed into silence while I waited. "Miss Ferber, I was a very foolish woman. I'm certain you've heard the stories about me. I'm sure I was the laughing stock of *that* crowd. Ava and Frank and…Alice."

"No, not true," I told her. "Max worried about you, as did the others."

"Well, I made a fool of myself. I let myself believe that he and I had closeness—but we did. We spent years as a team. But when he got married, it knocked me off balance. I felt—betrayed. I was a foolish, foolish woman. So I got bitter and I made things worse. I *walked* away. I'll show him. The bastard. He'll miss me. He'll beg…" She waved a hand in the air dismissively. "Sometimes you do something that you know is all wrong, like you can see yourself outside of yourself and you say, stop, stop, stop, but you can't." Her voice was strained and weary, almost a whisper.

"You miss him. Sophie." An epitaph for both of us.

Suddenly she was crying. "What do you think? He was such a good man. He gave me a life I thought I'd never have. On the outside it was nothing—the old maid in the front office. But we laughed and told stories and…" She closed her eyes. "He never made me any promises he didn't keep." She reached into a drawer and took out a tissue, dabbed at her eyes. The crumpled tissue dropped into her lap, but she didn't seem to notice.

"You shouldn't be so hard on yourself, Sophie. You're not the first woman who's tumbled like that. You were a woman who…"

"But foolish, foolish." She seemed surprised the tissue was not clutched in her hand.

"I need you to help me now," I said, and she sat up, a puzzled look on her face.

"How?"

"That night at the Paradise. You were there with friends and…"

"And I had a fit, stormed out of there. A birthday party I ruined."

"But why?"

She sighed. "Those are my friends, those three women. My only friends. We play cards together, see movies, travel to places for the day, shop and gab. But mostly we get on one another's nerves." Her laugh was brittle. "We're the only friends we got. Well, that night Mina, one of them, the most annoying, spotted Alice at your table, so, of course, she had to tease me about it. I took a little of it. After all, I'm used to the cruelty of other people who get something out of hurting others. But I simmered. A slow burn, let me tell you. The party went on, but I sat there quietly, nursing this one drink I always allow myself when I go out."

"Then you exploded."

She shook her head back and forth. "A class act, no? You three ladies had left there by then, and my mood was getting darker and darker. Ethan was in the booth with a drunk Tony, and he sent over a bottle of wine for the birthday girl. I'd been ready to head out of there, but that wine meant I'd have to stay longer. Nobody was ready to light the damn candles. After a half bottle of free wine, Mina chided me again about Alice—chubby Alice, not even a pretty starlet to intoxicate Max. And a murdering widow, a mob wife. It was getting late. I'd wanted to leave an hour earlier. When they lit the candles on the cake, I exploded and"—she laughed out loud—"ruined the evening for everyone."

"Well, it sounds to me like you enjoyed yourself. At the end."

A twinkle in her eye. "It did feel good to see frosting on that beastly woman. She hasn't talked to me since. Candles in her blue hair." Her voice got low. "Then I learned the following day that Max was shot to death, and…and I didn't know what to do."

"Could I ask you some questions?"

She shrugged. "I guess so."

"Did you see Liz Grable walk in?"

She looked perplexed. "The actress?"

I beamed. "She'll be happy hearing you call her that."

She grinned. "I'll bet. A first time for everything. She used to drop by at the office to pester Max. She was seeing…Tony Pannis."

"Not any more."

Sophie's face fell. "Yes, I did see her. Later in the evening, though. I was ready to get out of there. She walked in and stood in the doorway. Just stood there. We all looked up. She caught me looking at her and she backed up. She looked…I don't know… *hurt*. I figured she was there to see Tony, but I know she didn't like going to the Paradise because that's where Tony drank and got nasty and weepy and stupid."

"So she left?"

"I guess so. I turned back to my friends and when I looked back at the doorway, she wasn't there. Gone. What does she have to do with this?"

"I don't know yet."

"Well, you don't think that she killed Max, do you?"

I didn't answer her.

"Well?"

"I don't know."

She harrumphed, and then seemed to think better of it. "I'd be surprised. She always struck me as sort of pathetic." Then her eyes widened, frightened. "You don't think that I killed Max, do you?"

"No."

But her eyes were wary as she twisted in her seat, staring over my shoulders. "I stormed out of there but I didn't go to see him. I swear. I told the police that."

"Could you answer one more question, Sophie?"

That stopped her. A small voice, nervous. "What?"

She gave me the answer I expected.

◇◇◇

Late afternoon, refreshed from a pot of coffee at a diner across the street from Sophie's office, I sat by the window and watched Sophie hang a CLOSED sign in the door, lock up, and slowly walk down the sidewalk, headed in the direction of her apartment. A half hour later, a taxi dropped me off at Culver City where I mentioned Ava's name. As promised, she'd left my name at security, but the guard at first seemed hesitant to call her. I raised my voice. "She's expecting me, young man."

"Mr. Sinatra is here."

"So what? She's expecting me."

"Of course." He dialed a number and waited. He refused to look into my face, but finally said, "Here. She wants to talk to you."

Ava did not sound happy to hear my voice. "Oh, Edna, you did come, after all." Then she whispered, "Your phone call this morning jarred me."

"It was meant to." I stared at the guard who was biting the edge of a fingernail. "I have things to tell you."

"That's what I'm afraid of."

"Is Frank there?"

Surprise in her voice. "He's at a meeting. Why?"

"I'd rather see just you."

"I'll walk down to meet you."

I was directed to a small lounge that boasted one china plate on which one stale doughnut rested, centered on a table with magazines. I examined a freshly mounted poster of *Show Boat* on the wall. Perhaps, I grumbled to myself, in the future I'd best travel with a magnifying glass, all the better to view the teeny-tiny letters of my name buried at the bottom. I was but one degree of niggardly separation from the key grip and best boy.

Men's voices drifted in from the hallway, one of which was Desmond Peake's. I suspected security had promptly alerted him to my annoying presence, and he'd scurried from his warren to greet me. He peered into the room, eyes slatted. "Miss Ferber, two days in a row you're here. A pleasure."

"Are you sure of that?"

"I was until a second ago." He was tickled by his own humor.

I smiled. "Then there's hope for you yet, Mr. Peake."

"Ava expects you?"

"You already know that."

He sat down next to me, and twisted his body around to face me. "A banner day here at Metro. Frank Sinatra is back on the lot. The exile returns, at least temporarily."

"Another one of your favorite people."

He ran his tongue into the corner of his mouth. "I have so many."

"Mr. Peake, may I ask you a question?"

"You just did."

"Clever boy." But I wasn't smiling now. "Tell me, do you think Max Jeffries was murdered by some misguided patriot?"

He stammered. "What?" Then, back in full control, "Of course not."

"You say that with such certainty."

He took a long time to answer, as though weighing his words. "Admittedly there could be a crackpot out there, some vigilante, but I don't think so. Wouldn't someone like that—a victim of some delirium—target a higher profile name? Someone like...I don't know...an actor like Larry Parks, currently in the news. Someone who's already appeared before Congress. Max was a small-time offender, though I admit he'd been spotlighted in the press. But a hoodlum wouldn't seek him out."

"What about someone in your America First organization?"

He bristled. "We're patriots, and non-violent. We're theorists, constitutionalists, loyalists. We..."

"Don't murder?"

A thin sliver of a smile, indulgent. "Of course not. We want names...not obituaries. We're true Americans, Miss Ferber. We want apologies, recanting, and loyalty oaths. People *do* make mistakes, and we forgive them, so long as they acknowledge the error of their ways."

I shivered at that, but went on. "So who killed Max?"

"I assumed all along it was some personal vendetta." He stood. "Now if you'll excuse me, Miss Ferber. I have appointments. I trust Ava Gardner will take care of you."

"She already has."

A puzzled look on his face as he backed off.

"Oh, Mr. Peake, one more question."

He stepped closer. "What is it?"

"Larry Calhoun is a member of your organization?"

"You already know the answer to your own question." He started to walk off.

"I have a favor, Mr. Peake."

He turned back. "And what is it?"

"I'd like to talk to Larry. I have a question for him. Could you please ask him to call me?"

He deliberated, his brow furrowed, but then he nodded. Without another word, he disappeared into the hallway.

A few minutes later Ava stepped into the room. "I see Desmond has been here already. He sputtered at me as we crossed paths."

"Well, he actually served a purpose today. He told me something I wanted to hear."

Ava scoffed. "Edna, what?" But she didn't wait for an answer. She cradled my elbow under hers, our shoulders touching. The scent of jasmine, heavy and cloying. "Let's go back to my dressing room."

I accompanied her down the hallway, neither one of us speaking. Smiling, she bowed me into her rooms. I expected a familiar Broadway dressing room, small and cramped, the sickening smell of old stage makeup and mouse droppings. The lingering bite of sweat and spit. Instead Ava escorted me into a spacious three-room suite, with a stocked kitchen and bathroom. I swept my hand around the room. "I guess you're a star."

"That could change in a heartbeat, Edna. Tomorrow I can be back in a closet with has-been darlings." She looked worried. "Right now Francis is trying to woo himself back into the contract with Metro."

"Will it work?"

She shrugged. "He *can* be charming." She glanced toward the shut door, then up at a wall clock. "I expect him here in a bit." She moved around the room nervously, looking into a mirror, playing with lipstick on a tabletop, reaching into her purse for a cigarette. "He can also be a bumbler."

Determined, I reached out and held a hand against her shoulder. "Ava, stop moving." Both of my hands held her shoulders as I looked up into her face. "Ava, I want to go back to our conversation this morning."

She looked away for a second, her eyes lingering on the closed door. "Edna, you scared me." Almost a whisper.

"Did I really?"

A wistful smile. "I suppose not, but I'm…scattered. It makes sense, but I don't see how you can prove…"

I let go of her and she toppled into a chair. I sat down. "I think I can now. I need one more conversation. Well, maybe two. Maybe Larry Calhoun. But I need to talk to Ethan now. Can you reach him here?"

She picked up the phone. I listened as she chatted with someone in accounting, who at first refused to believe he was talking with Ava Gardner. Irritated, she hung up the phone. "He's on break in the commissary, Edna. But he's with Tony, who's looking for a job here. Ethan is trying to get him some work. God knows what he can do!"

I frowned. "This is not good. I want to talk to Ethan alone, without Tony. This is a wrinkle I didn't anticipate."

"You want to wait until Tony leaves?"

I shook my head vigorously. "No. Not this time. I seem to deal with the brothers Pannis together all the time. The whole world does. This time will be no different, though unwelcome." I stood. "Having Tony there is not good."

"Edna, I don't think it's a good idea…"

I raised my voice. "I never said it was, Ava. But it's the only thing I can do now."

She fidgeted. "I'll come with you."

"No."

"Edna!"

"No, Ava. If I'm wrong, I don't want you there."

"And if you're right?"

"Then the game is over."

Chapter Seventeen

Ava gave me directions to the commissary, one building over, and I headed there, though my steps dragged. Ethan and Tony. Tony/Tiny. He wasn't supposed to be there. Falstaff in sequins, begging for pennies from a miserly brother. But then, I thought wryly, neither should I be strolling the hallways, the wandering novelist shuffling through Metro with an I.D. badge and a purpose.

My progress was interrupted by an aide to Dore Schary who'd heard I'd invaded the hostile territory. She waylaid me as I turned a corner, standing in my path with a clipboard and pencil, her face grim. Trying to smile but failing at the simple human act, she questioned whether my being there had to do with tomorrow's premiere of *Show Boat* at the Egyptian Theatre.

"No," I said quickly, "I've already been accosted by Desmond Peake."

I tried to move around her.

"Did you see Miss Gardner? Where are you headed now?"

"To the commissary."

Suddenly chatty and bubbly, she confided that Dore Schary was out of town—"a man who respects you"—and would be unable to see me.

"I don't expect to see him." I raised my voice. "I'm leaving L.A. You will *not* see me tomorrow."

She looked relieved, jotted something on the clipboard—what? confirmation of my travel schedule?—and scurried off.

Out of the corner of my eye I spotted Peake waiting for her. My, my, such clandestine intrigue: Edna Ferber, the *Show Boat* herself, lumbering through the sanctified Metro hallways. Alone, adrift, and doubtless a danger in this celluloid canyon.

But I was stopped again. At the doors of the commissary, a voice shouted my name. "Edna, wait." Frank Sinatra, his face flushed and that Adam's apple bobbing, came hurrying up to me.

"Frank." I was confused.

"Wait." He stopped next to me, swung around so that his back was to the commissary door. He was out of breath, his face too close to mine. Those awful scars, those blue eyes so bright now. "Edna, Ava just told me what you said about…Max."

Another wrinkle, this. Why would she do that? I tried to step around him. "She shouldn't have done that. I asked her for secrecy."

For a second he closed his eyes. "Look, I don't want you to do this alone."

"I do everything alone."

"Not this." He softened his voice. "Not *this*."

"I do not need a protector, Frank."

He stammered, "I'm not here to…to protect you, Edna." He smiled broadly. "Hey, I've heard enough about you to know you can win your own battles. But I think you need to have a friend with you." He reflected on his words. "Yeah, a friend."

"A friend?"

He nodded. "I can be a friend, you know. I'm not always an ass."

Now I smiled, staring at the jumpy man, this short, scrawny scrapper with the red bow tie and the cowlick. Ludicrous, perhaps, but staring into those blue eyes I saw something I didn't associate with him—had *refused* to see: real concern. And despite what he said, that look also communicated something else—fear. He looked nervous, his fingers opening and closing quickly. All right, then. My rogue companion, though uninvited. The wisecracking man with the sarcastic tongue and the flippant attitude—the brazen brawler—the nasty man—all eclipsed for the moment by a young man who wanted to come out on the side of justice. I looked at this crooner with a kind of wonder, not certain if I trusted this gangly Galahad. An intriguing soul, this Francis Albert Sinatra, Ava's lover. A man who could surprise me. Even old ladies welcomed surprises.

Ethan and Tony looked up as Frank and I, side by side, approached the table. Tony rose, plopped back down, confused. "What the…" Frowning, Ethan kept his eyes on Frank.

"Boys." Frank addressed them warmly. "Miss Ferber would like to visit with you."

Ethan laughed in a high, unnatural cackle, while Tony folded his arms onto the table, hunched over, head bobbing as though he would drop his head down for a nap.

"We were just leaving," Ethan said. "I have to get back to work. Tony filled out an application…" He stopped. "What?" The word was almost shouted out, addressed to Frank. "Frankie, I only got a minute."

I pulled up a chair directly across from him. "Then my timing is perfect. Remember what you told me about timing, Ethan? You said everybody in Hollywood depends on timing. It's the key to everything out here. Bam bam, hit your mark."

A baffled look, first at Frank, then at me. "So what? You came here to remind me of things I said at a cocktail party?"

"Partly."

Tony roused himself. "I gotta leave."

Frank reached out and touched his sleeve. "Sit, Tony. We're friends here. Miss Ferber has something she wants to say." He spoke in a calm assuring voice. For a second, I thought he'd sung the words, so smooth and lilting were his syllables. The crooner, easing the way.

Tony darted a frightened glance at Ethan, who refused to look his way.

"Timing," I repeated.

In a clipped, hard voice, with a sharp glance at Tony, Ethan demanded, "What are you trying to say, Miss Ferber?"

Tony was fidgeting, rocking back and forth, but another look from Frank quieted him. It struck me as uncharacteristic of Frank, this wistful and hypnotic smile. The seasoned keener at your funeral. Tony stopped moving and closed his eyes.

I had trouble focusing on Ethan, suddenly forgetting the questions I'd planned to put to him. Distracted by Frank's suave maneuver with Tony, I considered how little I really knew about him, this smooth balladeer, how quick I'd been to condemn him, to draw him as a facile caricature. Yet Ava loved him, and I respected her. Indeed, so many parts of Frank failed colossally. Ethan's word: failure. Frank nodded at me because I'd not answered Ethan, intent as I was on watching this pacific ballet with Tony.

Now, spine erect and hands gripping the edge of the table, I announced ferociously, "Ethan, you murdered Max."

Tony squealed, flew back in his chair, nearly toppling it over, a gurgling sound escaping his lungs. Beads of sweat glistened on his face, in the creases of his neck. His eyes darted first to his brother, then to Frank, but not to me. Breathing heavily, he swayed toward Frank who put his palm on Tony's shoulder. The effect was immediate: Tony looked at him, pleading in his eyes.

I was staring at Ethan, who watched me carefully, unblinking. I waited a long time. He sat back, his body at attention, eyes narrowed, and seemed to be sifting through his thoughts, planning his sentences…or maybe judging the value of mine. Then, finally, speaking in a low, gravelly voice from the back of his throat, he spat out, "Preposterous."

The word hung in the air, explosive, thunderous. Suddenly he looked down at his hands, his expression troubled. I followed his eyes and saw a tremor in his right hand, a movement he tried to squelch by covering it with his left hand. He looked perplexed, as if he couldn't believe his body operated independently of his brain.

"Preposterous!" A hiss. "I won't sit here and take this."

Frank glared. "Of course, you will." The tenderness he'd showed Tony was gone now, the old spitfire back.

Ethan twisted his head slowly toward Frank, and I saw what I suspected these last few days, in bits and pieces: a fierce and massive dislike for the famous singer. I swear a sneer escaped from those tight, thin lips, and for a moment I envisioned Pete on the showboat, the vicious crew hand in love with Julie, whose love is unrequited and who turns her in to the sheriff. The dark melodramatic villain the audience rightly hissed. Ethan and Pete, two men at a moment of devastating reckoning.

Frank looked at me. "Prove it, Edna."

Ethan, in that split second, must have believed he had an ally in his old friend, Lenny's blood brother, because he nervously smiled at Frank. Prove it, lady.

"I shall," I trumpeted, but paused, collecting my thoughts.

"Go ahead," Ethan snarled.

"Timing," I repeated. "Ava prompted me to revisit the night Max died, especially what happened at the Paradise. That got me thinking about the night before—the disastrous dinner at Don the Beachcomber, the night Frank here"—I nodded at him—"got a little drunk, resented Max's idle flirtation with Ava, then hit him. Frank notoriously threatened to kill Max, a public declaration I gather he's in the habit of making, unfortunately"—Frank winced—"but so be it. The following day the tabloids ran with it—Frank's threat to commit murder. Timing. The next night Max was, indeed, murdered. The rumors grow, alarming Ava but not Frank…at first. Not until the cops took him in for questioning. It's logical to suspect Frank, especially with his hair-trigger temper and his overweening arrogance."

I glanced at Frank who had pulled his lips together, frowning. "Thank you, Edna."

"You're quite welcome."

"Christ," Ethan muttered, "This is…"

"Just a second," I went on. "Someone wanting Max dead might see this as an ideal time, especially someone who's harbored a long-standing, festering grudge that probably turned into outright hatred. Timing. It was also convenient that Max had become the poster boy for the blacklist, his name bandied about in the columns, the hate mail arriving on his doorstep. Even death threats. No one took such threats seriously, the product of loose cannons, crackpots."

"Crackpots," Ethan echoed me.

"But Max's murder would not surprise some folks. Max was obsessed with the blacklist—he and Sol Remnick spent long hours talking about it. Sol made an interesting observation before he died. The so-called-patriots don't murder; they torment, they deprive folks of income and reputation. Their cruel and unusual punishment is slow and deliberate. Desmond Peake, a leader in America First, got me to believe this, too. For all their absurdity and their misguided patriotism, his group believes in redemption, admittedly after coercion and appropriate public humiliation."

"Max was a Commie," Ethan seethed.

"No, he wasn't. And you know it, Ethan. When you said that one night, it made me wonder. You pride yourself on logic, precision, all the orderly trimmings you've manufactured for living your own life. Everything in its place. Regimented truth. So that remark made no sense. You *knew* better, though you'd like others to believe Max courted his own death."

"So how did I do it?" Cocky, he threw back his head.

"Just a minute. This is my script now, my storyboard. You're a man who prides himself on control, but that wasn't always the case. A drinker, a wife-beater, you reformed yourself, true, something that must have taken inordinate discipline. Severe, authoritative—a life lived with rigidity. Why? I wondered. Why so keen a transformation? Because, I suppose, you burned with a deep-seated anger, a desire for vengeance."

Tony made a blubbering noise, and for a second we all stared at him.

I went on. "It was clear the other night when you and Tony fell apart at Ava's house—you resent Frank and his success. It should be *your* success. Tony told us your comment about Adam and Ava—how they don't deserve what they've worked for. I listened to a man who is craven, bitter, seething. And thus dangerous."

"Your scenario is missing some elements." He gave out a false laugh. "Missing pieces."

"Circumstantial? You bet, Ethan. So far. But you resented your own failure. That's *your* word: failure. It burned you, ate you up. Ava and Frank, success, money, cynosures whose lives are documented in the magazines. Hollywood, the land of dreams and money and fame—it all eluded you. So close...but gone. Fame, power, money—they eluded you. And with Frank now disappearing from both your lives, you despaired. Hence the business of heading back to New Jersey. That's admitting failure, no? Back to staring faces, folks who'd point and remember the boy who left to meet his dreams."

Tony started to say something but stopped when Ethan shot him a look.

"To you, Max was the instrument of that failure. Tony's career was over. But yours never started. That script you gave Max—the one you've mocked and played down and cavalierly dismissed—it was the touchstone of your failure. In Max's journal today I found his summary of your final conversation, a description of how you fell apart, weeping, a little drunk then, when Max told you it was worthless. You blamed him, irrationally—then Hollywood, then, bizarrely, Frank. Three lines stayed with me. 'I have to do it for Lenny. He won't like it if I'm a failure.' Awful words. Max told you to get out and what did you say. 'I'll be back, Max.' An innocent enough threat, idle, but one you took seriously. You did go back."

"Crazy lady." Tony was sweating.

"You *believed* in the puerile script you peddled, sadly. It was your ticket to your name in lights. After Max's rejection, you played it down—mocked it with Lorena. But inside you seethed. Max squelched your most important dream. You were left with a penny-ante job and a life on the fringe of Frank's glory."

A whine, high and thin. "I make money in real estate..."

"Then Lenny died, the catastrophic event in all your lives, and you accused Alice of murder. That became your mantra. Alice the black widow. You let Tony believe she'd taken all the fortune

Lenny bragged about, but you, the numbers man who probably laundered cash for his brother, knew there was little left after the government stepped in. But it served your purpose to let Tony believe and whine and spout his nonsense. Because, frankly, at that moment you made a decision: you stopped drinking and like the Iago character you sometimes quote, you plotted revenge. Or maybe it solidified when Alice married Max—the ultimate indignity. Max, the man who single-handedly killed your dream of fame and fortune. It all comes together, no?"

Ethan opened his mouth but nothing came out.

"You also decided to make Tony your unwitting dupe. The genial comic, plodding, a little funny, the social drinker, a soft-hearted soul though not so dumb as everyone thinks he is—he became your tool. You whispered murder in his ear. Words like betrayal, dishonor, family. And Tony fell apart, losing himself, gaining weight, losing jobs, a binge drinker. I don't think you thought he'd get so out of control, and it might have scared you—this dissolution so quickly. So you coddled him, sheltering him at the Paradise where he could get plastered and not bother a soul. Except maybe Liz, who still cared for the young man she remembered fondly."

Tony started to say something, but stopped.

"You decided on revenge. Kill Max, and somehow blame Alice who got away with murder one time but perhaps not a second. Leave the pistol on the hall table so that Alice, returning, might pick it up, thinking Max had been careless with his gun. A possibility. Relying on chance. Alice feared guns, and, unfortunately for you, gingerly picked it up with index finger and thumb so that the cops immediately had doubts about her as suspect. She was still, of course, a possible killer. Chance."

"Alice did…" His voice trailed off.

"No, that plan failed. Lenny is gone, the brother revered and loved. A decision by you to avenge—cool, calm, collected. A deliberate man, waiting, waiting. Timing. Always timing, you said. And that night at the Paradise the stars came together. Alice is out of the house. You watched her having a drink and leaving for the movie with Lorena and me. Max, nursing his wounded jaw, at home alone." I looked at Frank who was entranced by my voice, barely blinking. "It was a crime of opportunity."

"Preposterous," Ethan growled again.

I shook my head. "You left the bar, headed down the street to Max's, a short drive, rang the bell, followed him back to his workroom on some pretext, and when Max sat down, you shot him in the head."

Silence at the table, Tony breathing hard. Frank's hand, I noticed, rested on Tony's shoulder.

Ethan's voice was thick with venom. "Ask Tony. Ask Harry the bartender. I never left. When you all stopped back for a nightcap, I was there, watching over a drunken Tony, our usual night at Paradise."

"Not so," I said, checking off one more point in my head. "One thing bothered me later that night. You spend a lot of time stopping Tony from drinking. I'd seen that before at Ava's. Yes, that night Tony was morose, having lost his comedy spot. But you let him drink. You seemed to encourage it. All right, let Tony drown his sorrows this one night. You knew Tony would drink until he passed out, which he sometimes did, slumped there in the booth until closing when it was time to drive him back to Liz's. That bothered me."

"Ask Harry."

"I don't have to ask Harry anything. I talked to Sophie Barnes today. She recalled Tony slouching in the booth, crumpled in a corner, snoring. And you'd disappeared. She considered you'd gone into the kitchen or backroom, which you probably did. But she recalled that she glanced back as she stormed out—some fifteen or so minutes after she'd first looked—and only Tony was still in the booth."

"You're right. I run a bar. I was in back."

"At one point Liz Grable came looking for Tony, walking in and spotting him drunk and passed out. She backed out, headed home. She'd had it with both of you. She told me this afternoon that Tony was by himself."

"I told you…"

"But I pushed her and she remembered that your car wasn't in the parking lot in its usual spot. She knew it because Tony doesn't drive and relies on you—you always brought him home. On the nights when she met Tony there your car was in its usual spot, right of the back door. Well, that night it was gone. But she paid it no mind. After all, you weren't inside with Tony. She wasn't surprised to see Tony by himself. Disgusted with him, she went home."

"I was…" He clammed up.

"Something else. When Larry Calhoun was handing you the papers for the sale at the Ambassador, he sniped that he'd chosen not to hand them over at the Paradise to a drunk. I wondered, by chance, if he'd stopped in that night and you weren't there. Desmond Peake is putting in a call to him and…"

He held up a hand. Spittle at the corners of his mouth. "You got it all figured out, right?"

"Yes, I do. You slipped out and murdered Max. You could accomplish the deed in less than a half hour. Considerably less, in fact. It was a question of timing, Ethan. You're right on the money. Timing in Hollywood is everything."

Ethan was biting his lip like a frenzied chipmunk. He reached for the empty coffee cup and rattled it.

"Ava told me to look at the players and where they were situated. And that led me to you, Ethan."

Ethan shot a fierce look at Frank. "Is that why you're here, Frankie boy? To take me in? To play the tough guy one more time? To catch a murderer and hand him over? The boy from New Jersey who made it big slapping handcuffs on the boy who never got a chance? Is that it? High muck-a-muck Frank Sinatra. Boozy kingpin. Shoot-'em-up crooner." He raised his voice, shrill, metallic. "I didn't come out here to pick up crumbs off your table. Lenny told me…it…it was all ours for the picking. I hoped they'd arrest *you*, Frank. Haul your ass off to prison. You, who threatened to *kill* him. Maybe Alice, but I thought…you. You or Alice—I didn't care. Big shot. You and Ava, two drunks.

Alice killed Lenny and what did you do? Nothing. She *murdered* him. You let it go because Ava told you to. Alice got away with murder. Murder! At that moment I knew what I had to do."

"All right, stop," Frank said slowly.

"I hated Max. He is everything Hollywood did to me that is rotten. He dashed my dreams—made light of my script. My blood was in there."

"Oddly, Ethan, in this dreamland out here, where everyone makes up stories, you still couldn't make anyone believe in you."

He smiled. "And there was that Commie sipping cocktails with Frank and Ava. Like he was one of them. It was all perfect, really, so logical. The pieces of a puzzle coming together, piece by piece. Exquisite, mostly. The stars in alignment. For once… with *me*."

Suddenly Ethan swung into me, a jack knife move, but Frank stood, moved behind me, and placed his hands on my shoulders. I could feel his touch, his fingers pushing into my flesh. A comforting move, and welcome. He simply stood there, not saying a word, as Ethan glared.

"Sure thing, Frankie boy. You know how you call everybody a bum? Well, you're a bum."

Frank measured his words. "I may be a bum, Ethan, done my share of rotten things, but I also know that Max didn't deserve to die." He lifted one of his hands while the other still rested on my shoulder. "Sometimes you gotta do the right thing. Right, Edna?"

"Yes."

Frank pointed at Ethan, a bony finger aimed at his chest. Ethan stiffened and wrapped his arms around his chest. "Edna's a smart cookie, wouldn't you say?"

Ethan spat out his words. "I would have gotten away with it if she'd stayed in New York where she belongs."

Frank's hand grazed my cheek affectionately. "Hey, welcome to Hollywood."

Chapter Eighteen

Ava and Frank smiled into the camera at the premiere of *Show Boat*. I folded my copy of yesterday's *Los Angeles Times* so that I could stare at the two lovers at the gala event at the splashy Egyptian Theatre on Hollywood Boulevard. Two days ago, July 17. The day before that event I'd sat with Frank in the commissary at Metro. Three days ago. Two days ago. Both lifetimes in the past. Worlds far from me as I sat in the first-class compartment of the American Airlines plane, headed back to New York.

Tonight *Show Boat* would premiere in Manhattan, though I'd not be there. I'd be in my bed with a tray of food, catching up on mail and friends.

Hollywood was history. The past is over.

Frank Sinatra told me that one night, but it turned out he didn't really believe it either.

Three days ago, the beginning of that long afternoon as Frank signaled to security to step in, then two police officers appearing, though Ethan, sitting there with his lips drawn into a straight line, his eyes filled with hatred, refused to move. Spine rigid, hands gripping the edge of the table, he demanded to be left alone, ordering the cops around in a fierce and chilling voice. He had to be lifted from the table bodily, his fingers pried off the edge; and even then, held in the air like an errant, spoiled child, his knees still bent and his fingertips curled, he set his face into a stony mask. He said nothing as the cops hauled him away, his body catatonic. He didn't look back when Tony plaintively called out his name.

Tony, that blubbering mass of grief. I'd not wanted him there, of course, because I did not want the sad man to witness what would happen. Poor Tony, twisted by his brother into a lost soul who railed at a world he could never understand. A victim, shattered. Even before the cops arrived, while security stood over his brother, Tony dissolved into a weeping fit, rocking back and forth in the seat, head rolling as though unhinged, sloppy wet tears gushing down those fat cheeks. "No, no, no." The rumble of his voice filled the large room where other diners, luckily not so many late in the afternoon, watched in horror, some backing away or standing by the entrance.

I sat there quietly. It was Frank who tapped Tony on the shoulder and nudged him to get up. And it was Frank, whispering in a small, demanding voice, who directed Tony away from the table. As I sat there, unmoving, staring away from Ethan, Frank began walking Tony around the room, maneuvering him around the tables, his right arm draped over Tony's broad shoulders, his head dipped into Tony's neck, whispering, whispering, a drone I couldn't hear except to know that it was someone soothing a lost and miserable child.

Frank walked Tony out, found a phone, and called Liz Grable. He later told me that Liz had told him to bring Tony to her at the beauty salon, which he did shortly; and that Liz, leaving work and embracing the trembling Tony, had taken him back to her home, from which he'd just been exiled.

"She'll watch over him." Frank told Ava and me later. "He's hurting. And maybe she's the one thing he needs now."

He also told us that Tony had babbled in the car that he'd suspected Ethan of the murder, though it seemed impossible, of course. He could never ask him...or even consider it, but he'd roused himself twice that night when he'd passed out in the Paradise. Both times Ethan wasn't there. Later, asking him, Ethan said he'd never left Tony's side. One night last spring, rifling through Ethan's bureau at his apartment, searching for singles and change, he'd spotted the .32 under some papers. Days after Max was dead, he'd checked again: the gun was gone. Still he fought the idea that Ethan could do such a thing.

Cold, cold—that was how he described his brother. "I knew he was burning with something from the day Lenny was murdered." So the gun was no surprise. "Ethan takes care of me. How could I say anything?" he asked Frank. "I thought he'd kill Alice. He *hated* her. Not Max."

The stewardess poured me more coffee as I stared at the black-and-white photo. She glanced at the newspaper in my hands. "Oh, Hollywood royalty," she gushed. I nodded. Frank was dressed in a spiffy black tuxedo with a dark bow tie. Ava wore a strapless gown with elaborate folds and twists of fabric, bunches of ruffles across the bodice. I wondered about the colors, though I assumed the dress was a vibrant assault of greens and blues and reds. Vaguely oriental looking. With her hair pulled back to accentuate those high cheekbones, Ava appeared exotic, the wild woman. Frank held a *Show Boat* program in his hands, as both smiled for the camera. Behind them Tony Curtis and Janet Leigh looked the proper couple, not like the glamorous woman in front of them. I smiled at that: Ava, Ava, the woman as temptress of the night. The article mentioned the success of *Show Boat* and of Ava's stellar performance. A film classic, it was called. A monumental achievement. Metro's Technicolor extravaganza.

I'd sat with Ava in her dressing room at Metro for hours, and she made a pot of tea for both of us, hovering, solicitous. "Thank you, Edna," she'd whispered, but I'd simply closed my eyes. Exhausted, I needed to fly away from Metro, get back to the Ambassador, and start to pack my suitcase.

But that night, kidnapped from my room, I sat with Ava, Frank, and Alice in Alice's living room, and we talked and talked. Alice wept, and then Ava did, and then I did, too, the three of us chain-linked to Max. A bond, we three women, a cherished closeness. Frank, I suppose, learned not to cry when he was a blustery boy in hardscrabble Hoboken, but he had the sense to be quiet. No, that is unfair: he made his feelings known by his gestures—touching Ava's cheek as he passed by on the way to the kitchen, squeezing Alice's hand as she sat on the sofa—and with me…a spontaneous hug as I stood to leave, so serendipitous that Ava and Alice both smiled.

Ava had told me he'd decided I had "class," a favorite word. Some women had it. That's why you loved walking into restaurants with them, their arms linked with yours.

So Frank wasn't always a cad and a bounder, this Francis Albert Sinatra, though I feared I might be too forgiving at the moment. That could change.

When both drove me to the airport and Ava held onto me for a long time, Frank simply shook my hand. "You know, Frank," I said, "I'm afraid I misjudged you."

A mischievous gleam in his eye. "No, Edna, you really didn't."

Ava smiled. "Keep dreaming, Edna. Wait until the next scuffle with a photographer."

The night before he'd sent flowers to my hotel suite, an enormous—and vaguely funereal—spray of carnations and roses. But when I leaned in to smell their bouquet, there was none. Of course not. In L.A., where sunlight covers you like a shroud, the flowers have no scent.

◇◇◇

Late yesterday afternoon, returning from a walk about the Sun Club Pool, I spotted Lorena Marr waiting for me in the lobby. She watched me approach, her eyes on me the whole time. I stood in front of her, looking down, and waited. "Edna, could I talk to you?"

"Of course, Lorena."

"Please sit with me."

I hadn't spoken to her since Ethan's arrest, so I began, "Lorena, I'm sorry it worked out…"

She spoke over my words, her head going back and forth. "Stop, Edna."

I sat in a wing chair next to her. "Are you all right?"

"No, I'm not." A feeble smile. "But it's not your doing. I've been thinking about what happened…Ethan…Max…and I need to tell you something." A rasp from deep in her throat. "Christ, Edna, I'm sorry. I let myself be blinded. That's the word—blinded. Ethan *had* changed since he was my husband. He'd stopped drinking. He was always rigid and severe but he got…deadly serious. I even thought we might get back together. I *liked* him. I used to love him. I suppose I still do. I wanted to believe I could have something with him. Foolish, foolish. I thought our friendship was sweet and cosmopolitan and enviable, very modern Hollywood, after the messy divorce." She fumbled in her purse for a cigarette and lit it. She slumped in her seat and closed her eyes.

"But you were bothered by something?"

She nodded quickly. "I *ignored* things. That driven personality. He masked an emotional upheaval, covered it over. I realize now everything had to do with revenge…on Alice. And Max. A double slap to his face. Alice killed the beloved brother. She ruined all their lives and took away a promised future. He plotted…and Max was the target. How best to hurt Alice! He hated Max, the instrument of his failure. There were signs, Edna— comments that slipped out, little vicious angers, ugly, mean, then simply smiled away as banter. I didn't know the depth of his obsession, though I should have."

"Lorena, you're not to blame."

"A part of me is. You can't talk me out of it, Edna. I didn't want to see it. He wished *her* dead. *Him* dead." She sucked in her breath. "I knew he had guns from Lenny. He kept them hidden from me, but I knew. Once, late at night, I woke up and heard him in the living room. Quietly I looked in. He was there in the shadows, in his pajamas, drunk, aiming his gun out the window and whispering, 'This is how you die.' He looked like he'd given himself over to evil, Edna."

"Lorena…"

She held up her hand. "When Max was killed, I knew in my heart that it was Ethan. I knew it. That's why I was so distraught."

"But you didn't *know*…"

A thin smile, haunted. "In Hollywood if you're not a character in someone's dream, you have nothing. A lonely life, a shell. Look at Sophie Barnes."

"But Ethan gave you only nightmares."

"It was better than…nothing." She bit her lip. "Nothing."

She stood, took one last drag off her cigarette, snuffed it out in an ashtray, and turned away. "I guess I could never be the kind of friend I wanted you to see me as, Edna. Like Ethan, I failed." An unfunny smile. "And now it's too late." She walked past me and out the door.

◇◇◇

I finished my coffee and put down the newspaper. The pilot was announcing altitude and clear skies. We were free of L.A.'s noxious smog. A nap, I thought: a rare nap. Six hours to go on the flight to New York. Instead, I opened the carrying case I'd placed on the floor, taking out some folders. Alice had given me a parting gift, which stunned me: the script of the 1936 *Show Boat*, much tattered and frayed, a working script, with Max's notations in the margins. On the title sheet an abundance of signatures, inscriptions to Max ("You're the best, Max"; "Sing a song for me, pal") and signed by Irene Dunne, Allen Jones, Paul Robeson, Hattie McDaniel. A sheet filled with praise and love and honor.

"Max would have wanted you to have this. He prized it highly." Then she'd added, "Even though Max told me what you thought of that movie."

I'd laughed. "It was one of our jokes, you know."

So I cradled the script to my chest, cherishing it. She'd also tucked into the script four black-and-white photos of Max on location, deep in conversations with Paul Robeson, with others.

Ava had also given me a gift, though she made me promise not to open it until I left L.A. Now, unwrapping the package, I found another photograph, an eight-by-ten of her with Max, arms linked around each other. Ava was dressed as Julie LaVerne, her head tilted backwards, her shoulders hunched, the beautiful mulatto standing on the seedy wharf. Oblivious to the intrusive camera, they were smiling at each other, and it looked as though they'd just shared a private joke. They looked happy, the two of them, the Hollywood backdrop behind them.

I thought of Ava and her dream of someday escaping Hollywood, perhaps making a life for herself in Europe, away from the glitter, the groping moguls, and the intrusive photographers. That dream was still possible for her. A woman who dazzled me, not so much because of her incredible beauty, but because of her wonderful humanity. You could see it in that photo, especially in the way she held onto Max, the way her eyes shone as she most likely teased him.

For a moment I choked up, my eyes moist. The pleasure of Max in my life—the way one human being can deepen your spirit and widen your vision—can add to the sweep of your heart. In that moment I closed my eyes and felt a rush of warmth and joy. He was gone, but what trailed in his dust was good. Ava always knew that. We both adored him. On the photo, scribbled in her carefree, loopy penmanship, she'd written a simple inscription:

Dear Edna,
You loved him, too.
Ava.